My Friend's Dream

Manisha Kaur Rathore

Copyright © 2018 Manisha Kaur Rathore

All rights reserved.

ISBN: 9781687181480

For the dreamers

PROLOGUE

KYARA

I look to my left. The balcony doors are wide open, wind gushes through and the curtains are blown inwards. I see the shadow. A figure through the curtains. I walk towards the balcony and gasp. Jen stands on the balcony rail, teetering on the edge. I can hear her shuddering breaths of anxiety and I hear her cries clearly past the roaring wind. My heart beats rapidly, forcing blood through my body and into my brain. I'm scared to call her, scared that she might slip. She pushes herself against the gales to stay balanced. She's… she's distraught. Not thinking right. God, what is she doing!

"Jen…" I breathe softly, frightened by what is happening in front of my eyes. Frightened of what she is about to do.

She turns her head only, still balancing, petrified and unsure of what to do. Her face is red and wet with tears, she finds her way into my eyes, crying. Then… her foot slips!

My feet move. My arms stretch out long. I leap. Her shriek pierces my ears. I close my eyes and for a split second, my whole world stops.

***

I can still hear the cry in my ears and I can still see the balcony when I close my eyes. For some reason, this image scares me more… more than anything that came after that. I remember it so clearly even though it's the time I want to forget the most. It's strange to think that it ever happened, because God and fate had different plans.

I remember the day I got my A-Level results. Results Day. It was warm and humid with crowds of students bunched into groups of lifelong friends. Some cried with sorrow, some cried with joy, some just stood still, shocked, looking down at the white piece of A4 paper they held, the results, which our teachers and parents told us our lives depended on. But my life depended on something else.

'Kyara Averoni' was written on my envelope. I just stared at it, lost in my own world. My heart was pounding in my throat, I swallowed hard to counteract the dull pain. My hands were shaking and I remember thinking how stupid I was because I always did well at school. I studied hard as usual, yet I was afraid of something. Then I realized, it wasn't the results I was worried about, it was moving on to the next step – the final step – of education. When I opened the envelope and unfolded my A4 piece of paper to reveal my grade 'A' final results, I recall mixed emotions. My results were good. Great in fact! I smiled, and then read the writing near the bottom of the page. I had been accepted into university – the final stage of education, the dream of academics, and the dream of my parents as the first person in our family to ever get to this stage. That's when my smile faded, my heart ached and my eyes filled with tears. It was like standing in a house not a home. My friends had chosen subjects they actually wanted to study. My friend Emily was a top student, her grades were exceptional. Teachers pushed her to apply for medicine because she had the potential, she did apply for it but then pulled out because she wanted to follow her heart, she wanted to be a school teacher, she wanted to teach six year olds mathematics and English and she did it. She followed her heart. At that point in time, I thought she would be the only person I'd ever meet who ignored the teachers – our guiders – to follow her heart and I admired her courage. However, with my mind set on pleasing my parents and taking the easy route that would make me reasonably rich, I accepted that I would study physics at university. But then, life took me on a different path, one much different from Emily's straight subject swap over. A path that still haunts me but a path that I cherished while on it, a path that I cherish today and a path that I will cherish forever.

CHAPTER ONE

KYARA

As usual, I'm the first one there. I make it up four flights of stairs to the fourth floor where I come on to a large square landing, with two doors to my left and one door to my right. The single door on the right reads '403' – my apartment. I take a deep breath and open the door with my newly issued keys and drag my luggage into a long narrow hallway, carpeted dark grey. The walls are tall and white and the smell of fresh paint fills my nostrils. As I walk further along there are two doors either side of me exactly opposite each other, 403A and 403B. My key reads '403A'. I step inside to find a decent sized room with a large window and grey curtains at the far side. A desk sits in front of the window. Next to the desk is a double bed and behind the door is a spacious wardrobe with a mirror. I like the room, it seems quite homely and efficient. I drop my luggage inside and continue to explore the rest of my new apartment. Next to 403B is another door which leads to a newly refurbished bathroom. At the end of the thin hallway is an arch which leads into an open plan lounge and kitchen area, all fresh with the same white walls following through. The kitchen is a decent size, with polyvinyl flooring and a rectangular breakfast bar that splits the kitchen from the lounge. Four stools are tucked underneath it. The lounge is cozy, with a hefty sofa, a chair and a low coffee table. There's plenty of space for extras like a TV and I can't wait to start making this apartment my home. But the best part is what lies beyond the lounge covered by grey curtains; as I draw them back, the evening sunshine flushes through the glass door and ignites the lounge. I squint and feel a smile taking over my face. I open the doors and walk out onto a small balcony with a rail that comes up to my belly button. The balcony itself is small but the view beyond is grand. Below lie the university gardens, carefully decorated with soothing water fountains, colorful flowers, freshly cut green grass, cute benches and carved footpaths. Beyond that, in the distance is a spectacular view of the city's high rise. The whole sight is magical and I take my time to admire it for a while letting the cool breeze brush my hair back. I'm enjoying the beginning of my new life. The moment is interrupted by the sound of the front door opening.

"Oh, hey!" A tall, slim girl with blonde hair and bright, green eyes walks in, her luggage toppling over as she gasps for breath. "They really need a lift up here," she laughs still gasping.

I empathize with her exhaustion and laugh with her. She's really pretty and looks girly, but who am I to judge.

"I'm Jennifer Kostigan," she holds out her hand.

"Kyara Averoni," I say, greeting her with a handshake.

"So we're room-mates? Flat-mates really, I mean we don't share a room, LOL," she says looking up and around the hallway.

From what I gather, Jennifer has her own type of humor, which surprisingly, I actually find funny. She walks further into the apartment, making conversation in a bubbly and confident tone. Not like me, I'm shy with new people, it takes me a while to trust them. Plus, she is beautiful and tall which makes me feel slightly intimidated because I know I'm not the obvious kind of pretty, but I try to let go of these stupid judgmental thoughts. It is weird how they just pop into my head when I don't actually want to be judgmental. Human nature is hard to understand.

"Wow, this is nice!" Jennifer says.

"Yep, it is, and it's a lot bigger than I expected," my confidence begins to settle in after I clear my thoughts and since I

My Friend's Dream

got here first, I have about ten minutes more knowledge than she has.

Jennifer unlocks and kicks her room door, shoving her luggage inside and following it in.

"Ooo, it's nice! Wait. Is that all of my wardrobe? It's small! Is yours the same?" she asks.

I take a look around, "Err, yeah, pretty much, although I think my wardrobe is a little bigger because the bathroom is on your side. Here, take a look," I say, leading her into my room.

"Oh man, see this is nice, I mean it is the same but that wardrobe space is bigger. Oh well." She doesn't seem to mind too much, but I don't need all the space and I definitely don't have as much luggage as she does.

"Do you want to swap?" I ask.

"Oh no no no, that's okay, mine's pretty much the same anyway," she politely backs away.

"Honestly Jennifer, it's totally okay with me, plus you've got more stuff, you'll have more space to put all…that," I point at her pile of bags.

She looks at them as they topple over and then looks back at me, "Are you sure?"

"One hundred percent."

We do a quick swap of keys and bags and then I give Jennifer a quick tour of the apartment.

A few moments later we hear chattering on the landing, so we head out to meet our neighbors. A tall, dark skinned, young man with a short afro walks out of the apartment opposite ours followed by another young man, light skinned with brown hair. Both of them look decent, confident and are actually quite handsome, again I get a little nervous.

"Hi!" says the first one, holding out his hand walking closer until we meet in the middle.

Jennifer shakes his hand, "Hey! I'm Jennifer, this is Ky…ara?"

"Yes, Kyara," I confirm shaking both their hands.

"Jennifer and Kyara, I'm Marcus Marley," says the first guy

in a strong deep voice.

"And I'm Brian Walker, nice to meet you, although I'm just telling you now, I'm not very good with names," says the second guy.

"Yeah me neither," Marcus thinks of something quickly, "Can we just call you Jen and… Kye?"

"Sure," I reply for both of us. I like it, nobody has ever given me a nickname and it's not like it's hard to derive one from my name. "So, what will you be studying?"

"Oh, actually this is our second year, I study medicine," Marcus says.

"Ooo Doctor Marcus, hey," Jen nudges him cheekily. I'm also impressed and I'm really happy for him, I know how hard it is to get into Medicine.

"Ah, yeah, I hope so," he smiles shyly, "And you guys?"

"I'll be doing physics," I say.

"English literature," says Jen.

"Really!" Brian steps forward, "I do lit too, Jen, I'm on the master's course, so I'll graduate at the same time as you."

"Nice! How's first year?" asks Jen.

"Easy," says Brian, "But if you need any help, I'll be right across the hall," he gestures.

An excited voice yells from below, "Well, well, well, there are girls on my floor!" A cute, muscular guy with his black hair tied up in a messy man bun stands a few stairs down. His tanned face glows in a cheeky smile. His facial hair is dark black and scruffy. He joins us on the landing. "What's up guys, I'm Rio Fernandez," he shakes everyone's hands and tells us he will be studying mechanical engineering.

Jennifer and I introduce ourselves as Kye and Jen. This is going to stick and stay with us throughout our university lives now. Rio is living in the apartment opposite ours and next to Brian and Marcus'. We're later joined by Dequan Lee or Deq as we decided to call him and Lia Davis. Deq is Rio's flat-mate and studies software and computing, his Asian features hide behind his glasses, he's thin with a clearly toned physique and looks rich, but sweet, but nerdy all at the same time. Lia is a home student studying Law, she's also pretty with brown hair and is a tiny bit shorter than me. Both are also in their first year and had met today on campus. I've already made six friends, which is quite a lot for me. They all seem good fun, genuine and different in their ways. I wonder how things will pan out. Usually people make better friends with their course mates but we shall see.

CHAPTER TWO

KYARA

We all decide to eat together in the evening, Jen and I volunteer to host since we have the biggest living room and we're keen to make friends. We order pizza and sit on the floor surrounding the low coffee table. I already feel comfortable, it seems as if we've all known each other for a lot longer. This new family of mine is relaxed and I'm enjoying their company. We're all hungry so the food disappears quickly and then we begin to get to know each other a little more.

"So, Marcus, you want to be a doctor?" Rio throws his pizza crumb in the box, "Is it something you want to do? Or is it something your parents made you choose?" he laughs, but seriously we all want to know the answer to that one.

"Well, to be honest I've always wanted to be a doctor, nothing else ever interested me. My parents might have had a bit to do with putting it in my mind, but in the end, it was my decision to take medicine, and, I don't regret it, it's hard, but it's interesting. I like biology and I want to cure people." Marcus does seem like a helpful, kind hearted person. "So yeah, I like it. I'd like to go into curing autoimmune diseases eventually. Unless, I become a basketball player," he laughs. "What about you guys? Engineering?"

Rio speaks next, "Nah man, like you said I wanted to play sport too."

"Oh, so that's where all the muscles are coming in," Jen chuckles.

The boys wink and smile at the compliment.

Rio continues to flirt, "Yep, I'm a sporty person," he gestures flexing his bicep. We all woo him on, "but it's a lot of competition, so I took what I'm good at, designing stuff and I think equations which is kind of engineering, plus I like my cars so mechanics seemed to fit. I just go wherever life takes me."

There's a rush amongst us as he mentions cars, of course the boys like them, Jen and I were interested too but not Lia, she sighs in boredom at the subject.

"Engineering is good," says Deq, "Good money, decent job and it's interesting. I've always been into computers and video games. Ever since I got my first game, the Nintendo sixty-four…"

There's another urgency of chatter as we all remember the classic from early on in our generation.

Deq continues, "Yeah, I know. So, I always wanted to invent my own."

"Cool. Like the *Dex* Box Live! I look forward to it!" Brian laughs.

"That would be great!" Deq cheers.

I love Deq's dream of designing his own game platform. It is impressive, video games and technology are our future.

Rio has a thoughtful question, "So can you hack stuff?"

"Ethically yes. Officially, you're not allowed too, but yeah, I sure could. I have programmed software and I once hacked GTA for seventy million dollars – in the game!" Deq explains.

As everyone exchanges fascinated looks, I begin to get nervous thinking about my turn and how I'll announce my dream, if it even comes up. I keep saying it over and over in my head to make sure it doesn't sound stupid, but the more I say it, the more stupid it sounds.

"Hey! That's illegal!" Lia interrupts my thoughts.

"What are you going to do about it, Judge Lia? Sentence me?" Deq replies cheekily, "Why are you studying Law anyway?"

"Well, to put it simply, I hate criminals, I hate crime and I like analyzing things to come to a conclusion, plus I was on the debate team for so many years that it's kind of become my hobby and I love it! I want to make the world a better, safer place."

Lia tells us it's her dream to become a barrister and she's almost there now. Law is interesting but it can be a headache – just like every job.

"Hey man, Brian, since we met, I wanted to ask, why the hell did you choose literature?" Rio asks.

Brian laughs, as if unsure what to say, "Oh man, don't ask, I don't know why I chose it. I wanted to be a basketball player too. My teacher at school said take literature, she was hot, and I took it. I still don't know what I want to do but that stuff is just a dream and-"

"Just a dream!" Jen yells cutting him off.

She's serious and we're all a bit shocked at her abrupt yelling.

"You don't think dreams come true Brian?" she asks glaring at him.

He falls silent and then she looks at each of us. Everyone shrugs or gestures in agreement with Brian, except me, I just sit there waiting for more from Jen.

"You have a dream?" Brian finally builds up the courage to ask her.

Jen's face turns red, she looks at the ground and hesitates before answering, "I…well, when I was…a kid, I wanted to be a… an astronaut," she looks up at us and forces a fake smile. The smile that I do.

"Really?" asks Lia as surprised as everyone else.

"I thought you were going to say something like a model, or fashion designer or something." Brian says.

"What? You think a blonde can't like science?" Jen argues a

good point, "How stereotypical for a guy that studies literature."

We all toot and mumble at the offense and tension between the two literature students.

Rio, as the person he is, makes things worse, "Ahh, I see a little something going on here."

"Rio!" cries Jen, "There's no *thing*, and this is an argument, a fight."

"That's how it starts," he whispers to the rest of us.

The atmosphere is alive and although they are arguing and Jen is trying to make a good point, there is laughter and sarcasm in their playful voices.

"Oh yeah, so why didn't you take astronomy or astrophysics?" Brian asks with a smirk.

Now Jen's smile fades, her voice quietens. We all fall silent, waiting seriously for her answer.

"I, err, didn't do very well in Physics, actually, I did, but in the retake and the retake doesn't' count when applying to university. They look at the first sitting grades only."

Brian's face fills with guilt, he apologizes gently and we all feel sympathetic towards her. Jen tries to call off the sympathy by saying she's over it and that she's fine and happy with literature, but I know that tone, she's far from over it. I know what she's going through. So am I.

"So Kye, what did you want to be?" Marcus asks me trying to move off the subject of crushed dreams.

This almost makes me giggle in a revolting way, "Well, since we're on the subject… I *have* a dream…I wanted…want… to be an actress." The words uncontrollably leak out of my mouth. A look of surprise fills everyone's faces, even I am shocked at what I just said. *How did I just say that? That's far from what I was rehearsing in my head!* I don't know if it was the topic we're talking about that made me spill the truth or the comfort of the people surrounding me, but it's out there now and the silence is embarrassing me. "What?" I roll my eyes.

"Like a movie star? Like Hollywood?" asks Rio intrigued.

"You have more stereotypes? A tanned girl, long black hair,

not too tall, not too pretty, needs glasses to read, studies science...can't be an actress?" I really don't know what I'm saying now, I'm just trying to hide my nerves.

"No, no, it's not that, it's just, why are you taking physics? Why don't you go to acting school?" says Marcus.

That is indeed a question on everyone's mind, and I have my reasons. "Well, I am the first person out of my entire family to go to university, to get this far in education. It is my parents' dream to see me graduate and hang a graduation picture on their wall. To add more pressure, they tell me that my brothers look up to me! I have tried becoming an actress. I really have, but we all know that a key factor in this industry is luck. Pure luck or fate. I don't need qualifications to be an actress, I need destiny to be on my side and luck, which by the way, I don't have much of. So I just chose what I was good at - physics."

"Do you still want to be an actress Kye?" Lia asks.

I nod.

"So you are here, in the final stage of education, at university, studying a degree in physics, wanting to become an actress?" she finishes on a question but really it's a statement. A statement that hits me hard.

I realize just how stupid I am, I got completely carried away! I am so stupid, and my stupidity has been exposed in front of a bunch of people that I just met! My face burns with the heat of embarrassment, I can almost see how red my cheeks have turned from the bottom of my eyes. My palms and forehead sweat. *What was I thinking?* I try to explain myself further, "As I said it is luck. If I take drama or go to acting school and still don't become an actress, I'd have nothing. I wouldn't even get a good job, and why the heck are we all at university anyway? To get a job, to earn a living, for the money. This way even if I don't become an actress..." *which I will*, I think to myself, "...at least I'll have a degree to fall back on. Right?" I end my justification impatiently waiting for someone to think that this is the right thing to do.

"I like that way of thinking," says Jen.

I'm relieved that firstly someone spoke, and secondly that

they agree with me and my way of thinking. She even nods at me. It's like she's reassuring me.

"Not everyone has the mind frame and the courage to pursue their dreams." Jen makes a statement.

It literally feels like God himself is talking to me, telling me to follow my dreams. This is strange. I feel exposed but relieved. Is it good? Bad? I really don't know. I don't know what just happened in the last few moments. I feel numb, the air around me feels thick, yet the atmosphere feels spiritual. These mixed feelings confuse my brain.

Thankfully Rio breaks the silence by standing up and taking the empty pizza boxes into the kitchen, "Well, I don't mean to break your hearts but honestly, dreams don't really come true."

"Yeah, realistically, I agree," Brian adds, "Dreams don't come true to people like us. That's why they're called dreams," he finishes off his drink and follows Rio to the kitchen.

"I have to agree with the guys," Deq joins in the negativity while Lia nods along.

Marcus also agrees and I nod along, humming, but thinking the complete opposite, trying to forget all that I have just said. As we tidy up, I notice Jen is lost in thought, her forehead is scrunched up and she's quiet. There's something about her that I really empathize with.

"Anyway, tomorrow is orientation or fresher's fair as some people call it, so we can show you guys around if you want?" Marcus finishes picking up the cushions off of the floor.

"Yeah, maybe you could join the drama society? The school of acting is quite big here, you could make it a hobby," Brian advises pointing at me.

Hobby? I hate that word.

We all agree to meet at eleven a.m. in the hallway, and on that note, they all leave. Jen shuts the front door and I switch off the kitchen lights. We walk towards our rooms making eye contact and giving each other a sympathetic smile.

"That was fun," she says opening her door. "Although that Brian guy is a little too much."

I laugh tiredly, "Yeah, it was fun,"

"Hey Kye…" Jen calls turning her head to look at me just before closing her door, "…don't ever give up on your dream."

CHAPTER THREE

KYARA

I'm up early, I never sleep well in new places, nevertheless, I like my room and I will get used to it. Plus, we have a whole new day to look forward to.

Jen is a deep sleeper, I had to go into her room four times to wake her up in time for the tour and thanks to my early habits we were ready on time.

We finally reach the ground floor and take a few minutes' walk from the halls of residence to the campus. The walk is pleasant, it's a sunny day with a slight breeze brushing the loose strands of my hair back. There are students, parents and professors all around the university. We approach the Center Square where all sorts of stalls are lined up, each one selling a different society to join, handing out flyers and freebees. There is a colorful buzz in the air, some stalls are extremely busy and others are quiet. The societies range from sports, such as basketball, hockey and polo to choirs, religious societies and entertainment to subjects groups like the mathlete club. Deq takes a leaflet from the gaming society and Lia stops at the debate club. Marcus and Brian are already part of the basketball team from last year and Deq and Rio are interested in joining too, but as with most sports or performing societies, they have to complete the trials tomorrow. I walk through middle of an aisle, not really sure on what I'm looking for. It is weird because in my whole academic life I've always joined societies and taken part in extracurricular activities from rock-climbing to the choir, but now, I am lost. Everyone has scattered out discovering new activities. I turn to search for them, as I do, I see a huge golden man printed on a poster, his arms crossed. Oscar. Goosebumps wave over my body. The sign above it on top of a stall reads 'Drama Society'. I subconsciously walk towards the stall. Leaflets are laid out with photos of previous plays and performances. The stage looks huge as does the auditorium. The costumes and set look professional and the photos are from actual theatre performances showing crazy expressions, great characters and exaggerated posture. I mean why wouldn't there be, this university has its own acting school! I hear the girl behind the stall giving me some more information, but I am dazed in my own thoughts. I can feel the excitement turning into sweat. *Should I? Should I not?* A rush of emotions flow over my body, crashing at my heart. I locate the sign-up sheet, which has a gridded table printed on it, numbered one to thirty and on top, the heading reads, 'Actors/Actresses' up to number twenty six has been filled in and only four spaces remain. Beneath that are two more headings, 'Extras' and 'Tech' these had no numbers so I guess they have no limit. The extras section has only a few names but the tech section is heavily filled. I notice I suddenly have the pen in my hand. I just touch the paper with the tip when a group of four girls push in front of me. They laugh between themselves, loud and full of attitude. The one at the front has blondish, brown hair, she wears a skintight skirt and a small crop top finished with posh heels that must have been at least five inches high; if she wasn't wearing them she'd probably only be a little bit taller than me, but right now she looked like the Eiffel Tower; tall and beautiful and overpowering. Somehow she made her trendy but strange outfit look glamourous, with a milkshake in one hand.

"Girls! This is it! The drama society!" she says with

excitement but her confidence is way too much. Obviously she is the leader because the other girls are yelling her name and making supportive comments.

The leader introduces herself to the rep, her name is Betty Johnson. She will be studying Drama at the School of Acting. She too wants to be an actress and from my point of view she probably will. She has it all, but I've always been told that overconfidence is a defeater of confidence. The rep starts looking for the sign-up sheet. I take one last look at the empty spaces on the list and then hand it over. After all she did go through the struggle of auditioning for acting school and then was actually good enough to be selected. It is only fair for her and her three followers to fill the last spaces. As I hand the rep the sheet, Betty's rather short friend with shoulder length brown hair snatches it from my hands and then they all turn their attention to me. The other two girls; one as tall as Betty, fair with long red hair and the other tanned with bright blonde hair look me up and down. Their faces show disgust. They look at each other and sarcastically laugh. *At me?*

"Oh look! Four spaces!" says the short girl holding the sheet.

"Quick get the pen," says the bright blonde.

They sign the sheet in a hurry, while Betty's eyes stay fixed on me, she slyly glances back to check if her girls have signed it, once they have, her strong gaze is back on me. I try to avoid her eyes, I feel uncomfortable and am now getting defensive too…so I just stare back at her.

She finally opens her nude lips, "Oh I'm sorry, were you going to join the tech team?" she takes the sheet from her friend. "Give me that! Here you go," she hands the sheet to me with a pitiful smirk whilst turning to lead her girls away.

They leave and I am left holding the sheet with the 'Actor/Actresses' column now full.

"Would you like to join the tech team?" says the rep from behind.

Now that was genuine.

"No thanks," I put the sheet on the table. As I turn around,

I bump into Jen who stands right behind me. Before I can think of words and before she could ask me anything from the frown she wears, I'm relieved as Brian calls us for a tour around campus with the rest of our crew. I hurry along nervously and quickly trying to get away from Jen who follows behind me still frowning.

"So this area is the center of the university," Marcus begins the tour from where the fair is held. "We call it Centre Square or Clock Tower because of that," he points to a large tower with a clock on it. "And basically all the buildings surround this part. It is big, but there's shortcuts to each building through side roads, but be sure to look left and right when crossing. Oh and there's the student car park," he points to an outside carpark. "If any of you have a car or if you can actually afford the monthly parking charge because it is a rip off for rich people."

Brian continues from Marcus as we walk further down, "This building here is the School of Engineering and Applied Sciences, it is the biggest school in the university."

It is definitely grand and a mixture of new and old, modern and antique. It has quite a few entrances and exits and ramps to underground floors. Here, all the Engineering, Physics, Science and Astronomical Sciences take place. The building is connected to the School of Computer Sciences at one end and at the other end it is connected to the School of Medicine and Dentistry.

"Do you guys want to look around, they do have some pretty cool equipment in the labs underground?" Marcus asks.

"Yeah, the labs are awesome and the equipment is really expensive. Only students of this school are allowed down there. They have to scan their ID cards to get in, but it should be open to everyone for a taster today. Have you guys got your cards yet?" Brian asks me and Rio.

We both nod. The building is huge inside, the reception is spacious with benches and stools. Corridors spring left and right, there are lifts everywhere and it looks modern and neat. The lecture theatres are all sorts of sizes, some huge, other are small and some of the rooms are classrooms with tables and chairs. There are a few labs on each floor, people are in them wearing white coats, goggles and gloves, performing cool experiments. The underground laboratories are much bigger and they do have a lot of security, there are cameras everywhere! These labs have special underground entrances and tunnels where vehicles can drive in and bring goods to the store rooms and workshops. They really do have expensive material here for the engineering department and the equipment seems quite technical. I feel a little overwhelmed. This university has so much to offer! Rio is already touching things that are labelled, 'DO NOT TOUCH'. Models and prototypes of all sorts of projects are on display, in fact everyone was interested in seeing the workshops and labs even the non-science students which explains why it's really busy down here.

"Hey! Look! A space probe! Jen exclaims with excitement. We all take a good look at it. It is highly intricate and looks almost real... *it might be*. It's someone's final year Astronomy project. Jen glares at it lost in her own thoughts. I notice that she reads the accompanying information booklet thoroughly, then she softly touches the materials and moves the probe carefully to see every little detail. I'm surprised she knows what it's even called, though she did want to be an astronaut.

We move on, checking out the School of Medicine and Dentistry, 'The School of Rats' as Marcus calls it, because of the amount of dissections they have to do. Then the Business School, which is fancy and new, as is the School of Social Sciences. The Law School, on the other hand, is an old building, full of character, like a cathedral. The library is enormous and there are plenty of open places to study and chill with friends. There are cafés scattered around campus and a few canteens too, this literally feels like a mini city. Next to the library is the School of Languages and Arts, Jen and Brian's school, it is also quite traditional and old. We enter the building to show Jen around. We walk through reception and then pass a long corridor following Brian towards the classrooms. To my left, I catch a glimpse of what I wasn't hoping to see...*or was I?* Pristine, transparent double doors end the Languages area and above the doors a sign reads 'The School of Acting – All the World's a Stage', without realizing I'm already opening the doors and walking through. The hallways are lined with quotes, Shakespeare and photos of productions and plays. I look through the windows of the rooms as I walk by, there's not much in them, just lots of empty space waiting to be filled with movement and creativity. I walk past a door labelled 'Costumes and Props' and another labelled 'Tech'; both are locked. Around another corner and down a long corridor with a bar and coffee area on one side, I see huge doors and between them a large horizontal glass window. I peer through it. The School of Acting is remarkable, it's a theatre hall! A massive one! The one in the pictures at the fair but the photos do not do it justice! Many rows of seats stepping downwards lead to a lit up stage, bright and spacious with red curtains draped back. The current set seems to be post war and looks so professional that they must have spent lots of money on it. Students hang around on the stage, with scripts in their hands, chatting, reading and rehearsing. The delicate hairs at the back of my neck stand up, I am so happy and so overawed to see this that, it makes me feel sad.

"Woah! Damn! Actors have the sickest life ever!" Rio leans on the window and looks down in amazement.

I breathe out a laugh but I'm not happy. My laugh is sorrowful and my eyes are fixed sharp on the stage…where I belong.

CHAPTER FOUR

JENNIFER

Later that night, we decided to eat out and well, go out. After all it is fresher's week! We had a good dance and I have to say, the guys dance pretty well; Brian and Marcus seemed to be quite popular at the club and Rio was hitting on any girl he laid his eyes on. Kye's a quiet one but man she can move! She knows all of the coolest dance moves like the viral ones in memes! I'm more of a two-step dancer, but I still had a great time!

We get back at about four a.m., Lia had left earlier to go home. We are all pretty tired from the long day. The boys are out of it and head straight to bed.

After changing into our pajamas, I find Kye in the kitchen finding a midnight or early morning snack. She goes for the milk and I open up a pack of cookies, good thing we went grocery shopping together yesterday after meeting because students snack all the time.

"Tonight was fun!" Kye says as she pours milk into two glasses, "I've never been out before."

"Oh my God! Really? You cannot tell at all, girl your hips don't lie!" I say, surprised by the fact that this was her first time clubbing.

"Me? No, I'm not that good. I had to do a Latin dance in a play once so I just picked up some of the moves from there. And my brothers are always dancing around to those viral meme things and they force me to dance along too, so, yeah!" she bites into a cookie.

"Well, it looked awesome," I say taking a sip of milk.

The cold milk washes away my tiredness, I hear chatter and giggles coming from outside, we walk towards the balcony.

"Wow! It's almost five a.m. and people are still out," Kye says, as we carry out our milk and cookies through the double doors and out onto the deck.

The air is warm and the university is lit up. Small bulbs light up the garden blow. A few huddles of people walk along the paths. I soak in the view and breathe in uni life.

"How are you finding it so far?" Kye asks.

"I like it more than I thought I would," I reply. "I like the people, the place, I love the apartment! And the guys opposite are lovely too, though they are all guys."

"Ha! Yeah, but I guess, it's a good thing, lots of protection," Kye says.

I laugh, "Or none at all!" *Why would I even say that?* I think to myself after blurting it out like an idiot. Kye laughs with me anyway. There's no awkwardness between us, she gets my silly jokes.

"Speaking of the apartment, we need to decorate our rooms," she says.

"Oh yeah! We need to personalize them and funk them up," I begin to picture my room decorated to my taste. My brain quickly forms an image, "I need to have a huge poster of ...of..." I pause briefly and then spit something out, "...of Shakespeare..." I realize I'm getting carried away with my thoughts. *Shakespeare? Really?* That was the expression on Kye's face too.

She reads my mind, "You were going to say a rocket or the solar system or something weren't you?"

I keep quiet at my embarrassment and puff a smile.

My Friend's Dream

"Hey, that's fine by me Jen," Kye continues, "I would have a red carpet going through mine and a poster of the Hollywood sign."

"The red carpet would be cool. I'd have rocket ornaments in mine!" I dream.

"Yeah, and I would have an Oscar!"

"Oh, the famous golden naked man!" I say.

We laugh for a while until silence falls and neither of us know what to say next. Nothing I could think of really makes any sense to come after that. So I just finish off my milk.

Kye finally breaks the silence with a question I don't know how to answer, "Jen, you still want to be an astronaut don't you?"

I feel stupid, I want to say yes but I would sound like an idiot. Saying no would be lying and she is asking so sincerely that lying would be betraying the dream. *Why is it so damn hard to admit?* My brain and my heart fight between themselves; saying 'yes' would be stupid and would hurt me, but saying 'no' would kill me inside. No one has ever asked me that question before, not so sincerely. No one ever asked me what I wanted to be! I am taking such a long time to answer that actually saying 'no' now would be stupid. I look into Kye's eyes, which seem somewhat hopeful, trustworthy and as if they already know the answer, she's just waiting for confirmation. Words don't come out of my mouth, instead I just nod. I already trust Kye, we are going to live together for the next few years so she might as well know the truth. Kye doesn't react much, instead of surprise, I see understanding in her eyes… I see pain…a similar pain to mine… the pain of an uncontrollable dream. Her dream of becoming an actress. Strangely, I feel more comfortable – just knowing that someone is in similar shoes – I always thought I was the only one.

"And, you really want to be an actress, like really," I tell her. "And you're still going to try? You don't need qualifications for that," I answer my own question.

"I don't know," says Kye, sounding fed up of her dream. "I mean, I've been trying my whole life. Agencies have scammed me, I haven't been picked out from theatre shows and online auditions for movies have rejected me. Maybe now I should just concentrate on my degree," her voice shakes.

My frustration kicks in, "Yeah, so just concentrate on something you don't even want to do! Because that makes sense." And my sarcasm too.

"You're one to talk," Kye raises her eyebrows at me.

"My situation is different, I would have studied astrophysics if I passed the entry requirements. My grade in physics messed it up, my parents were breaking up at the time – it's not a big deal, it happens and everything's cool now. Anyway, I knew a 'C' grade wasn't good for university so I retook the test and got an 'A', but when I actually applied to universities I found out that they don't look at any retake grades, they only consider the first sitting grades."

"Ah, yeah you're right they changed the rule this year. Damn, that's annoying! I'm so sorry Jen. But, why did you chose literature? Why not something mathematical at least?"

"Well, I got really angry at the time and decided to go for the subject that I scored highest in which was English literature. The thing is Kye, I understand everything mathematical and scientific, I remember everything too, it's just that at that time with everything going on, I don't know what happened. It's like it wasn't meant to be."

"Have you asked the admissions office to see if they might be able to change your subject?" Kye asks.

"Four times! Email, calls, a letter and even face to face. They say that they can't break the rules," I shake my head in frustration. "Anyway, back to you, all actors face rejection at first and I don't care how stupid it sounds that you're at university, I want to know someone who's dream came true."

"Hey, you read my mind. I would so love to know that person too."

It's true, I have never met anyone who's dream has come true, it's always 'I *wanted* to be, *but*', there's always a *but*.

Kye looks towards the stars in in the sky, "You know what Jen, acting is so diverse, it's all in the imagination, I've always had these crazy imaginations and story ideas, some completely fictional to do with aliens and some very realistic, about life."

I smile as she speaks, interested in each and every plot she tells me. I picture a new world, a world of imaginations and stories – Kye's world.

"I had this idea of the sun reaching its red giant phase – as you would know – and then it gets closer to earth about to suck it in, ha! I also had an idea of a dance themed film based on flash-mobs and a mix of genres…" she continues with her adventurous ideas which range from fantasy to war. "I once created a film about two girls who get lost in an unknown forest and have to find diamonds and fight bad guys to get home – this was an imaginary game me and my friends used to play when we were like eight years old. The film was for a school project, I had never studied film or media, so I pretty much made it from research, wrote the script, directed it, edited it and acted in it. I remember my teacher telling me not to do it because the project too big but I proved her wrong of course and even got an 'A'."

"Woah woah woah, wait, you have got to show me this film!" I yell with excitement. "That's awesome, it takes so much courage to do something like that."

"It is way too embarrassing, the video and sound quality is shit and I didn't have the proper equipment-"

"I don't care, you're showing it to me. No excuses," I force.

"Alright! But I have to get to it first, it's on my dad's old computer at home. So you'll just have to wait… for now," Kye giggles.

"Man, a film, against your teacher, that's great!" I'm amazed, Kye seemed like a goody two shoes but I can totally see why she did this, it's her passion.

We continue to express ourselves, Kye tells me how she used to pretend she was a power ranger at school and I tell her how I used to wrap toilet paper around myself and then pretend I was an astronaut, I used so many roles of toilet paper, my mom was furious. Kye isn't surprised by my stupidity, instead she laughs and admires the fact that I had the imagination to do such a thing. She tells me how she *places* herself in films that she watches, she creates a new role (obviously to be played by her), she gives the character a personality, a name, dialogue and explains how they fit into the storyline, she places them in the movie and in each scene of where they would come in. In Pirates of the Caribbean she created a female pirate character, one of Jack's friends and previous servant of the Governor. In The Avengers she's an agent with extreme knife throwing and rope handling skills. In the Fast and Furious franchise she's Letty's younger sister – cheeky, feisty, strong, the glue that holds the team together. Her made up roles seem so real and are so well defined that I can actually picture each and every one of them, they all fit in just perfectly. She speaks with excitement and is lost in her own world of imaginations taking me with her, I can see into her imaginations the same way I see my own imaginations of being an astronaut. I am seeing a world outside ours.

"You're such a dreamer Kye," I place my hand on her shoulder and let out the most sincere smile I've ever let out, "I've never met a dreamer before."

Kye's smile fades and she places a hand on my shoulder looking deep into my imaginations, "How badly do you want to be an astronaut?" she questions.

"It's the only thing I want. Kye, if I could just wear that suit once, sit in a rocket, see Earth as a globe, see the universe above and do one spacewalk – my life would be complete." My voice shakes as my honesty spills out, "I'm scared of getting old without my dream coming true, I'd rather die before I see the end of my hope." My eyes fill with tears and so do Kye's. I don't mean to sound depressing to someone I've just met, but I feel comfortable talking to Kye and never have I ever expressed myself so clearly to anyone before – especially verbally – the only other thing that knows me properly is my diary.

I take a moment and then try to joke my way out of the tears, "I wanted to be Neil Armstrong but I'm going to end up being Shakespeare." I see Kye blinking tears away too, "Kye, why don't you still do it?" I ask her.

"Do what? Act?" her voice sounds like an engine running out of gas, "If only God would help me," she begs looking up and then around as if calling God himself.

"Do you believe in God?" I ask.

"Yeah, well...I have faith in him. He's got the controller, he's the only one who can make my dreams come true. I talk to him just like this, I don't get much of a reply but I believe he's everywhere, watching, listening... just not listening to me... yet!" she cries, smiling like a child talking to the air around her.

"You have faith?" I'm intrigued, I've never thought of God in the scenario of my dreams but the way Kye is talking around her makes me feel a little mystical.

"Yes I do, I think faith and hope are the two most important things in surviving life. Faith gives us hope and hope keeps us going." says Kye.

"So you are a dreamer and a believer, yet you're still planning of letting go of your dream?" I question her. I am confused, her thoughts and words motivate me, but here, she is the one backing down. "Kye, what you just said and the ideas you have, prove that you can be an actress. It might take longer than getting an agent or being *noticed* but you'll get there eventually!" I feel a rush of excitement as an idea crosses my mind.

Kye squints at me, "What do you mean? And what do you mean *eventually*? I don't want to begin my career in movies playing someone's grandma."

"Well, we better get started then!" I yell. With Kye still confused I begin to explain my brilliant idea, "Look, you have these amazing ideas and I study literature, in other words story writing," I focus on Kye with all seriousness. She raises an eyebrow. I expand, "So, I will help you write your ideas in the form of a story, a book, or even scripts, which we'll publish! And then like a lot of books nowadays, hopefully some producer will turn your book into a film and then ta da!" I spread my arms, "You're an author and an actress of your own book slash movie!"

Kye's confusion turns into a thought, "Really?" is all she manages to say.

"Look, I know how much you want to be an actress and I just think now that you're here and while you've got the chance, you should try it out. You've tried everything else, right? So you might as well try this too," I beg. I really want this to work for her.

An impulsive sparkle lights Kye's eyes, "Fine!" she says with excitement. "Let's do it, but I warn you I'm no good at writing so you have to help me."

"Yes of course I will Kye! And so will *he*," I look around holding my palms up indicating her God. "It is like destiny intended for this to happen; me studying literature, you studying physics and us meeting-"

"Destiny?" Kye questions with another glint of energy, this time she squints in thought, a cheeky thought. She looks at me.

"What?"

"If it is destiny, then surely I can help you become Buzz Lightyear!" Kye exclaims.

"Yeah. Kye, I actually *do* need a degree and a certain amount of knowledge and experience to do that." I say.

Kye reminds me of how well I did in my physics retake and I see the whole fate situation before me, but I actually need to study some sort of science to even think of realistically becoming an astronaut.

"Okay Jen, you are going to do two degrees," Kye explains.

I'm baffled by the idea. As if doing one degree isn't hard enough already.

She continues, "Most of my physics classes are mixed with the astro-science classes, so you are going to independently study astronomy, astrophysics or whatever-"

"Astrophysics," I nod with all certainty. "Astrophysics."

"Yes, astrophysics, by attending lectures and learning independently and then with my help, you'll take exams and you'll graduate. I'm sure you won't even need my help much, you know it all anyway and you'll understand it when you study it."

I like the idea, but how is that going to be possible without being enrolled on the course, I hope Kye has a solution to this, and she does.

"Don't worry about how you'll sit exams," she says. "We all have to register for our examinations online anyway and you can register for the astrophysics ones as well as your literature ones, you only need your student number!" Kye's excitement is overflowing, it's amazing how much joy we're getting from carving each other's paths towards our dreams.

"I know it's going to be hard, I know," Kye controls the excitement but doesn't lose determination. "The science school here have so many internships and work experience opportunities from people like NASA! You could get selected *if* you study the subject. You have to be in it to win it," she insists.

I like Kye's keenness and she's quite right - *in it to win it* - that clicks a thought in my mind. Kye didn't join the drama society. They have all sorts of opportunities like performing at top theatres where you could possibly get seen by directors and producers. I have a deal to make.

"Alright!" I say. "But on one condition."

"Condition?" Kye's eyes narrow.

"I'll study astrophysics and literature and you'll write your stories, but, you have to join the drama society."

Kye closes her eyes and sighs but before she can reject the offer I persuade her.

"Like you said, you have to be in it to win it. You could get selected too! That Blondie and her Co. pushed in front of you, I saw, but who cares, they can make adjustments."

"Blondie?" Kye looks surprised.

"What? I can say it. I'm blonde. I wouldn't mind if you said it too."

Kye giggles and then takes a moment to think, she opens her eyes and then, "Deal!"

We shake hands and embrace each other. The deal is sealed, on faith. We have the drive to make each other's dream come true. I feel happy and overwhelmed to have met a friend who feels what I do, who dreams like I do, who is actually pushing me to achieve my dreams rather than the general push of 'get a good job, good money, live well'. I need her as much as she needs me to get our dreams. It really is as if fate has planned this. We are both average girls, leading normal lives and we have decent middle class families. There is no sympathy towards us and we don't need it. We really do have everything yet there is something missing, a *want* not a *need*. Sometimes the things we *want* in life are the things we have to chase and with the sun rising we are just about to do that. This is the beginning of the journey to our dreams.

CHAPTER FIVE

KYARA

After a rather crazy night I wake up at midday from the noise of chatter in the park coming through my window. I wonder if Jen remembers our deal or whether it was just a thing of the moment and in real life motivation only lasts a few minutes.

"Kye!" Jen bursts out of her room and into mine, "Come on we're going to sign you up to the drama society!" She opens the curtains blinding me with the sunlight and then heads into the bathroom.

I am relieved to find her motivation still at one hundred percent. Nervous but excited, I get out of bed and get ready for the day. I style my hair in half a braid and then braid Jen's hair, we eat cereal in the kitchen as the boys join us wearing shorts and vests ready for sport.

"Are you guys going to the gym?" asks Jen.

"Nope, Deq and Rio have basketball tryouts today and Marcus and I are club members so we're heading down too" says Brian. "Do you want to come Jen?" he teases her as she pulls a face at him.

"Oh nice, speaking of societies, I err..." I make a start, but feel way too uncomfortable to finish so I look at Jen for help.

"Kye wants to join the drama society," Jen completes my sentence taking a spoonful of cornflakes into her mouth.

The boys look at me and then at each other in surprise.

"I knew you were a drama queen!" exclaims Rio.

I giggle shaking my head, "Rio, that's not a good thing and I'm serious, I really want to join but the spaces got filled up yesterday, I saw the list," I look at Brian and Marcus for some advice.

"Well, that's not good. I mean, usually if the lists are full they don't take on any more people," says Marcus, still trying to think of a solution.

"There's got to be something we can do!" Jen puts her spoon down, "Kye's different, she's a scientist not a typical drama student, do they not want that mix up and diversity or whatever?"

"That's a fair point, and you are like… tanned…you know…for diversity…not an all-white cast," adds Deq.

"Yes, that's true. You should ask and tell them what you study, they might change their minds and let you join," says Marcus.

"Who do I ask?"

"I know a guy who might be able to help," Brian says, "Dwaine. The president of student activities and societies."

"Dwaine – the basketball captain?" asks Rio.

"Yep, he likes having authority," nods Marcus. "But he's alright."

"Yeah and coincidently his girlfriend is chair of the drama society," Brian adds. "You can come down with us now if you want, he'll be at the tryouts."

"I'll just go grab my bag," says Jen cheekily nudging Brian with a grin. "I would love to come along, thanks."

I agree to that offer. I feel a little relieved that the guys know this Dwaine guy, but his grand authority makes me nervous.

* * *

We take a short walk through the colorful gardens in the heat of the sun and approach the sports grounds – a huge outdoor basketball court lies in front of us. Next to that is a tennis court and then a football pitch. Behind is a building, which I'm assuming holds the shower rooms and indoor sports courts. All the sports fields are busy with people, there must be tryouts for quite a few different sports today. There are cheerleaders doing their thing, boys and girls throwing, catching and kicking, people cheer and shout. It's a vibrant environment. I like it. We make our way onto the basketball court, there are guys of all builds on the court warming up and chatting. Some are muscular, some are tall, some are confident, others seem nervous; this is their audition and I know that feeling.

Rio and Deq grab a ball and start warming up, Marcus starts mingling with old friends while we follow Brian to Dwaine, the president.

"Dwaine!" Brian calls.

Dwaine turns around, a tall, slim man, with dark skin, his every muscle toned in the number twenty three vest he wears accompanied by a bandana tied around the circumference of his head. His jawline is a piece of art and his eyes are bright, his hair is styled into braided cornrows. He has a striking confidence about him. He smiles whilst walking towards Brian.

"How you been man?" Brian asks.

"Brian my man!" he calls shaking Brian's hands as they bump off each other's shoulders. "I'm blessed, I'm blessed. How are you?"

Brian goes into a quick catch up conversation and then introduces us, "This is Kye and this is Jen," Brian points at us. "They're freshmen. This is my man Dwaine, the president of student activities."

We shake hands. He seems nice.

"Basically Kye wanted to ask-"

"Brian!" someone calls from behind hitting him with a ball.

"Ow! Toby!" Brian calls bouncing the ball back to this Toby guy, he jogs toward him and gives him a manly hug, while Jen and I are left awkwardly looking up at Dwaine.

"He was saying you wanted to ask me something?" Dwaine

breaks the silence with his deep voice.

I can feel my heartbeat in my throat and my cheeks giving off heat. *Why am I so nervous!?* "Yeah…actually…err I wanted to join the… err… Drama Society…" I halt.

"And…?" Dwain asks for more information, although I feel like he's really not cooperating.

"And… at the fair all the places filled up, so I couldn't sign up." I feel embarrassed and as if all eyes are on me.

Dwaine frowns to the point where his forehead wrinkles up, "What makes you think I can get you on the team, I mean signed up?" he says.

I'm already nervous and embarrassed and now I'm being questioned, "You're the president of all student activities." A slightly different me is now speaking, my face turns red as I try to get my point across, I can feel sweat everywhere.

"Yes I am, but we have rules bae, I can't just let you sign up out of nowhere," he gestures with his hands making him look more confident and overpowering.

I have no come back, the sweat is turning into a drench and I just keep telling myself to calm down. *You want to be an actress? Stop being so damn awkward.*

Jen butts in, "Hey! Dwaine! Listen, rules are there to be broken and Kye is different, she's not studying drama like everyone else in that society, she's studying Physics, a science. Don't you guys want that whole diversity thing? Isn't that why we have societies – so you can do something other than your subject?" Jen makes a good point. "She wants to be a Hollywood actress," and then she completely ruins it.

Dwaine is a poised man, he's not shocked by Jen's sudden outrage, nor is he amused at my vulnerability and craziness of becoming a Hollywood actress that Jen just exposed, he simply frowns in thought.

"Well, why don't you study drama or go to acting school if you want to be an actress?" he says looking down at me. He doesn't sound sarcastic, he seems to be straight up truthful. He's actually being so genuinely straightforward, that it's hard to hate him even though he's not helping. But that is a question that haunts me and I am sick of people asking me it.

"Acting is not something you study, you just do it. All you need is an opportunity and luck maybe." My cheeks burn and right now, if I make a fist with my palms, surely sweat would drip from it like water from a wet cloth. However, I stand my grounds. I continue to argue my point before I lose the confidence, "I guess you want to be a basketball player…captain?" I step forward, "Isn't that why you joined the team? Do you *study* basketball?" I make my point.

Dwaine laughs, thoughtfully, his hands on his chin. I pretty much offended the guy that I came to, to ask for help. So stupid.

"Woah, Okay, okay, you are right, anyone can be an actress, but for this…" he points at the basketball hoop. "For this you need skill and training, acting is easy, shooting a hoop, now that's hard, you have to know how to do it, you have to be tall."

Did he just insult my height? This guy is now annoying me. I laugh spitefully, "Firstly, acting is a skill and secondly it works the same way as a scout *picking* you out of a *game*. Actors also get *scouted* from *plays* or *films*. Like I said, it is an opportunity. Oh and by the way, you don't have to be tall to shoot a hoop." I roll my eyes.

Dwaine pouts his lips and raises his eyebrows, "Err yeah you do."

"Err no you don't!" He annoys me to the point that I now imitate his gestures and his voice without even realizing.

Jen laughs behind me but she soon stops when we realize that everyone is staring at us. Balls are no longer bouncing and the chatter has disappeared.

"I'll tell you what," says Dwaine acknowledging the audience we have created.

I look at Jen anxiously.

"You shoot one hoop… one hoop…and I myself, will take you to the drama society," he smirks. "What do you say?"

What the heck have I just got myself into? This is typical of my kind of luck. I have to fight for everything! Absolutely everything.

The pettiest of challenges always come and block my path and I always struggle before overcoming them. To top it off basketball really isn't my sport. *This is just brilliant, thank you very much God. What the heck are you doing up there!* I feel awkward standing in front of the audience. I don't usually feel awkward in front of an audience, but this is different. *Don't back down Kye.* I could say no and go away looking like a fool and then will probably cry later on, or I could shoot, miss, look like a fool and then still cry later on. Either way I'm going to look like a fool and cry, so I might as well try it. I feel so scared right now, that I begin to act.

"One hoop?" I confirm pretending to be confident.

"You've got one shot," Dwaine's gestures the number one with his forefinger. "If you miss, no drama."

"Fine." The word slips from my tongue and the crowd begin cheering.

Jen takes my arm and pulls me back slightly, "Kye, can you do this?" she whispers.

I just stand still and quiet in disbelief of what is happening in my first few days here. I'm not that tall, I definitely don't look sporty in my ankle boots, leggings and checked shirt. I don't look girly either, I look like a nerd. Now, I'm more afraid of being embarrassed than not getting into the drama society. I cannot believe what I've got myself into!

"Yo! Ball!" shouts Dwaine.

Someone throws him a ball.

"It's all yours," he places the ball in my hands. "Win or lose, its life. I'm glad you're up for the challenge, Kye." His voice softens and he moves me back a step and into position. "From where you are, we call it a three pointer. One shot, Kye."

I look at the black stripes on the orange ball and then at the net, far... far away. I'm already popular now, thanks to this, so now it's about my reputation. People stare at me intrigued, even Rio, Brian, Deq and Marcus are staring. Now is the time to become the cool, popular girl or the idiot, wannabe actress. I look at Jen, then the ball and then the net squinting as the sun catches my eyes. I look above the net to the sky, *God help me please.* I swing my arm right over my head and squat before a slight jump letting go of the ball, not even being able to see it because of the blinding sun. I wait for the embarrassment to come. The orange ball swings straight through the net not even touching the rim or the board! I did it! The crowd go mad! The guys are shocked. I am shocked! But I hold my real expressions inside. I act cool and smirk at Dwaine. Then I look behind at Jen with wide eyes gasping for a breath with total astonishment.

"Thank you God!" I mime, closing my eyes.

Jen runs up to me with a hug and whispers in my ear, "Beginners luck."

"Fricking hell," I whisper back in a shaky voice before putting on a feisty look and turning to face my audience.

The boys run over to me praising my fluke – which deep down, they all know of. I catch Dwaine in the corner of my eye who is pleasantly surprised and claps sincerely.

"Nice shot," he compliments.

"Thanks," I reply.

"You know, you're not the kind of girl I thought you were."

I laugh, "Well, never judge a book by its cover."

"I won't. You're alright Kye, you're alright," he nods to himself, "I'm glad you got it in. The drama society have their introductory meeting on Thursday. Meet me in the Centre Square, outside the main building at four p.m., I'll take you there."

"Thanks Dwaine," I blush as my nerves calm down. My body relaxes. I overcame the obstacle. I don't know why God makes me do such things, I mean what the heck!

Brian pushes forward, "Yeah okay, you're welcome! Are you girls done now? Shall we start the trials?" he yells as people cheer him on.

One step at a time.

CHAPTER SIX

JENNIFER

"Kye, are you sure about this?" I ask from my room with the door slightly open, changing out of my pajamas. This is not something I planned on doing, ever, but it has to be done.

"Not really," Kye replies sarcastically popping her head through her doorway while she makes her bed. "It'll be fine Jen, there's like two hundred people in my lectures, no one knows anyone and no one will even notice. Trust me," she reassures.

"You wouldn't do it," I mumble.

Kye overhears me, "You're right, I wouldn't, I've always been a *good* girl, but right now, we have made a deal, so the choices we make from now on will be different from the normal crap. So right now, in our situation, yes I would."

"Would what?" Brian bursts through the front door with Rio trailing behind. "Would what?" he repeats.

They walk down our corridor.

"Wait!" I yell nervously toppling over my jeans, "I am changing!" I slam the door shut. I hear Kye and Rio gigging, "Man! Can't you guys knock?"

"Well, you're the one changing with the door open," Brian

yells back at me through my door.

He is such an idiot. I shout back at him, "I mean the front door you ass!"

I finish changing in a rush and pull the door open finding Brian imitating me in front of Kye. Brian is against everything I say and he is getting on my last nerves. He stops the act when he sees me glaring at him in anger. Lia, Marcus and Deq knock at the door and then walk in. I gesture to Brian, indicating what a knock sounds like.

"Anyway, 'would do what?'" Rio comes back to the point.

I look at Kye looking for an answer. *Should we tell them about our deal?* We both know we're stupid but they don't.

"Hurry up, we have to go to class," Lia insists.

"Oh yeah, Jen I can walk you to your class, I'm going the same way," Brian teases me.

I blurt it all out, "No thanks, I'm not going to that class. I'm going to Kye's class."

"What?" Deq asks me.

"What?" Rio asks Kye.

"What?" Kye asks me again.

I give Kye a look and then explain the whole situation as quickly as possible to our friends. We get asked a lot of questions and we try our best to answer them but everyone is still muddled and slightly amused.

"So let me get this straight," Rio says leaning on the wall in thought, "Kye's going to study physics and somehow take part in theatre stuff and become an actress. Jen's going study literature just to stay in this university and then you're going to sneakily study astrophysics, get a degree and become an astronaut," he finishes and folds his arms.

It sounds terrible when someone says it back like that.

Kye awkwardly nods.

"That's the plan," I say.

"You guys made a deal?" asks Deq.

We both nod. Silence.

"That's not going to last," Brian breaks it.

"Even if it did, how are you going to pay for those extra exams? And Kye, theatre and acting training can cost a lot too you know," Rio makes a good point.

"We'll find work, get jobs," Kye finally says something.

Marcus sighs, "I see what you guys are trying to do and I understand what you want, but I agree with Brian, you'll do it for a few weeks and then you'll forget about it. Trust me. You might as well not get your hopes up. That's the reality. You don't want to lose out on your current degree if things go wrong. Then you'll lose out on both your education and your dreams," he tries to put some sense into us.

But I am not willing to make sense of things right now, "Guys, we are going to do this. I mean, we don't really know each other that well, but thanks for the advice." It is weird saying that, it feels like we've known each other for a lot longer, but that's the truth.

"You two have also only just met!" adds Brian, scowling at me.

"Guys," Kye steps in, smiling, "It's not about how long we've known each other, this is about opportunity, this is our last chance and a good one too, we've found a path, one that's a little odd, yes, but it's a path, and we've been searching for one for years, so we have to take it." She speaks softly yet persuasively, "We're young, we're students, and we don't have responsibilities like children to feed or a mortgage to pay, so if we want to do something for ourselves then this is the right time. We might never get a chance again. When we look back at our lives twenty years from now, I don't want to think, 'I wish I'd done this, because maybe I'd be in a different position now.' No! I want to be sure that I've tried everything and have taken every opportunity, so that when I look back at my life, I have no regrets. Besides, what do we have to lose?"

Well, Kye did that brilliantly. There's silence in the room. She really does make you think and creates that movie kind of atmosphere, I can hear some kind of sad-ish motivational music playing in the back of my head.

"Okay fair point but what if you fail and not graduate

because of this... deal?" Rio asks.

"Well, like Michael Jordan says; 'I can accept failure, but I can't accept not trying.'"

The boys all look at Kye in awe.

"I have two brothers," she explains.

Kye makes another straight to the point, point. She is either amazing at motivational speeches or a damn good actress. Everyone is in deep thought, warming up to the idea, Rio and Lia are smiling already.

"Literature and Physics are our backup. We won't fail. That's what you guys will help us with. Then we will be able to pay our mortgages, feed our children and help our husbands." I close the discussion with a light laugh.

They all agree and giggle with some conviction and then we leave for our lectures and my first astrophysics class.

* * *

We walk down the long hallway, through two sets of large double doors until we reach the lecture theatre. Kye had told me to act *normal*, I suppose the *acting* part is easier for her, but I think I'm doing pretty well. People wait around the doorway, some in groups chatting, some daydreaming, and some staring at their phones. Kye introduces me as an astrophysics student to a few people she had met at the introductory sessions – that feels good.

We enter a lecture theatre that can easily seat around two hundred people. We take our seats near the back in the middle of the row. People have their books and laptops out. Kye pulls out a notebook, a fancy calculator and a textbook. I take out my notebook and pencil case. Soon, everyone is seated but the chatter remains loud. The door opens again. An old man, around the age of sixty walks in. He has a slight hunchback and holds a black brief case. His clothes are a combination of neutral colors such as creams and browns. He places the briefcase down on the desk at the font of the room, pushes his round glasses up and brushes his grey, turning white, wispy hair back with his hands. He takes a few minutes to sort out his desk and then stands looking up at everyone. He waits for silence. I'm nervous, I know my cheeks are flushes like a red apple in a basket of green apples. Silence finally falls. He then hands a sheet of paper to a student at the front and asks him to pass it around for us to write our names on it.

"Professor Kyle Kennedy," he says in an old, wise but strong voice whilst writing it on the board. "You may call me Professor or Dr. Kennedy. I have been teaching here for thirty years and have completed three PhD's in astrophysics, mathematics and cosmology. You will see me quite a bit during your time here, as I teach quite a few modules and I am the dean of this school. You may be studying slightly different subjects but all your first year classes consists of the same content, hence this will be your class for the year. In your second and final year only a few modules very specific to your subject will be studied separately depending on your subject." He pronounces every syllable in a posh tone, "You have all chosen tough subjects therefore I expect you to be the brightest students of your entire generation. I expect you to work hard and be proactive and to read and research instead of watching online TV shows."

I think he tried to be funny, but his face is still serious and so is the class.

"All assignments are to be handed in on time, if not before the deadline. Answers in exams are to be clear and well written with no excuses. I will not waste my marking time trying to decipher terrible handwriting."

I feel scared, it feels like he's only looking at me when he talks.

He continues, "There will be plenty of opportunities to gain internships from various companies and even to secure graduate work throughout your time here, but that shall depend on you as an individual as the competition is extremely tough. You are all mature adults but I will make clear to you my two rules; no chatting and most definitely no use of phones. I will learn your names but for now forgive me if I pronounce them incorrectly."

My heart skips a few beats.

"Any questions?" he asks.

My Friend's Dream

Silence.

"Alright. Welcome to Introductory Physics," he says, turning to his notes neatly laid out on the desk. "Now, a top grade question to test your abilities; what are Kepler's three laws of planetary motion?"

Silence, no hands.

He looks around, then pushes his glasses down and randomly reads from a piece of paper, "Ki… Kyara Averoni," he moves his eyes scanning the room. Kye's eyes widen, she flushes red and sinks into her seat.

"Miss Averoni?" he asks again.

Kye looks at me thinking *shit* and then slowly raises her hand.

"Ah yes, Miss Averoni, do you know what they are?"

Kye seems lost for words, she 'errs' and then tries to make a thinking face. She doesn't know the anser. But I do! I know exactly what he is asking and have already finished writing the laws down in my notebook. I nudge her as she's about to give up, I point at my writing, tapping on the paper. She needs to trust me. Kye looks down, she hesitates for a few seconds looking confused and then reads it out.

"The first law…" she begins reading from the notes I point at with my pen, "is the law of orbits – all planets move in elliptical orbits with the sun at one focus. The second law…" her eyes widen, she pauses to understand what I've written, "…the second law is the law of areas – A equals L over two M ($A = \frac{L}{2M}$), and the third is the law of periods where T squared equals open bracket four, pie squared over G, M, close bracket r cubed ($T^2 = \left(\frac{4\pi}{GM}\right)r^3$)…. I think." She finishes nervously.

"Well, that is correct!" Dr Kennedy acknowledges her with a nod. "It can also be…" he continues to explain the concept further.

Kye sits back in shock. She turns to me and mouths 'what the heck' with a wide eyed smile. I just wink at her.

The lecture is intriguing and I know a lot of the concepts already from my own reading and research. I'm surprised that I actually am on the same level of these physics geeks, if not higher. Maybe it is meant to be, maybe I will become an astronaut, yes I will...

CHAPTER SEVEN

KYARA

It is Thursday afternoon, I leave early since I have to walk down the four flights of stairs and then all the way to Centre Square, plus I need to make a good impression, after all Dwaine is breaking the rules for me. It's a busy afternoon with lots student activities going on. The boys have gone to basketball practice after making the team, Jen is in the apartment catching up on the literature class she missed and Lia is also in our apartment doing some reading. It is now one forty two p.m. and Dwaine is not here, I suppose I am early. I stand for a while outside the main building, then awkwardly sit on the edge of the fountain. I try to look busy on my phone swiping across the screen but honestly I have nothing to do on it. It's almost two p.m. and he still hasn't arrived, these eighteen minutes feel like eighteen hours. Then, some thoughts cross my mind; *what if he's forgotten? Or worse, what if he was lying?* I feel uneasy and as if the passersby are staring at me, giggling at me being fooled, but I know it's just my brain playing games with me.

Someone taps me on my shoulder, "Kye," it is Dwaine.

Thank God for that, now everyone around me seems normal.

"Hey!" I say.

"Sorry I'm a little late, basketball introductions ran over. I hope I didn't keep you waiting too long."

"Oh no, its fine, I just got here," I lie, leaning casually on the fountain wall.

"Cool. Shall we?" he asks.

I nod and follow him. Dwaine has stood up to the genuine guy expectation I had of him after our first meeting. He's still confident and true to his words. As we walk, I notice he dresses well and blends the old traditional menswear with the new *swag*. He is most definitely a popular guy, he greets many people along the way with poise and I feel popular just walking alongside him – the complete opposite of what I was feeling five minutes ago and a few people if point me out as the 'basketball actress girl'. Wow, things spread quickly around university. We end up at the same theatre hall that I had seen on the tour with the guys. I am late – and that was something I hate being and therefore I never am – but this is different so I try not to think about it too much. We walk through the doors at the back of the auditorium and then down the steps. As I follow Dwaine, I see the girls who took the last four places in the drama society, they stand tall in their crop tops and made up faces with the yellow blonde one, Betty, still clearly in charge. Dwaine leads me onto the stage. I take a good look around. It is huge! The audience seats look grand from here. The stage lights are on and I feel that power, that energy, that special force of air gliding over me. I'm in the right place. People chatter amongst themselves, most glance at me once and then continue talking as they anxiously make new friends. It looks like they haven't officially started yet. Dwaine walks towards a tall, black girl with beautiful frizzy locks of hair. She sees us and then comes toward us walking sarcastically straight past Dwaine and greeting me with a handshake.

"You must be Kye, right?" she says.

"Hi, yes I am," I say.

"I'm Sheera, Dwaine told me all about you and we don't usually allow this, but since you put Dee in his place, we can make exceptions," she sarcastically nudges Dwaine.

Sheera and Dwaine make a perfect match. She is simply gorgeous, a natural beauty, and she seems like a really nice person too and Dwaine is a tall, confident, handsome man with a great, genuine personality.

"Yeah yeah okay, she's just jealous because she couldn't shoot a hoop," he tells me laughing, "Well, I'll leave you guys to it."

"Alright, see you later," says Sheera cuddling Dwaine.

He kisses her on the head and then makes his way back up the stairs saying, "Have fun Kye!"

"Thanks!" I call out in appreciation.

"So you want to be an actress?" she asks knowingly as she walks to a desk at the side of the stage.

I honestly did not want that to spread and right now it is spreading like fire in dry grass. To try and calm the truthful rumor down, I reply saying, "Yeah, I mean who doesn't?"

Really not the best of casual jokes to be making when I've broken the rules to be standing here, but Sheera smiles and agrees with my joke. She is mature and sensible and I feel protected by her leadership of this society, especially as those girls – *Blondie and co* – have now noticed my presence and have begun to obviously gossip about me.

Sheera calls everyone to sit in a circle and begins introductions, she introduces herself first with her name, her favorite play and the type of acting course she is studying. There are lots of freshmen and women and a few people from Sheera's year. Most people seem humble as we go round the circle until it is Blondie's turn.

"Hi, I'm Betty Johnson," she says flicking her golden hair back while pouting. "My favorite play has to be all of the ones that I have been in," she smiles as we all giggle, "Oh and I'll be studying drama at the acting school."

Everyone here was from either the acting, media or film school. Lastly, my turn approaches, time to break the trend.

"Hi..." my voice shakes, I control it and get it over with

quickly. "I'm Kyara. My favorite play is The Lion King and I study physics."

Murmurs and gasps fill the air, some surprised expressions and some confused. Betty mockingly laughs with her three followers of which; the short one with brown hair was Maya – she studies acting with Betty, the red haired one was Abbey – she studies dance and acting in a combined honors and the light blonde was Ellen – she studies Film and Theatre. I smile at the surprise in the room as people begin to seem more interested in my choice rather than being disturbed by it.

Sheera takes over, "Cool, thanks guys! So this society is one of a kind. It is fun but take it seriously when it comes to auditions and rehearsals because our school has a reputation for itself in the industry, a good one too. Before we start with some traditional drama games, I have some important information to tell you. Next month we will be holding auditions for our annual play and this is a big deal because we do invite casting directors from the movie industry to watch it therefore you could get selected for something if they see potential!"

Casting directors! Thank God I got the ball through the hoop! And thank Jen for forcing me to do this! There are whispers of excitement around the stage.

Sheera continues, "Exciting right! So if you would like to audition then we'll be giving out scripts next week, read them thoroughly and practice! Because there will be a panel of judges who will decide on which role you will get and whether you will be part of the ensemble or whether you will play an individual role. Oh and the judges are tough! I'm an assistant judge but I don't get much of a say. Backstage people, you need to make a portfolio if you don't already have one to show the judges if you want to be part of the crew. Rehearsals will start soon after the auditions and we will be showcasing at the end of the year, which if you think about it, it isn't far away, take out the holidays and breaks and we're what, like six or seven months away? So don't be lazy!"

This is an opportunity of a life time! I can feel the excitement in my heart, I look up subtly, *Thanks for this opportunity God! Please help me stand out in front of these industry casting directors!* I need a good role first. I need to brush up on my acting. I can't believe this is what the society can get us, I am so glad I joined! *Maybe this is my time?* I'm thrilled but my competition is tough and I can see it already.

"Alright! Stand up! Let's get started!" yells Sheera as someone hits the music from behind.

Maybe this is how it's going to happen. Maybe this is how I'll become an actress.

CHAPTER EIGHT

KYARA

The audition day came fast. I prepared what I could and gave more time to that than I did to physics. I want to get a really good role that helps me stand out, I need to make statement as I'm the odd one of the society, a *geek*. I had been learning my lines with everyone so they had their hopes up too and now I have to live up to it.

Jen and Brian walk me to the audition, on the way Jen spots Betty driving a white car into the expensive car park that the guys were telling us about on the tour. Of course she can afford the parking fees and of course she drives into university. I ask Jen and Brian to leave halfway so that I could get focused and so that it doesn't look like I'm being dropped off by my parents. Sheera is at the door of the theatre, she signs us in one by one. The stage is set and the lights are on. There's a couple of people dotted around the auditorium and a panel of judges sit in the front row. We walk on to the stage in single file and line up. The judges introduce themselves in turn consisting of; the head professor of the School of Acting, a popular theatre director, the script writer and the manager of the costume department. Without saying much more they take their seats and we begin.

My turn to audition was somewhere in the middle. I was a little shaky but I kept telling myself that this is what I want, so I went out and just gave it my best. I got no comments from anyone after my audition, we simply left once our audition was over. One thing I realized in the waiting room is that the more you really want something and the more it means to you, the more nervous it makes you and the more chances you have to mess it up. Whereas when you're not really bothered about something you tend to just go there with no nerves and get the job done. It's an ironic part of our nature.

* * *

Later that evening we're all called back to find out which parts we've been cast. I stand next to my new drama friend Jake, he is a nice guy and wants to be an actor but he prefers theatre to film. To be honest drama is one of those classes where you pretty much get to know everyone, up close in just a few days since we're always sharing stories and sharing space, lifting each other up and forming one body. There's minimum personal space in acting and performance, everything is just out there and for that you have to be confident with yourself. Most people are pleasant and I am actually popular being the only scientist. But then you always have the odd few who seem to feel more superior than others. We follow Sheera in and stand in a line on the stage opposite the judges.

The head judge begins to speak, "Welcome, now we haven't had much time to decide on who plays who, but I am sure we have made the right decisions." She walks from side to side, "First of all, I would like to emphasize just how important this play is, not only is it fun but for some of you this could be an opportunity of a life time! Casting directors will be watching and even a few agents, so make the most of it, represent yourselves and our university. Practice, be on time and attend every rehearsal no matter how big or small your role."

There is some mumbling however surprisingly Betty is silent, she's focused and really *really* wants a good shot at this.

"Now onto the parts…" says the head of the school of acting. "Starting with the leads, the lead female role of Natasha goes to…"

Numbness fills the air around me, silence fills the auditorium. It feels humid as my heart races to find breath. Here we go…

"… Betty Johnson!"

My heart takes a steep drop, Betty's reaction is composed as she flicks her hair back looking at her besties though you can tell she is relieved and proud. I on the other hand, am disappointed in myself, I really wanted the lead. *I thought this was my time God?* There's still a few decent supporting roles left, so I listen for my name carefully. The judges assign the parts and I don't hear my name. A traffic of thoughts cross my mind; *my skin is tanned, my hair is black, I'm short, maybe I'm not pretty enough, she's tall, pretty, blonde and white…*

"And the maid will be played by Kyara Averoni," the head's voice reaches my ears.

Maid!? What the heck? God seriously? I stand there in shock. I didn't even know there's a maid in the play. Maya laughs out loud while Abbey pinches her to be quiet. Betty smirks making eye contact with me.

"You have a long monologue, so good luck!" The judge says. She reads out the final few roles and then heads off.

A monologue?

I know what that is but I've never performed one before. *How long is it? A paragraph or two? Is it an emotional one? It must be, they all are! Is it just one monologue?* We sit down to get familiar with the play as Sheera hands out the full and finalized scripts. As soon as I get one, I rush through the pages to find my lines, as does everyone else, flipping from beginning to end and back again. About half way through the play I finally find my character – *The Maid* – and underneath are my lines, which continue on for two whole pages! I take a gulp, this is theatre, not film! I actually have to learn all these lines by heart and there's no conversation which means there's no lines to bounce off.

"Woah!" says Jake, who has been cast as *The Farmer*. "That's a long monologue!"

"Aww, are you only in it for one scene Kyara?" asks Betty Blondie smirking.

I choose to pretend not to hear her, that way, she's the one embarrassed because she got blanked. *I am a little let down though. I'm in one scene only and there's sixteen scene's in this play! The casting directors won't even remember me, they won't even notice me!*

Sheers joins me and Jake, she announces that she is directing the play and that she didn't want to tell us before to maintain objectivity.

"That's a good role Kye, you have lot to remember," says Sheera.

"Thanks," I reply.

"Now, try and develop your character, you know what I mean? You've got comedy written all over this. Try and make the audience laugh, exaggerate every action and dialogue. I see the maid as an old, flat footed, hunchback, southern, maid. Make her real, like bring that evil but silly cartoon character to life."

"Yeah! I see that!" I laugh with her as she leaves to help someone else. I can see my character and I feel a lot better about my role after talking to Sheera. *God, I'm sure you've done what is best.* Maybe this is my stand out role and it isn't exactly a small role, it's actually huge, I have a whole scene to myself, to stand out. This could work. Whether it is my stand out role or not, I'm going to give it my all. *Southern.*

CHAPTER NINE

JENNIFER

"Alright, I'm ready," says Lia posing in her outfit in my room.

"Damn girl! You look hot!" I say, looking at her through my mirror whilst trying to find some earrings and running slightly behind schedule.

Today is Kye's play in the big auditorium. It is the opening night and Kye has been there all day for a final dress rehearsal. The play starts at seven prompt, and it is half six already! So I was trying to hurry the heck up and hurry the boys too. I storm across the hall into Brian and Marcus' apartment putting on an earring. I find all the guys there, almost ready but not quite. Rio sits on the sofa completely indulged into a video game dressed dashingly enough for the time we have left, whilst the other three boys search frantically for something.

"Damn it!" shouts Brian, "Kye is going to kill us!" he searches the sofa working around Rio who ignores the shouting. Marcus searches in the bedrooms and Deq rushes out into his apartment looking for something.

"Have you found them?" Deq yells from across the hall.

"No!" Marcus and Brian yell back.

My Friend's Dream

Brian runs past Lia and I towards our apartment finally noticing us, "Woah! Aren't you guys a *little* overdressed?"

"Well, Kye said people from Hollywood might be there, you know casting directors, actors..." I get lost in the compliment for a moment.

"Maybe Zac Efron or Chris Hemsworth...maybe." Lia finishes the sentence cheekily, taking some lip gloss out of her bag and applying it.

"Yeahhh...oh...kay," he says thinking we're stupid. He continues into our apartment and starts shuffling around.

I snap out of it, "Guys what the heck is going on? What are you looking for?" I ask frantically. "We need to leave like right now!"

"Wait wait! We err...lost our tickets. Quickly help us!" says Deq.

"What!" Lia screams at Deq. "You lost your tickets?"

I try to calm my anger, "You know what, you lost them, so you find them. Come on Lia, let's go." I walk towards the stairs in my heels. Lia nods and leads the way.

Marcus speaks running into Brian in the hallway, "Guys, Kye will be pissed off if we're not there, please help us, it'll be quicker! Plus, you're going to need support walking down in those heels anyway."

Lia lets out a sigh of frustration and we know Marcus is making a good point, so we start searching.

"Guys! This room is a mess! You sure would lose shit in here!" I say looking in their kitchen.

"I don't get it, we've looked everywhere." Marcus is confused, but still relatively calm.

I look at my watch – six forty three p.m. – I let out a restless scream.

They all start searching faster except Rio who smiles in excitement at the TV, he moves the pad in all directions quickly just wanting to win, unware of his surroundings.

"Rio! Brian shouts, "Get of your ass and help us!"

"Shh!" Rio hushes him, glances at the clock and then presses a combination of buttons, "YES! Oh my fricking days! Did you see that?" he roars in excitement as his opponent dies on the screen. Deq is the only one who appreciates Rio's disgusting behavior at this time.

Rio turns off the TV, stands up and then says, "Let's go!"

"The tickets!" Marcus reminds him of the frustration we're going through.

"I've got them, let's go!" Rio cheekily heads for the stairs; "Come on or we're going to be late. Its six forty five, it'll take us ten minutes."

We all take a second of pure silence and utter disgrace as we watch him go down the first few steps casually. My anger has boiled and now it is time to pop.

"THAT IS IT!" I shriek, running after Rio.

Brian runs after me, holding my arm, "Okay, okay, now is not the time. Calm down."

Deq and Lia follow us followed by Marcus who locks up.

* * *

We make it to the auditorium just in time. Perfectly on time actually. My perfectly, not Kye's, but still can't believe the audacity of Rio. We are about half an hour into the play and Kye still hasn't been on stage. Betty Blondie on the other hand has not left the stage for more than a minute and that was for a dress change.

"Err is Kye even in the play?" whispers Marcus.

"Maybe she's a prop? You know, like that tree." Deq points to a large cardboard tree.

"Shut up! She had a speaking role dumbass," I say.

"Guys, I don't know where Kye is, but that blonde girl... the main one... with hair like yours Jen, she is hot!" Rio says with excitement looking at the boys between me and Lia.

"Man, you read my mind!" replies Brian, fist bumping Rio across me.

Hot? Is my initial reaction, but then honestly she is noticeably pretty and does have nice hair.

Lia shakes her head, "Not hot, she's just about room

My Friend's Dream

temperature."

"Hmm, maybe a little higher, I'd say body temperature," I join the judging.

"What?" Deq says extremely confused by mine and Lia's comments. "She's just hot," he sets things straight and then winks at the boys.

Lia pinches him. The boys make faces at each other.

"Girl talk," says Brian.

"Excuse me? Girl Talk?" I say louder.

"Guys, we're in a play, and the steward is looking at us, so shut up," Marcus tells us off. He is the mature one. "She is hot by the way," he says quickly. "Kye should be coming on soon," he changes the subject and finishes.

I'm about to make my point again but Lia nudges me to shush, the steward *is* looking at us. We all hush, waiting for Kye to appear. Just a few moments later, there's loud sound effects and then…the curtains close. The six of us sit there still for a few seconds, very confused.

"Is that the interval?" asks Marcus as the audience applaud, some people start to leave, and others stay seated chatting to each other. "Don't tell me that's the end!"

"Oh please tell me it's the end!" Deq cries. "This is so boring!"

"Mate, would you look at Blondey! She' fire!" Rio says.

We are really half way through now, and Kye still has not been on stage. It's a bad impression on the guys, we are trying to get their support in our dream swap, but this is going the wrong way. I feel bad for Kye, I mean what if there are casting directors here, Betty is right in their eyes, and Kye is not even in the show yet! She worked so hard for this.

About fifteen minutes later, people return to their seats and the curtains open once again. We all pray for Kye to come on soon. The play starts and Blondie is center stage again. Lia is the only one actually interested in the play, I'm just waiting for Kye, Deq is on his phone, Rio is watching (but I doubt he's listening), and Marcus and Brian are dozing off. *Kye's God, please bring Kye on.* I say in my heart to Kye's so called friend – God. And to my surprise, Betty exits the stage, the lights dim down and to our right spotlights light the stairs of the auditorium. From the back of the theatre, an old, wrinkly woman with a hunch back and grey beehive hair stomps down the stairs. Her buttocks stuck out from her red long skirt which matched an apron and a blouse. She speaks in a loud, old voice with a strong southern accent. Lia and the boys sit upright in their seats, we watch as this character makes her way scarily down the stairs, with big movements and loud dialogue. She catches everyone's attention. All eyes in the audience follow her steps and move with her. As she awkwardly scrambles onto the stage representing her old age and making the audience laugh to stitches, we catch her face in the light. It is an old version of Kye! It is Kye! We are all in complete astonishment!

Kye looks completely different, old yet strong and southern! Her actions are incredible, her body shape, the way she walks with her hand on her back swinging her hips; her every move is hilarious! The audience clap and laugh as she brilliantly delivers a long monologue. I could watch her forever. She literally changes the feel of the play. She wakes everyone up! She even spots us and continues acting without even a smirk back at us as we laugh and clap and wink and wave at her. She has so much to remember and is confident, she fits right in on that stage, in fact, no, she is standing out! She is a different person completely! And she has proved our point to the guys, this is wicked!

Kyara Averoni can act!

CHAPTER TEN

KYARA

The twenty performances are over and I already miss it! It was one of the best things I'd ever done! And even though it was hard work for only one scene, I do feel like I made my statement – at least that's what the guys said. Rio thinks Betty is *fire* as I gather from Lia and Jen and even I think she gave a great performance and actually she did fit the role well – much better that I would have. Her boyfriend Nick James – obviously like one of the hottest guy in our year that all the girls die over (not my type though) – came to more than one performance of ours and popped backstage now and then, throwing the other girls off their lines. He is on the baseball team and though guys don't seem to have much rivalry in this university, the baseball team and the basketball team don't seem to like each other very much. He has an overpowering aroma about him that I really don't like. The drama society still meet up once a week to discuss next year's plans and obviously Nick pops up too and lingers around the back with his friends waiting for his girlfriend. Anyway, so far no one has been *selected* by a casting director or an agent. Not even Betty. She hates me even more now for some reason, maybe I'm getting more popular with the drama school or something, but I can feel her hate growing toward me.

Floor four, the guys, Jen and Lia are like family. I haven't missed home once yet. I love the challenges here, the people and just life! *Thank you God.* To add to this I have written up four of my story idea outlines and have started writing my first novel, the newest addition to the ideas, which of course Jen is helping me with and the story involves a similar character to hers. Speaking of Jen, she is doing well in her astrophysics modules and is working towards passing in literature. She plans her time well to catch up on classes she misses for both subjects. Speaking of passing, exam season is now upon us all. Deq managed to use his expertise to enroll Jen onto the astrophysics exams. Lia being the law student, wasn't too happy about this and actually none of us were too keen on the cheat but sometimes in life you have to take a little bit of a shortcut as long as it doesn't cause anyone harm – like my parents say these days are not like the old ones.   Jen is working her ass off for these exams, after her retake, she doesn't want to leave any room for disappointment now. She only has one English exam but a lot of coursework and four astrophysics exams. I have four too and everyone else also has about four or five exams each, except for Brian who has one. Studying is hard especially during exam season, the stress is building up, however so far we've worked hard to keep the peace between us and our books. Sometimes we study together in the living rooms, sometimes alone with our doors wide open shouting across the hallway talking to each other. Sometimes Jen asks me questions which are annoying and then we end up having a big argument – and a pen fight. Brian plays music out loud most of the time and just types whilst the rest of us do practice questions, make posters, use sticky notes and other weird revision techniques. I have only just begun my revision because of the play but I try not to stress and just want to get them done quickly so that I can move onto better things – like writing my book. Jen on the other hand can feel the pressure, she has a lot to learn and revise, and has coursework to complete before the deadlines. She works day and night and you can see it in her that she wants to do exceptionally well in astrophysics. In literature she just wants to pass but today even that is proving difficult.

We all quietly study, the balcony doors are open and the warm summer breeze brushes lightly through the living room. Lia is in the kitchen reading, I sit on the floor with my notes, books and laptop laid out in front of me. Jen is in her room with the door open and the boys are in Brian and Marcus' apartment. We study quietly in deep concentration until an accidental loud sound of R&B music shudders and vibrates through our bodies. My hand slips causing a scribble across my notes, Lia jumps out of her seat and Jen roars with frustration.

"BRIAN!" she screams charging out of her room.
Lia and I follow her into the boys' apartment, who seem to be having a fricking party! They dance around locking and popping and rapping along to the loud music. Marcus holds a wooden spoon as a mic, Rio and Brian do the wave and Deq's break dancing spin on the floor comes to as uncontrollable halt as he finds the pause button on his laptop. They all freeze.

"Argh!" Jen shouts in pain and anger eyeing all of them.

She is upset and angry and it is clearly showing on her burning red cheeks and watery eyes. I totally understand how she is feeling right now, this stress and pressure is added by us, me, and her... herself. It is unnecessary, she would be doing great with only literature to concentrate on but she has the supplementary stress of astrophysics and that too at her own will (and mine), so it would feel stupid to fail at both especially when we have no one but ourselves to blame. Despite knowing this, and despite how annoying the guys have been over the past few weeks Jen has been patient and has been controlling her anger, trying to stay calm.

I step in front of Jen, "Are you guys fricking crazy!" I shout at the boys. "Huh? Are you? We have exams tomorrow, we're freaking out, aren't you?"

"This time I swear it was Rio's idea..." begins Brian.

"What!" exclaims Rio.

"Yes! And jeez chill guys, we're taking a break, it's only music and they're just exams." Brian says.

"Brian, they are *just* exams for us!" I yell. "Jen has a lot more than us, a whole extra course and one where she hasn't even attended all the classes. Have some sympathy!" I talk to the boys in my non panicky stern voice. Rio's uncontrollable smirk at my - *mom like* - telling-off catches my eye. He really does make anyone laugh in any situation even me, but I had to stay strong for Jen, I force my anger through, "Rio! You better stop laughing right now, because if you don't, I swear you'll never laugh again!"

Until this point we were all frustrated but were only joking with each other however after around fifteen mins of Lia and I arguing with the boys, it was no longer a joke to Jen.

Jen puts her face into her hands, "I shouldn't have done this," she says quietly and completely serious. "I should never have taken astrophysics, now I'm going to fail that and literature, then I'll be kicked out." With an upset tone she leaves us standing in silence. The pressure of her dream has got to her.

Lia breaks our silent stares after some thought, "Maybe this whole dream thing is too much for her," she leaves too and heads back into our kitchen.

I suddenly feel guilty. This is all my fault. I feel numb and have a lump in my throat. I just wanted Jen to live her dreams but I don't want her to get kicked out and lose what she has already – literature. I don't even know what to do right now. Should I console her? And tell her everything will be fine? But I don't know if it will after seeing her so upset.

"Man, I've never seen her so angry before," says Marcus.

All four of them stand there feeling guilty and unsure of what to do next. I'm unsure too. I leave their apartment in silence and head towards Jen's room, where she slams the door shut. Brian follows me and just as I reach for the door he holds my arm back.

"Wait," he says in a soft tone. "Let me," he is truly sorry but looks strong and mature enough right now to handle the situation. He is a man that will admit his mistake and apologize if he genuinely feels bad and I'm going to stop that. I nod at him, he lets go of my arm and I continue to study in the kitchen.

Brian knocks on Jen's door, "Jen," he calls tenderly opening the door and entering her room.

My Friend's Dream

He leaves the door slightly open and since everyone is silent after the commotion, Lia and I overhear Brian's attempt to apologize to Jen.

At first Jen doesn't speak.

Brian sincerely apologizes, "Jen, I'm sorry, I know I've been an idiot. We're all sorry." Before Jen could tell him to leave he sighs and says, "Look at me, I'm really sorry. I didn't realize how hard this is for you, I know, you're doing two courses and we're not helping so I promise, we won't, I won't, distract you again. Promise. Okay?"

Jen still doesn't respond, but Brian's soft voice and apologetic tone melts mine and Lia's hearts.

"In fact we won't even rap again until your finals are over..." he continues. "And you know Rio can't go a day without rapping or singing or even humming for that matter."

He is trying to make her laugh, it isn't working on her but Lia and I on the other hand giggle along.

"So true," Lia whispers to me.

"You know what, from now on, right now, I myself, am going to help you," Brian finishes.

Our giggles in the kitchen stop. Lia looks at me with raised eyebrows and I look back at her eyebrows raised and my tucked chin in.

And finally Jen laughs, "Ha!" albeit sarcastically. "You? Help me? No thanks Brian."

"Jen, I've been through a year and I'm doing the same thing as you. Plus no lie, I'm alright at lit and I only have that to concentrate on. Trust me. I can help you," Brian speaks honestly and is offering a great hand indeed.

But Jen is being Jen, "I don't want to cheat," she replies.

A not so funny but funny joke pops into my head and I'm pretty sure it is in Brian's brain too – she is already cheating the whole university by hacking into the astrophysics classes! But I'm not doing any better of a deed by persuading Jen to actually do this.

Luckily Brian doesn't say anything stupid at this moment. "You're not going to cheat, I'll just help you with your assignments and you can use my work as a guide. I can review your work and edit it too, this way you have more time for astrophysics."

Me and Lia exchange impressed looks.

"Is that a deal?" Brian convinces her, "I promise you'll get through this and I...*we* are all going to help you."

After a few minutes of thought Jen agrees, "Alright, okay, deal – you can start on this, read it through and edit it please, it's the creative writing module."

"Already! I was just going to take a quick break...I'm just kidding, ha! Send it over on email."

Jen slaps him with what sounds like a book, they both laugh and so do we. As Brian walks out of Jen's room we pretend to be indulged in our work, as if we never heard a word. He looks at us and winks as he heads off to his room proud of his consoling skills.

* * *

I am so easily distracted when I have exams. I seem to go on my phone a lot more and scroll through Facebook, Instagram and Twitter every five minutes even though the newsfeed is still the same, or I end up on YouTube watching some random vlogger do the cinnamon challenge for hours. I basically do anything that isn't studying. The most distracting of all was feeling more inspired than ever to become an actress while trying to study! I spend hours dreaming about being an actress in movies and then I spend ages watching blooper reels and interviews, and more film ideas would form perfectly in my head when studying than when I had nothing to do. I feel more stimulated to write my book when I'm doing exam practice but there's just no time! Maybe it's because when I try to study, my heart realizes how much I want to be an actress. I don't know what happens to me in exam season, but I just feel so much more determined for my dream yet I have no time to actually do anything about it. The more I study the more I want my dream to come true – and that is totally ironic. I search for online auditions and casting calls and guess what? In exam season, everyone opens online casting calls! *Nice timing God*. Luckily I have Jen to help me out with the self-tapes, but they still take a long time. I have to learn short pieces from a script, get the camera ready, film it (and that's hard enough with the boys coming over every two minutes), and then make a video and send it. There was one where the role required parkour which they would train but the actress would have to demonstrate decent movement skills such as dance or acrobatics. I didn't have a recent dance video – the last dance video of mine was from a school talent show - so during exam season I had to come up with a dance routine, learn it and then film it along with a self-tape and submit it by the deadline which was within three days of me finding the casting call. My mind was all over the place! I was just so thankful for having everyone there to help me with this one, even though I still haven't heard from the casting department. I'm not going to lie, it was very hard to get it done in three days and it's hard overall just trying to do so many online casting calls while studying but there's one rule in the life of dreamers that I stick to with all my heart - take every single opportunity.

* * *

There is only a week of exams left to go, we all have one each left except for Rio who's last one was this morning and Brian who finished last week. We have powered through and time has flown by. It's a quiet night, we three girls sit in the living room, studying and listening to the radio.

"I'm so tired and fricking starving," Jen yawns as she begins to pack up.

"Me too," says Lia also closing her big book.

That was the understatement of the year.

"I need to get my book from Rio," I say getting up and feeling the pain from my stiff legs where my nerves have been squished. I make my way to the boys' apartment. Marcus and Brian sit glued to the PlayStation.

"Oi! Last game! Last game!" Marcus yells in excitement, "I need to study."

"Haha! Weak!" Brian laughs back.

"Guys, where's Rio?" I ask.

"Err, in Brazil," Marcus laughs nudging Brian who also laughs at the joke.

"Ha. Ha. Very funny," I say sarcastically while thinking about how we got through a whole year without making that joke. "That's actually a good one," I realize. "Seriously, where is he? He has my book."

"Oh, well you aren't getting that back," Brian says looking at the TV screen.

"Oh shut up Brian," I say.

We hear Rio and Deq walk up the stairs, they stop in the hallway holding takeaway boxes and look down the corridor to where I stand.

"These are for us and you girls, those two have eaten," Rio calls out to me.

"Well, that's a surprise. You fatsos usually eat all our food!" I call back to the boys.

"Okay, so don't thank us woman!" Deq sardonically shouts back.

"Haha! Thanks. Rio where's my book?" I ask him.

"In my room on my desk."

"Cool. I'm coming."

They turn and make their way into our living room surprising Jen and Lia. I find my book in Rio's mess and then join them for a much deserved takeaway.

"I so needed that! Thanks guys," Jen says tidying the kitchen with Rio.

"No worries dude," Rio replies.

"Well, as long as you're happy Jen, then we've made up for the whole distraction thing," Deq mutters.

Rio giggles whilst heading towards the corridor with the rest of us following behind, "Well, I'm off to bed guys," he says.

Lia walks in front of me.

"Lia it's late, are you not stopping over?" I ask.

She turns around and stops, as do Deq and Rio with the door open.

"Actually, I'm err... going to... well, we are..." Lia's words don't come out clearly. She blushes.

"We're kinda going out. Me and Lia," Deq blushes as he tries to put on a cool guy act to cover up his cute shyness.

"Oh my gosh! You didn't tell us! How long has this been going on?" Jen exclaims.

"Just a few week," Lia responds touching her hair.

"A few weeks!" I yell. "And we didn't even notice!"

They both giggle – in love.

"Woah! So, Lia, you are stopping at ours tonight…eyyyy!" Rio teases in typical Rio fashion.

"Hey shut up." Deq smiles pushing Rio through the door and rushing out quickly along with Lia trotting behind as Jen and I make faces at her.

They leave and the door closes behind them.

Jen takes out a twenty from her pocket and holds it up in defeat.

I snatch it from her hands, "I told you. I knew it! You could totally tell." I smile in my victory.

Our door opens slightly, Rio's head pops through, "I could tell too," he says cheekily as we both push him out and close our door.

CHAPTER ELEVEN

JENNIFER

Summer. Vacation. It was not a holiday for me. It was the most productive summer of my life! And I'm proud of it! Kye and I only went home for two weeks to see our families. I didn't tell mine about the whole extra astrophysics course, I didn't know how they would react, I'm sure they'd be happy about me studying my choice of subject but not so happy about the way I'm studying it, also I didn't need the added pressure of getting their hopes up. Kye told her parents about her book writing but not in much detail, her parents are really supportive of her dream, however she just wants the cap and gown for them. The rest of the guys went home for a little longer than us and truthfully, we did miss them.

    Kye hasn't heard back from any of her online casting audition yet and she tells us that when you don't hear back it usually means you got rejected. *I think that's stupid.* I know they get lots of applicants but a simple email saying, 'Sorry' would allow Kye to move on quickly. She sits there refreshing her emails every five minutes and with her phone battery on one hundred percent charge until a few weeks pass by. I guess that's just how the industry works. Moving on from the online auditions, she auditioned at local amateur theatres and then voluntarily joined one for their summer play. The play was quite a small amateur thing, and she played many different roles such as *Customer 1, Doctors Wife and a door*, but she only appeared on stage for a few seconds at a time. Her highlight was still playing the maid at the drama society's play. She was moving at a decent speed with her book writing, but for a modern girl she prefers to write her first draft by hand rather than typing it up. Kye has almost completed her first draft in three chunky notebooks and now it is time to type and edit.

As I said, my summer was super busy! Kye and I joined the gym to keep healthy and look fit but I also needed to improve my cardiovascular health as it is crucial for astronauts and for Kye, well, she is keen on playing an action role in movies so she needed some muscles. The boys gave me a great birthday gift by paying for and enrolling me onto a simple medical course (like a first aid course) which I completed successfully. Then I searched online for other mini courses that would enhance my knowledge because astronauts have to know everything – from how to be your own doctor to looking at how plants grow to being able to fix a mechanical issue. One thing that every astronaut needs is flight experience so to get ahead of the game and after a lot of searching I found a flight course! It was expensive but I got a good deal because I found it on a voucher website. To pay for this and some other expenses Kye and I also found ourselves jobs over the summer and we now work at The Mirage, an on campus bar/pub/restaurant as waitresses. We started off as summer temps but they've kept us on. It pays well and has some perks. With my work pay, some help from my parent and my friends, I went on the flight course. It was unreal! I'm not going to lie, it was hard at first, keeping a helicopter steady in the air is very difficult! But after just a few hours I did it, I kept it steady! Then there was straight line flying and all sorts of other training. The control panels are delicate and flying is a vital responsibility. I loved it! And to add to the medical and flight courses, I studied my ass off for year two modules making sure that I'm ahead in my own game.

CHAPTER TWELVE

KYARA

Year two is flying by and my book is taking forever to type. There are so many things I have missed out while writing it and paragraphing with speech marks is irritating the hell out of me. It's so…technical.

"Jen!" I call from my room frustrated, plunging my head into the duvet, "How the heck do I write speech marks properly!"

She enters my room, "Huh?"

"Am I doing the speech right? Should there be an indent when a new person talks?" I ask pointing at the screen. "And what if it's from my point of view, so I describe my actions before a person talks, can that go on the same line?"

Jen sits on the bed and takes the laptop. She reads from the screen and expresses a thoughtful look.

"You know what Kye, I've never thought about that before, I'm actually not too sure. There's definitely a new paragraph line for new speech, but that bit…hmmm…" she reads on. "Let's ask Brian."

"Brian!" we both call empowering our voices so that the sound could reach his ears, across the landing. And to our surprise he arrives quicker than expected.

"What's up?" he asks leaning on the doorframe, in his

charming attire, looking smart and as if he has come to the rescue of two distressed ladies.

"We need some help with speech marks," Jen explains.

He makes his way over and sits on the bed too. I sit up making space so that they can deal with the issue. Brian reads through a paragraph on the page and then starts fixing my mistakes showing us both, but more so showing Jen what he's doing. He explains it clearly using examples from my written piece, looking at her every now and again while she stares at the screen making sense of it all. I suppose he's used to helping Jen with literature stuff. I just sit back and take note.

"Understand?" he asks Jen forgetting I'm there.

"Thanks!" I say taking the laptop from him, cheekily interrupting their moment.

"Anytime!" he turns his attention to me and then casually leaves the room.

Jen takes the laptop from me again, she leans back, "This looks great Kye! Let me read some more," intrigued by the story she innocently reads… and blushes.

* * *

Another drama society session finishes, we did some immersive theatre training today. This is a small part of our end of year musical dance play this year, in which I have another small but decent role of 'Lana the Choreographer'. Immersive theatre is different, I'd never heard of it before, but I actually enjoyed it. It is more fun being an audience member than the actors in this one and the creepier, the more fun it is. The acting part is difficult though, you really have to play off the audience as you don't know how they'll react but you still have to stay fully in role.

I walk with Jake down the hallway towards the exit, we halt when we find photos of the play last year displayed on the corridor wall.

"Kye there's you!" Jake says pointing at a funny picture of me, my character.

There's three photos of me in my crazy old woman outfit,

three quite good ones actually. My posture is great and my expressions are better than I thought. I take a good look around and let the throwback sink in.

"Man, I need some of these for my portfolio," says Jake.

"That's actually a good idea," I reply to Jake's comment, thinking about how great they'll look on my portfolio too.

Jake is on the wall a little bit but Blondie is spread over it like butter on toast. And speaking of her I can hear her shrieking with excitement running towards the wall.

"Oh my gosh, oh my gosh, oh my gosh!" she screeches with her girls running behind her. She stops directly in front of me. "O M G! I am everywhere!" she points out. "Do I look good in that one? Do I look fat?"

"Betty you look gorgeous!" says Ellen.

"Girl, you got it going on the whole wall!" Maya tells her.

"Well, obvs," Betty responds.

Abbey, the dancer admires her only picture, "Hey look, there's me-"

"Look at that one over there! I killed that stage," Betty cuts Abbey off and points in a different direction completely.

"I wonder if they have it recorded, I could do with a video of the dance, ah it was such a good time," Abbey talks but no one is really paying attention except me and Jake.

"Yeah yeah the dance was good… ahhh look at that one!" Betty rushes a response to Abbey before moving on to some more self-absorbed compliments.

Jake looks at me wide eyed with raised eyebrows as he begins to leave. I feel sorry for Abbey her dance was actually quite intricate and was worth compliments, she choreographed it too.

I think I should at least compliment the poor girl, "Abb-"

"Hey beautiful!" Nick James, cuts me off. He walks toward Betty in his cool guy apparel, tall and broad. He looks at me for a while as he walks towards us, before finally turning his attention to Betty. Before I get left with the group of haters, I follow Jake out and head back to the apartment.

I hear the boys laughing and discussing something in

My Friend's Dream

Brian's and Marcus' apartment as I make my way up the last flight of stairs.

I hear Deq saying, "Weak man! Why are you so scared?"

I drop my bag in their hallway and walk towards the living room.

"I don't know man, I just…KYE!" Brian exclaims out of the blue as I enter the living room. "Hey, how… how you doing? What…what…what brings you here?" he asks nervously hiding their conversation.

I stare at him confused and then walk towards the kitchen for some water, "What is the matter with you?" I ask. "Can I not be here, you guys are always hogging our living room."

"Haha, you're funny!" he continues acting weird.

"Jeez! It's only Kye, Brian," Marcus says indicating to carry the conversation on.

Brian gives him a rushed look saying 'shut up'.

"Yeah, it's just me Brian," I say smirking.

"Yeah, it's just Kye, she's one of the guys," Rio says smirking even more than me.

My smirk fades and I pull a face at Rio to combat the insult, "Excuse me?" I say, not taking it too seriously as I make my way over to the sofa where Deq and Rio slouch.

"You know, I mean you're cool," Rio explains himself.

Brian makes faces and gestures at the boys to indicate them to stop talking.

"So…Brian…" I say as I drop in between Deq and Rio on the sofa. "Why don't you just *ask her out*?" I cunningly smile at the boys who all look shocked, especially Brian.

There's a short silence as they all look at each other and then Brian tries to play dumb. He laughs a sigh, "Who? I mean…what are you talking about?"

"Oh come on! I think she knows," Deq yells.

"Yeah, it's quite obvious," I say.

"Really?" Brian asks turning serious.

I nod, "Look, you just need to do it man, it'll be fine,"

"It will?" he asks, "What does she say about me?"

"Oh no no, I can't tell you that," I say sipping from the glass.

"What! Kye!" Rio shouts in my ear.

"Why not?" Brian asks as he kneels behind the table directly in front of me – looking cute.

"Because, I can't."

"What kinda fool-?" Marcus says to himself annoyed that I won't tell them any gossip.

"Come on Kye!?" Deq urges.

Brian tries, "Kye, how will I know what to do or say if you don't tell me stuff… like what you guys say…about me."

I shake my head.

"Kye!" they all exclaim.

"No! Because, she's my girl, you know, we can't tell you our inside…stuff."

"But we're your boys," Rio says.

I look at him dully.

"Nice try," Deq quietly compliments Rio.

"Thanks man," he whispers back.

Marcus cunningly asks a question, "Okay answer this; should he do it?"

"Yes," I say.

"But how, like what should I do? Hints Kye, hints. You can give me some advice."

"What would you want, you know, as a girl?" Rio questions.

"Me?" I put the glass on the table. They all come closer, take seats and actually listen in like I'm about to tell a story. I begin, "I would like to meet someone unexpectedly, for example on a long boat trip or something, but we go to the same college or school. In our first meeting at school we notice each other but don't really give it much interest. Then we actually get introduced and we have a little friction between us, you know, like we don't get along that well or something, like you and Jen." I pause and nod at Brian. "Anyway, then something happens, I don't know, say the waves get extremely rough, night begins to fall and rain forms a thunderous storm. The boat capsizes and I get hurt or something.

He swims forward to help me and then we see an island in the distance and head towards it in the storm. We hold on to each other tight so that we don't slip away in the monstrous waves. In the rough of the storm, that hate turns to something else. We finally make it to the island, his wet shirt sticks to his body revealing a heavenly physique but then I notice he's hurt. He tears off the sleeve of his wet shirt to reveal a deep cut running from his shoulder to his triceps. I immediately attend to it and tightly wrap the torn sleeve around it. Then we find a cave, were we…" Eyes widen around me. The boys are intrigued and totally engulfed in my fairytale as I now stand and walk around the room providing actions to my fairytale. "… Where we… TALK and wait the storm out. We share stories of our childhood, our families, our first impressions, our dreams. The storm finally dies down and we spend the next afternoon finding wood to light a large fire to help the rescue team to find us. Meanwhile we sit and wait by the now calm waves and the warm fire under the romantic sunset where we realize our bond and then finally realize where fate has led us. He holds my hand and then asks… for my hand in marriage."

"Marriage! And then what? You live happily ever after," Rio breaks my story. "Jeeze Kye, Brian wants to ask Jen out on a first date not her fricking hand in marriage!"

"Is that the 'stuff' you girls talk about?" Marcus asks genuinely.

"Damn! No wonder you write books," Deq thinks out loud.

"Okay, that's very nice Kye but Jen?" Brian rushes.

I sigh at their attempt to hide their actual interest in the story. I then begin again, "But Jen, Jen's different. She wants something a little simpler…"

"A little?" Brian asks worried.

I smile and walk to their smaller balcony as the sun begins to set, "Jen loves the stars, so she would definitely want something outdoor. Not a fancy date in an expensive restaurant, no. Just a view of the stars, with nature, some food, peace and-"

"Cheap! So you don't need to take your wallet with you," Rio laughs.

"Ha, I like that," Marcus adds.

"Yeah me too, though it's very weather dependent," Deq mentions.

Brian is lost in thought and doesn't really take much notice of their stupid comments.

"There's no winning with you guys is there? You have an excuse for everything," I say disgusted.

Brian flashes out of his thoughts, "Carry on," he gestures to me, waiting eagerly to know more.

* * *

"Yo! Guys!" Brian calls walking into our living room, where all of us sit around trying to catch up on work, letting in the breeze of the clear evening from the balcony. He looks casual but I can tell he's up to something.

"Hey, where have you been?" Jen asks.

"Oh, just, you know, in my room. Yeah. Why?" Brian responds awkwardly, he's not a good actor.

"Hm, nothing. Man, this essay is driving me crazy! I mean it has a two thousand word limit and I've written three thousand with two more questions yet to answer. Plus, we have that class test in physics to study for," she says a little frustrated but more amused.

"Oh, when are these due in?" Marcus asks.

"Both next week, there's so much going on!" she says.

Marcus nods and then winks at Brian.

"Yeah there is a lot going, but don't worry we'll get through it," I say, also looking at Brian then looking outside, giving him the heads up – he has definitely chosen the right day. He looks nervous, bless him, he really does like her.

"So anyone want to eat… something?" he finally builds the courage.

Rio is quick to respond, "Yeah man, I'm-"

"No! You don't," Deq quickly raises his voice and slaps Rio a few times on his back laughing loud until Rio the dumbass gets the point – which he does quite quickly, chuckling , so that makes me wonder whether he was just playing around in the first place.

"No thanks, we're… I mean I'm not hungry," I say casually, eyeing Rio.

"I'm good thanks," Lia adds, getting the point too.

"I'm hungry, are we going to order?" Jen asks completely fooled.

"Err, sure, I…err," Brian is stuck.

I help him, "Jen, don't you need to like take a break?"

"Yeah, that's why you've over-written. You need some fresh air," Marcus says.

"You too Brian, haven't you been working on that essay of yours? Just go and get a takeaway," Rio finally helps out.

"Yes, I have been working all day. Come on." Brian man's up and before any of us needed to say anymore Jen is already on her feet.

"Alright, let's go, anyone want anything?" she asks grabbing her purse and jacket.

We all say no and then they finally leave to go on an unplanned but planned date. The night grows darker and the stars begin to shine brighter. We all cheekily smirk and raise our eyebrows at each other praying for the weather to stay like this.

CHAPTER THIRTEEN

JENNIFER

I can't believe what just happened, well, actually I can. Brian, is so sweet! He finally asked me out! That whole quick takeaway thing turned into the best date of my life! We left the apartment and took a short stroll into the city. The sun started to set and since it was a Monday evening, it was very quiet. The weird thing is, I didn't even have the slightest clue that this was going to happen, but thinking back to how everyone was acting, now I get it. When we left I was wearing a very casual dress with slightly ripped tights, and my hair was in a mess – I mean I did go thinking we were just going to grab food and come back. Anyway, Brian and I walked for quite a while and every takeaway we came to he came up with an excuse and then walked onto the next one. It was getting darker and I insisted that we buy food at the next one; whatever it may be. It turned out to be McDonalds, we went in, cued up and then out of nowhere Brian ordered my usual along with a few extras, apple pie and mc flurries, and he paid. That's when I realized something was going on in his mind.

"Shall we?" he said turning around holding the food in a paper bag.

All I could do was nod at him, still trying to read his mind. Then another random move - he started to walk in a different direction to the way back.

"Brian, shouldn't we be going this way?" I pointed.

"Come on," he replied gesturing with his head so I followed him.

About ten minutes of walking up what felt like a huge hill and me pestering him about us going the wrong way, I started swearing at him for making me walk so much. It was a hill indeed, and when we reached the top, leaving the city center behind, we entered a grassy terrain. The grass was neatly cut, it was like a park and few yards down I could see a lake shimmering in the distance, but the most spectacular thing was what I could see all around that. The crescent moon shone brightly in the dark sky. I could see it twice - reflecting and in reality. And a cosmos of glittering stars lit up the velvet night. The light wind brushed my hair back as I stood on the hill taking in the breathtaking scenery and just dreaming about those stars and how glorious it would have been if I had brought my telescope.

"Wow!" I gasped, totally lost in the universe. I didn't even know about this place and had never been there before. We just always looked at the steep hill and turned back.

I spent a good few minutes just staring into outer space. When I turned around, I saw a small picnic blanket and my McDonalds spread out neatly, and Brian sitting there smiling shyly. I'd never really seen him shy before, he's always loud and annoying. But his blushing made me blush and then I went all shy.

I giggled, "Aww Brian," and then walked over to him and took a seat opposite him.

"What! The others have already eaten!" he tried to hide his smile. "Plus we need a break," he mumbled taking a sip from his coca cola. He handed me my drink and then we began to eat. I felt really nervous eating in front of him, especially a burger, usually I just dig in and don't give a crap but this whole situation made me act weird, I guess I knew what was coming. I tried to eat as ladylike as possible and for a while we were silent. Then we began to talk about university and how the past year and a half has gone by so fast, my confidence increased and then I, or we, were both back to normal. We spent over two hours just talking and laughing and then pausing to look up at the stars and the moon before making another joke or beginning new conversations. It was just relaxed and totally up my street. I loved it, I loved it way more than a fancy restaurant date, or a trip to the movies, we were under the stars, outside, it was just perfect.

The city grew quieter and shops began to close, we were talking about how Lia and Deq were secretly dating thinking that none of us knew, when we did, well Kye did, then Brian stopped and looked into my eyes, I waited, dreaming back into his.

"So," he said in his manly voice. "Would you like to go out…on a date?" he smiled giggling to himself at how he totally messed that line up.

"Was this not a date?" I replied smirking.

"What? This? Maccy's on the grass? Well, if you want it to be then-"

"I loved it," I cut him off touching his hand.

He smiled gorgeously at me and then asked the real question, "Will you be my girlfriend?"

I laughed in a shy manner, blushed and then nodded. Brian then held my hand softly before tensing his muscles and pulling me forward so that our foreheads touched, he pushed my hair behind my ears and then…

Yeah, you know what happened, use your own imagination.

But anyway *God, as Kye would say - thank you! He's just one of a kind and this was totally unexpected but I really wanted it to happen. Thanks!* I suppose opposites do attract.

* * *

"Kye!" I scream, as I hear her walk in with fresh laundry. I tuck my diary down the side of my bed and then run into the hallway practically jumping on her, dropping socks on to the floor. She knowingly smiles and hugs me back.

"What happened?" she teases.

"Shut up, it was all you," I reply still hugging her.

"Well, you're welcome," Kye says as I dismount her and pick up a few socks that I dropped from her basket.

I hold the front of her basket and pull her into the living room, "Kye, thank you! I just knew it was your idea!"

"Well, actually it wasn't entirely my idea, Brian did find the place, and did most of the planning, I just got him started."

"Well, it was just perfect, he is really sweet isn't he?" I ask her, helping her fold clothes.

"Says the girl who hated him," Kye replies. "But yes he is. What did you guys eat anyway?"

"MacDonald's," I mumble.

"Hahahahaha!" Kye sarcastically laughs thinking it was a joke, then realizing it wasn't, "Really?" she realizes.

I nod.

"Dumbass!" Kye yells.

"It was actually really good. And I officially now have a boyfriend."

"Yeah well, at least someone has," Kye says.

"Ahh, don't worry, your Tarzan will come along one day," I joke.

But Kye takes it seriously, she sighs, "Ah, I hope so Jen. I hope so soon."

I freeze for a moment. She seems sad. Kye does have a lot going on right now with her book taking a long time to type and Betty was irritating the hell out of her, but all this just gets her stressed out – she doesn't look stressed, she looks sad, just sad. I wait in silence until I gain her attention. I squint at her encouraging an explanation. I know there's something in her head.

She speaks, "Sometimes I feel like my acting dream takes over so much of my thoughts and my life that I forget how I also want the normal things in life. Like a loving husband, a home, a family. I want someone to love too, and sometimes I feel like I miss out on that because I'm so indulged in dreaming. I just think it'll happen when it's destined to happen, I'll meet the man of my dreams when fate wants us to, but I'm twenty two, single and not even close to love. Guys don't seem to be interested in me and I'm too scared to make a move. Am I not attractive or pretty? Like, should I wear more makeup? Is it because I'm tanned?" she pauses for a moment. "I want to find young love, like I want to be close to marriage at like twenty five years old, I want to be a young mom. That's in three years by the way. So I have got three years to graduate, publish a book, become a Hollywood movie actress, find someone, know them well enough and then get engaged," she laughs out of pity and I giggle in her sorrow too. "Oh God! Are you listening? What are you doing up there?! Come on man! I hope you've got all this written for me in the next three years! I would like the little things in life too you know!" Kye woefully laughs looking up and around her for her God.

    She is right. We are so caught up in our dreams that we forgot about the little things in life, like how we want to find love, marry, have children. We still would like to fulfill our duties of being a human – an animal, survival of the fittest kind of thing. I've never told anyone how I feel about the little things in life, but Kye's right, I do think of that stuff too.

    "Kye, I know exactly what you mean. We're dreamers and we want the little things in life just as much as our dreams. It's just that the little things are the norm, which is why our farfetched dreams somehow seem to take more effort and priority in the eyes of others and our own, only we feel what we want," I say what's in my heart. "Having said that though, I never imagined Brian coming into my life, I never imagined anyone coming into my life right now, it just happened. Like fate. From experience, most things happen when you don't really expect them to happen or when you don't have an urge for them to happen. They just…happen."

CHAPTER FOURTEEN

KYARA

"Alright! Settle Down." Dr. Kennedy begins his class.

I have two lectures a week with him this year as does Jen but she also has him for another astrophysics module. Luckily, Deq managed to hack into the system to get Jen an astrophysics timetable and put her name into the astrophysics list so the teachers know her name but she still has to be careful as she's not enrolled onto the course. We've got some new lecturers for the second year modules and we hoped not to get Dr. Kennedy again but unfortunately he teaches all three years of physics and astrophysics so we're stuck with him throughout our time here, unless he leaves. As it stands we still sit near the back hiding from him.

He finishes the lecture slides and then pauses peering up from his glasses, "Also, your class tests have been marked and are available to collect from the school office."

There's a sweep of whispers amongst the class, this counts for forty percent of the module so it is a big deal. We begin to pack and leave walking past him. He looks over his glasses with a squint watching us leave.

"I would take great care with these class tests because some of you have stumbled in your performance," he says quite distinctly looking at me and Jen as we walk out.

"Oh my God! Kye, I've failed haven't I? Shit!" Jen says running down the stairs to the school office.

"No, it'll be fine Jen. He just likes scaring people. Slow down!" I yell running after her.

"I knew it Kye! Whenever I think I did okay in a test, I actually do really bad. When I think it went bad, I do well. And this one I was sure that I'd done okay when we walked out, remember? Damn it! Ahh this is really important too!" Jen continues to stress as she gallops down.

"Calm down. I'm sure you'll be fine," I say panting as we reach the school office and join the queue to collect our test results.

When we get to the front, I hand in my student card and Jen fakes that she forgot hers - since it says her course - English Literature- on it and it's a different color - so she just gives her name. Fred, the school office administrator hands us our tests and we move out of the queue.

"What!" Jen yells.

"Shit!" I shriek.

"I got eighty eight percent!" Jen is ecstatic with her result. "Damn that's good! I knew it went well! What did you get?"

I stare at my paper in shock.

"Kye?" she takes my paper from me.

"Forty two percent," I breathe out.

Jen ruffles through my paper and through hers trying to compare the marks and answers. I stand still trying to figure out where I went wrong. I feel a bit numb, I don't know how to react or what to do. I've never done so badly in my entire academic life!

"Don't worry Kye, you had a whole lot going on with the drama society rehearsals, your online auditions, your book and all that."

"Yeah but how? Forty two percent!! We both had a lot going on, but how the heck-"

"Kye, it's alright, it happens, you passed!"

"I passed, oh my God, I just passed! Just!"

"Calm down. Look you can still make it up, okay. It's a one off and it happens," Jen explains. "And can you let me have the limelight for once please," she laughs.

"Yeah, sorry, eighty eight percent! Girl, well done," I cheer up and forget about my disappointing result. She's right, she did really well and if she does well then I feel like I did well. So it's a win-win. "Ah shoot, I have a rehearsal in ten minutes I need to go, but we can chill tonight I'm sure you'll want to celebrate… with Brian," I mumble.

"Ya, that's true," she says.

"Idiot," I murmur as I head off to the rehearsal.

"Ten minutes early ass freak," Jen whispers as we part ways.

"See you at work, I'll be there straight after rehearsals!"

We begin our rehearsal with a quick warm up followed by a rehearsal of the dance scene. I personally love dance and this scene expresses all kinds of dance with Abbey really choreographing the dances and playing the main dancer, I'm just 'Lana the Choreographer' in the play. Sheera and Abbey discuss the dance routine while Betty, Maya and Ellen gossip about them in a corner. Myself, Jake and a few newbies from first year rehearse lines from a scene. I see Nick – Betty's boyfriend – walk in from the top entrance with a few of his friends. He grins at Betty, waves at her friends, sticks his middle finger up at Jake and winks at me, before taking a seat right at the back.

"Are you on his bad side?" I ask Jake, looking away from Nick.

"You could say that, I mean, I do talk to his girl over there and he's over protective, but I don't really know him if that's what you're asking," Jake replies.

"Kye!" Sheera calls.

"Yep," I jog over.

"You dance right? What do you think about the unison part or should we use cannon?" She asks me.

Abbey begins to explain, "Unison is when you do a move in sync and cannon-"

"I think we know what unison and cannon are Abbey," Betty cuts her off. "I think the cannon looks better here." She voices her unasked for opinion.

"Yeah me too," copies Maya.

"Hmmm maybe, I think it depends on what impact we're trying to achieve," I say.

"Yeah, like if we can get the unison perfect I think the robotic movements will have a more forceful impact," Abbey adds.

"Yes, I like that Abbey," Sheera thinks out loud.

"Cannon would look good too, but from experience robotic dance sequences are more…uniform, you know," Abbey explains, she does have a great dancing background and I can totally see what she's saying.

"Alright, unison it is," Sheera makes the decision. "Guys, dance scene please!" she calls.

The performers get into position, I'm not in this scene so I watch with Sheera.

"Alright, so we're doing the robotic bit in unison, all together at the same time, timing is really important here so listen to the beat, one count of eight beats, let's just practice that. Can someone count the beats plea-?"

"…I will!" Betty now interrupts Sheera.

"Okay Betty when you're ready."

This dance sequence involves a street style dance with robotic moves in the background and Abbey slightly in front performing a dynamic sequence. Betty's role in this scene is to stand upstage performing simpler moves, which she suggested herself but honestly I think it's just distracting.

"Alright, stop there guys," Sheera calls, "That's a lot better, but Betty, I don't know if you should be upstage."

"Oh, I can be downstage," says Betty.

"Oh no, I mean, we have a really good dance sequence here I think the audience might get a little distracted. So maybe you should be off stage for this one. What do you guys think?" Sheera asks us all.

Abby smiles to herself at Betty being told to go off stage, and so do I, while the cast and crew seem to agree with the idea. It's not usually embarrassing for actors to be told what to do because that's our job, we're always told to go off or on stage to compliment a scene, but for Betty it was embarrassing.

"Yeah, I think that would be less distracting. However, maybe Kye should be on stage, her role in the play is the choreographer," Jake suggests.

"What?" Betty questions shocked.

"Hmm, I don't know, that might be distracting too," I give my opinion.

A newbie expresses their opinion, "Maybe, but that makes sense actually, the choreographer should be there, it is supposed to be a practice in the studio right? So maybe she should like stand and watch or count beats or something?"

Others agree.

"Alright let's try that, Kye on stage please and count beats or follow the moves, you know them," instructs Sheera.

Betty struts off into the audience and I find a fitting place on stage from where I see Nick standing up and glaring down at me. Nick leaves half way after meeting Betty in a short break we take. With this dance scene and three other scenes perfected we finish rehearsals for today. We only have a few more rehearsals left until the opening night and I have a lot going on especially now that I have to work harder for exams after flopping my class test and with a job at the same time, my schedule is getting hectic, however me being me, likes a hectic schedule. I find my bag and take out my work shoes and shirt. Abbey stands next to me searching for her bag amongst the many.

"There it is," I point towards her bag, buttoning my shirt up over the top of a vest top.

"Thanks," she smiles. "It's coming together really well."

"Yes it is, thanks to you. You're such a great dancer Abbey," I say. I've never actually spoken to her properly before, so this is nice and it is the first time I actually complemented her.

"Haha, thanks! I just love dancing so much. Way more than drama!" she says with passion that I didn't know she had.

"I can tell!" I say, putting my shoes on. Abby has already packed but it seems like she's waiting for me. "Wait, don't we do dance offs here at uni or something like that? You should do it."

"Oh yeah, we do, well the dance society do, I was going to join but…" she pauses. "Well, it clashed last year with this drama society and then… then I just didn't join." She seems lost in thought as we now stand in deep conversation.

"You chose drama over dance?" I ask sarcastically.

It isn't funny for her though, "Yeah well, Betty wanted to join drama and then you know, it's better to stick with your friends."

"I think it's better if your friends support you in what you want to do." I feel very sorry for her. Betty must have forced her to join the drama society but she has the right to make her own choices. Abbey was someone I didn't really like because she followed Betty around and did everything Betty told her to, but now I actually kind of feel bad for her. She seems hurt on the inside and still tries to pulls off a fake little smile.

"You're great at acting too," I say. "I'm just saying, I think you're great at dancing and you love it, it's your passion, so you should pursue it."

"Ah, it's too late now Kye. Maybe it's just not meant to be."

"No, it's not too late. Look, maybe it was meant to be that you wouldn't join in first or second year because you were meant to be part of this great dance play that we're putting on this year and you were meant to choreograph it. However, you've still got next year. Join the dance team next year, you still have a chance and I am one hundred percent sure they'll take you on. Plus you'll have an experience of both."

Abbey's smile turns more real. She thinks for a second, "Yeah, yeah, you're right, I will join next year. It's only a few months away now. Yeah. Thanks Kye."

"Don't thank me yet, join the team first," I begin to walk. "Sorry, I've got to go to work. I'll see you arou-"

"Abbey! Come on!" Maya yells from just a few steps away with Betty and Ellen staring at us with annoyed expressions.

Abbey shakes her head a little and then walks towards them. She looks so fed up of them and although I feel sorry for her, it annoys me that she accepts how they treat her and her dreams. Everyone should be able to and have the confidence to stand up for themselves. Maybe she just needs reminding.

* * *

The sun is setting but it's light outside, usual for summer. I make my way down to The Mirage, nice and early as usual. This job has helped us pay for the gym, my online talent memberships, Jen's extra learning courses, her astrophysics exams and general stuff like food. The timings are decent and fit around our timetables but they do ask for a lot of shifts especially after major examinations when everyone wants to just party and get drunk. I don't understand why students do that. The guys and Jen do too and even Lia! But not as much as other people, in class people are always talking about how they *need* a drink to celebrate or *need* to get smashed to embrace freedom from examination. It's crazy. People are supposed to have something sweet to celebrate like cake or sleep-in to embrace the freedom. Like *why*? Why do you *need* to destroy your liver to celebrate and be free? It doesn't even taste good. And then you'll hear people talking about how they got wasted on seven point five percent alcohol cider. What would happen if they had a shot of Grey? Yet, I still serve it (the cheap stuff, we don't have the expensive stuff at the bar) to people here, because I get paid to and alcohol is our highest selling product.

With my five minute walk coming to an end so do my thoughts on alcohol. As I shuffle through the door I see Jen tying her apron. Marcus and Rio sit at one of the tables near bar with work.

"Why are you here early?" I ask Jen, walking to the back and hanging up my stuff.

"Well, Bobby's sick, Nat's not in till later and Chef called saying he's stuck in traffic so I had to come and put the ovens on. It should be fine though, it's a quiet day today," Jen explains.

"Alright, and you two?" I ask the boys, putting on my

apron.

"Well, Brian and Deq are playing Fortnite," Marcus replies.

"Which is the biggest distraction ever," adds Rio.

"Yeah and we have studying to do," says Marcus.

"So we followed Jen here, and I'm hungry," Rio finishes.

"Of course you are," I eye Rio sarcastically.

"I hate that Fortnite game," says Jen.

I nod in agreement. It is the buzz right now and possibly what this whole year will be known for in history.

"Don't diss the game!" Rio frowns.

"You hate it because you've never played it," Marcus says fist bumping Rio.

"It's got no storyline, I like games with storylines like Assassins Creed." I act smart because that's the one I've played - more like watched the cut scenes on YouTube – and I genuinely liked it. I imagine myself playing the characters and hope that one day when the movies are made, I will star in them.

"Yeah but Fornite man," Rio dreams for a moment. "Can we get this done quickly and then go play?"

"Yep!" Marcus quickly responds as they both agree on that and then get straight into their studying.

"Do you want to sort out the tables Kye? I'm going to try and get those ovens fired up," Jen makes her way into the kitchen.

I make a start on sorting out the tables which involves checking and wiping, placing menus and cutlery on them and basically making them look neat. I hear laughter and conversation approaching and then the doors open letting in a group of people who have never been here before and I'm not particularly fond of. Betty, Nick and some of Nick's friends, the ones that were in the rehearsal earlier. My heart suddenly starts beating faster.

"Hey! Betz, look who it is!" Nick over-smiles with his arms wide walking right into the middle of the restaurant area.

I pretend not to hear and carry on placing menus on tables. I'm a confident woman and I know they're stupid, so it's best to just ignore them.

"Oh gosh! Are you wearing an apron?" Betty questions

laughing sardonically.

"What's her name Ky..Ki..Keira? Kyra?" Nick spits.

"Kyara Averoni, but everyone calls her Kye," Betty helps him out.

"Oh yeah, sorry. So, is this where you work, Ky…Ky…ara?" Nick asks taking the absolute piss.

Are they making fun of my name? And the fact that I work here? I have to stand up for myself. I freeze for a moment staring at a menu thinking about what to say. I keep looking down ensuring that I'm facing away from them, which moves them and Rio and Marcus out of sight. I wonder what Rio and Marcus are thinking right now. How embarrassing!

I lift up my head for more of a confident stance but still look away from them and say as fiercely but calmly as my voice possibly could, "*Kye* is fine Nick and it's not that hard to pronounce."

There's sniggering amongst them.

"Oh wow! She talks too," Nick smirks.

"She knows your name bruh," one of his stupid friends murmur in the back.

I still face the other way and move on to the next table continuing my job. My hands feel sweaty and I feel uncomfortably warm. I don't know what to say or do right now. *Why are they even here? Did they just come to see me? What if they stay to eat or drink? I'll have to serve, that's my job and there's no shame in that.* I try to reassure myself. I can't believe this is happening. I don't want to even see Rio and Marcus and what their expressions are. *Maybe they can't hear?* Of course they can hear! They're right there, sitting just in front of where Nick is standing. I bet they're thinking I get bullied. I don't. This is just stupid! Where the heck is Jen?

"Wait a second, babe, didn't she play the maid in that play last year?" Nick asks loudly, knowing exactly who I played in the play.

And to add to the whole situation Blondie actually responds in her sweet voice, "Yes she did babe."

"Well, I guess she didn't have to do much acting for that part. It looks like that's what she was born to do!" Nick's voice is viciously harsh and the rest of his gang literally laugh out loud.

I try to control my anger but he has crossed the line, not only is he dissing my acting and my role of that maid that I fully respect but now he's also being racist. My hold on one of the menus turn into a fist causing the card to crumple in one corner.

"That's right! You clean those tables sweetie, like you should. And some free advice – don't try and force your way onto the stage when it just doesn't suit you. You suit better here, being a maid in this run down student place," he laughs with the others. "Come on let's go someplace… more sophisticated."

That is enough! I grit my teeth and half turn around so that I can only see them and not Rio and Marcus, "Well, at least I make my own money rather than feed off my parents' bank account to go someplace *more sophisticated*!" I shout out in anger not knowing exactly what came out of my mouth.

Nick and his gang stop walking towards the door. They all turn around. Nick is in rage. He furiously strides towards me. My heart pounds in my throat. I don't know what to do. Shit! I hold my breath.

"Dude!" Rio stands up right in front of Nick, blocking his path towards me. Rio folds his arms. His wide back and stance partially blocks my view of Nick.

I'm in shock as to what is happening and what is going to happen. I find Marcus standing up next to me and a little behind Rio looking ready. My muscles tense and my body stiffens.

"Why are you getting involved in the girl talk bruh?" Rio questions him, he's calm and cool not angry or scary in anyway.

"Who the hell are you?" Nick moves his head forward to intimidate but Rio doesn't move, "Oh wait a second you're that Brian's mate from the basketball team right? Is that your girl?" Nick indicates me with a nod of his head.

Rio still stands cool as ever, "She might be," he says.

Marcus' head swings down at me with a surprised and muddled look, I'm shocked too. I shake my head stiffly at Marcus and shrug my shoulders.

"Ooooooh," Nick lengthens his neck to look at me over

Rio's shoulder and then looks back at Rio, "She's not all that, but she could definitely do better than you," he hoots but I can see his anger behind his daunting sarcasm.

There's some 'oooo's' and 'ohhh's' from his friends. I feel extremely anxious. *I really don't want this to turn into a fight, God*! Then I notice Betty holding tightly onto Nick's arm in a way that's trying to hold him back from conflict.

"Ha, she probably can, but what about your girl? You and I both know that she could a lot better that you. In fact, she might be already." Rio stings him back with a cheeky wink at Betty.

I am lost for words.

Nick steps ups closer to Rio, his pretty face turning bright red with fury boiling through his skin, "What did you say bruh? Huh? You wanna have it off!"

He's right in Rio's face now moving from side to side, fiddling uncontrollably and trying to threaten Rio. My senses tell me to stop this, I try and get to Rio to hold him back but before I even lift my foot, Marcus grabs my wrist and holds me back to safety whilst moving forwards to threaten the goons and assist Rio if he needs it.

"I'm not the one flinching," Rio says sternly looking deep into Nick's eyes, his arms still folded, he doesn't move an inch even with Nick's red face just a few centimeters from his. He stays strong in his stance and with his words.

Betty pulls Nick back, "Just stop Nick, let's go," she says quietly but harshly. She looks sacred, upset and annoyed.

Nick gives Rio a last strict look in the eye and then turns away, Betty looks at me in anger and takes Nick away as he shoves her arm off in anger. His boys follow him out as he bangs the door open with force so that they bounce back to a close. I stand numb and frightened not fully understanding what just happened. Marcus lets go of my arm. Rio turns around still looking serious, he slaps Marcus' hand in accomplishment and then finally smiles.

"I had your back bro," Marcus says to Rio patting Rio's shoulder.

"I know," Rio says.

Marcus taps me on the shoulder in a comforting manner before sitting back down at the table. I'm still uncomfortable with what just happened and don't know how to react. I never imagined a situation where I'd get bullied or humiliated especially in front of my friends and on top of that I never imagined that it would be the cause of guys almost fighting! I gulp hard in my very dry throat, I can feel the frown on my forehead as my low eyes search for clarity. *Am I going to cry*? I hope not, I swallow harder to hold back my startled emotions.

Rio walks towards me, he loosens his tense arms from folded to by his side, "Well, I definitely don't like her anymore," he jokes, smiling confidently.

I still look down at the floor, my whole head is bowed down. Rio stops right before me and then pushes my shoulders back so that I look up.

"Hey, don't worry Kye, these things happen, especially in Hollywood, you better get used to it. You're probably going to need a bodyguard when you're an A-lister actress – Hollywood's sweetheart."

That makes me think and scares me a little more. I feel a brief rush of adrenaline pumping through my heart and all over my body. Rio's right, I will be putting myself up for all sorts of drama, the media *is* crazy. However, I have already come to terms with that, I know what my dream consists of, the good and the bad and I am prepared for it. Maybe I'm alarmed because I've never experienced this before. Rio's voice is soothing and the way he talks just makes you giggle and feel better even though what he says holds some truth. The adrenaline dissolves quickly. I want to thank him for standing up for me and for being so calm and collective not angry or stupid, but words aren't finding a way out of my mouth.

"You know, I don't mind being your bodyguard when you're famous," he says cheekily. "If you pay me well of course."

Marcus laughs in agreement and I finally giggle too, closing my eyes hard, Rio kisses the top of my head after he successfully helps me out of the misery.

"I'm serious dude," he says folding his arms again as we

continue to laugh.

Jen walks out from the kitchen and into the bar area carrying a tray of glasses, I almost forgot she was in the kitchen.

"What's so funny?" Jen asks. "And you guys are loud. I thought we had a few customers," she looks confused as she empties the tray of glasses laying each one on to a different tray in the bar.

"Ah, well you did have customers but they left after an incident," Marcus confuses her even more.

She pauses and raises her eyebrow at Marcus as if he's just winding her up. We hear a clang of the back door from the kitchen.

"Sorry I'm late guys!" Chef calls from behind.

"Now," Rio smirks, looks down at my eyes and leans in, "Why don't you be a good bae and get your handsome, loving guy some food. Please," he winks cheekily.

"Bae?" Jen's expression is now a picture of confusion.

I push him back grinning at his acting and his attempt to confuse Jen more, "What do you want?" I ask.

"Bae – that looked serious?" Jen questions again with her mind puzzled.

"Whatever's fastest and no salad stuff, I need like proper protein," says Rio as he makes his way to the table.

"I'll have the same," says Marcus.

"Errr hello! Did I seriously miss something?" Jen yells.

"Yes you did, I'll fill you in," I say as we both head into the kitchen.

My confidence came back and I feel a lot better having realized that these things happen. I am glad Rio and Marcus were there and I'm kind of happy that Rio stepped in. I don't know what will happen when I next see Betty or Nick but I'm not afraid. Betty looked afraid too, and maybe she was just having a bad day and then went and spilled it all out to Nick who did what he thought was right for his girlfriend - it wasn't right - but anger and pride can stop us from seeing the difference between right and wrong.

CHAPTER FIFTEEN

KYARA

I wake up to a hot summers morning, made uncomfortable by my thick duvet, quite early for what I thought would be a lie-in from my last second year exam that I took yesterday. I hear and smell breakfast being cooked, I usually do the cooking but it is my lie in day so I don't care who is cooking as long as it is being cooked. I make my way to the kitchen to find Lia cooking bacon and Jen and Brian making toast. Lia and Jen both have their last exams today; Jen's Literature exam, everyone else has finished.

"Morning Kye!" says Lia, "Bacon?"

"Morning," I yawn, "Err in a bit, you guys carry on, I'm going to brush my teeth," because that's what I usually do first thing. I struggle to open the bathroom door.

"Err, Rio's in there!" yells Brian

"Argh!" you have your own bathroom you know!" I kick the door.

"Deq's in ours and Marcus' is in his," Rio shouts from the bathroom. "Good morning by the way!"

I grit my teeth in frustration and bang on the door to try and get Rio to hurry up, "Why are you guys up so early? You guys never get up early!" I yell.

"Too hot and bright," calls Brian.

I take a deep sigh as Deq walks in through the corridor with his abs on display putting on a vest top. He realizes instantly what I was waiting for.

"Morning Kye," he pats me on the back as I run into my room to get my spare toothbrush.

I'm organized and pretty much keep spares of everything. I run into Deq and Rio's apartment to use their bathroom. When I return freshened up, Lia and Jen are halfway through breakfast and Rio is just getting out of the bathroom. I shake my head at him for taking so long and he whacks the back of my head causing my hair bun to fall open, I slap him back and tie my hair up into a high messy bun as we head into the kitchen. Marcus is already here, eating fruit and cereals faster than usual.

"Woah, what are you in a rush for? You don't have a test today, do you?" Rio asks pouring coffee.

"No, but I have that last assignment to hand in by noon and I need to read it through, it's fifteen thousand words long," Marcus replies.

"Argh, I can't wait for this exam to finish," Jen exerts her frustration on the ketchup bottle.

"Oh I know, this year they've really dragged it out," Lia agrees.

Lia has been doing a one day a week internship this year with some local lawyers who deal with compensation for car accidents. She wants to gain experience in various law industries, last year she did an internship with civil and domestic lawyers. I bet she's the most intelligent student in her classes. She knows everything, makes good decisions and judgements and even has experience. I admire that she does love what she does.

"Kye did you get an email about a random class today at twelve?" Rio asks.

"Yes I did," I say. It is a weird one, the email was sent out to the Engineering, Astro-sciences and Physics departments.

"Are you going to go?" Rio questions.

"Yep. You?" I fire back. "It is the last lecture, we might as well go, it might be important."

Rio sighs, "Fine, we'll go."

The girls finish up their breakfast. Lia takes a quick look at her revision cards she made while Jen checks her pencil case.

"God, I hope we do well." Jen closes her eyes and tilts her head back as she speaks out loud.

"Ready?" Lia asks, walking towards the hallway still looking at her cards.

"Yep, let's go and get this over with," Jen says excited and nervous.

They grab their bags on the way out and kiss their boyfriends as Brian and Deq wish them good luck. Marcus, Rio and I also wish them luck. I adore the cuteness of the couples while the single boys cringe and then make jokes. The girls leave. Marcus leaves shortly after to read through his assignment. I'm left with the other guys and a whole load of mess which I forcefully order the boys to help me clean up before our extra class.

Rio and I arrive outside the lecture theatre. There are around six other people waiting outside, looking deep into their phones.

"Great timing Kye, we're ten minutes early and no one else is here," Rio whispers.

"Better to be early that late," I confidently say.

Rio leans against the wall. Ten minutes later and after more people than I expected turn up from both our courses and others, all questioning what this class is about, we finally are let inside. Someone from Jen's astrophysics class asks me where she is, which I instantly reply, "In an exam…" then with a quick nudge from Rio I realize that people still don't know that she actually studies literature and all the astrophysics exams are over so hastily I change my sentence to, "…exam recovery session." Jen can deal with that one when she gets asked later.

I get my usual notepad and pen out while Rio just sits their slouched in his seat almost falling asleep in the cool, air-conditioned room. The heads of each course are present at the front

My Friend's Dream

of the class along with the daunting Dr. Kennedy.

"Settle down," Dr. Kenner speaks with his usual authority. "For those of you who made efforts to attend today, I assure you, you will not be disappointed. Today's brief meeting is regarding an excellent opportunity. A paid internship. With a spectacular organization."

Rio leans to one side almost asleep and I sit with my face on my arms on the desk also sleepy and bored already. I don't need an internship, I need an audition.

"Please welcome Dr. Nigel Hadfield."

A man well dressed in a suit and tie stands up from a chair near the front and smiles giving a short nod at the few of us. Rio gives me an annoyed look for bringing him here.

"Dr. Hadfield is a space Astronaut from NASA and this internship is indeed out of this world with NASA themselves." Dr. Kennedy finishes applauding the man.

My eyes pop open, my head lifts up like a meerkat and my spine straightens making me taller than everyone even those sitting behind me. I look at Dr. Hadfield and locate his badge on his blazer collar. He is from NASA!

"Dr. Hadfield, as some of you may know, is an astounding astronaut," Dr. Kennedy's face was lit up too, I've never seen him so happy or excited.

He's an ASTRONAUT! My whole body illuminates. My eyes widen and adrenaline gushes through me. All I could think about was Jennifer, who currently, is probably finishing her literature exam. Rio also sits up, he grins at me and my huge smile, knowing exactly what I'm thinking. The others in the class also seem suddenly more awake and interested. One boy gets out his notepad whilst a girl next to him pulls out her glasses.

"NASA have an excellent opportunity for our students, whereby a paid yearlong internship will be offered to one of our exceptionally talented students," Dr. Kennedy informs us as he pulls up a presentation on the screen. "Dr. Hadfield will now provide you with some further information and criteria."

Dr. Kennedy and the other teachers clap. I quickly clap and then get my pen and scribble on my notepad to ensure it is working, ready to note down information.

"Thank you very much Dr. Kennedy," Dr. Hadfield takes center stage. "As introduced I am Dr. Nigel Hadfield, just a very brief introduction about myself; I graduated in Mechanical Engineering and I have worked for NASA for over fifteen years as an astronaut, mission specialist and flight engineer, I was also commander of a recent undersea mission that I'm sure some of you may have done some research on."

The slides of the presentation flow along with his words.

"We acknowledge that many young people like yourselves dream of becoming astronauts and with the advancing technology that the present day and the future has to offer we require young people like you, who have the ability to pioneer that future. Hence, at NASA we have set up a Young Astronauts and Scientists Training Program – YAAST Program, where we have fifty internship places available. We have selected twenty five top universities of which one of them is yours. From each university only two exceptional students will be offered an internship, which will begin in the summer of next year after you have graduated. Anybody from each of these scientific disciplines listed may apply for this internship."

A list appears on the board, it includes all the engineering disciplines, physics and all the astro-sciences.

Dr. Hadfield continues, "Now, you must be wondering what the application consists of? Well, it is not as simple as it may seem, this will require hard work and innovative ideas. To be considered for a place at the internship you are required to use your skills and knowledge gained from your studies as well as individual research and experiment, to fully design and build a prototype piece of equipment that can be used in space."

The room waves with gasps and whispers.

"Now, of course the design will not be perfect, we do not expect you to know everything but we are encouraging you to be as innovative and creative as possible with a concept of realism taking into consideration the use of equipment, the economics, the hazards, transport, size etcetera. You will be allocated with a supervisor from your school which I am sure Dr. Kennedy and your lecturers will be more than happy to assist you with. Your supervisor will not only guide you when and if needed but will also form a reference for your application. A detailed project brief will be provided to yourselves by your supervisors," Dr. Hadfield nods at Dr. Kennedy as Dr. Kennedy nods back. "You have from now, one year to complete the design and build of your project including an information pack in the format of an essay to describe and explain your project. Furthermore, this time next year I will return with a panel of judges from NASA who will assess your project and your skillset in the form of a presentation that you will conduct to explain your creation. Each presentation should last between fifteen to twenty minutes. More details on what to include in the information essay and presentation, and a checklist can be found in the project brief. Now, I shall hand back to Dr. Kennedy, but before do, I would just like to say that this is a truly incredible opportunity. You will gain a brilliant experience from this internship and if your design is innovative and practical it may be developed further by you with a team of our experts. Moreover, you will have the opportunity to work alongside experienced and admirable scientists at NASA and will be trained in an area of your choice whether that would be a mission specialist, flight engineer or one of the many roles we have at NASA. In addition to all this, there are prospects for a full time position with ourselves once you have successfully completed the yearlong internship. So do take part. Be imaginative. Be practical. Think like a scientist. Think like an astronaut. This is a challenge and yes, it may seem difficult and unachievable but years and years ago we once thought going to space was unachievable or landing on the moon was impossible however, after research, creativity and innovation, Yuri Gagarin made it to space and Apollo 11 landed on the moon with Neil Armstrong with Buzz Aldrin. There are many of you and only two places. This is not for the faint hearted but if you put your mind to it, anything is possible. We have already proved that. Good luck."

Dr. Hadfield finishes with a roaring applause from us and the teachers.

Oh my God, that finish was intense! He could be a motivational speaker, he could. I've got goosebumps, wow! He shakes Dr. Kennedy's hand, takes a sip of water and begins to put on his jacket.

"Thank you very much Dr. Hadfield. Can we please just take a moment to thank Dr. Hadfield as he now has to go and speak to another university," Dr. Kennedy applauds again.

We applaud again. Another lecturer leads him out as he smiles with his eyes looking at us on his way out.

"So yes, this is the fantastic opportunity NASA have to offer and we, as an institute are truly honored to have been selected," Dr. Kennedy begins. "The project briefs and further information have been uploaded onto the online virtual learning center. Read through it carefully. If you wish to take part in this *competition* as such, then please do contact myself or one of our school heads and you will be allocated a supervisor with whom you may discuss your project and ask for advice. We understand that equipment and materials for these projects will be very costly, therefore we are allowing you to use the school's equipment and material from the science storage labs on level minus two. Please note that the usual material extraction procedure will still apply; you must sign in and out of the labs and you must record the equipment and or material you take from the labs in the record book with your student number as you should be aware that each storage item is counted regularly. The usual rules apply to the storage labs and you must seek permission before taking out equipment from your supervisor. Equipment is very expensive therefore please ensure your project plans and detailed designs have been thoroughly checked with your supervisor before you go ahead and build. Also, you will be restricted to how many of each piece of equipment or material you may take, therefore think through this before hand. Everything that you need should be available in the storage labs however, if there is something that you require which we do not have in the labs and if it has a high cost, you may fill in a material request form which can be found in the brief and submitted to your supervisor.

Now, this is a great opportunity however it is a very difficult application process, designing and building a piece of space technology is not an easy task and therefore I advise you to only take part in this if you are very serious about taking this internship with NASA. This is not a game and you must take this seriously, deceptive swindling use of equipment or school materials will not be tolerated. Hence, and as I said previously you must confirm your designs with your supervisors prior to building. Any designs that we believe will not meet its theoretical application, that are insufficient or impractical will not be given permission to move forward and you will not be authorized to build.

Nevertheless, you have one year to design and build your projects, please think about this carefully and read through all the material provided online before making the decision to take part. Once you have thoughtfully decided to take part, you must request a supervisor before the end of this week. Once allocated, I would recommend making a start on your designs right away as this will be the longest and hardest part of the project. Staff will remain available over the summer to assist, however appointments must be made in advanced as we also have families to see to. You may use the school's resources over the summer, the library for example will be open twenty four hours a day and you all have access to the labs via your student card, nonetheless we would advise you to work in the labs when staff are monitoring for health and safety purposes; over the summer this will be from nine a.m. until six p.m. Monday to Saturday.
Are there any questions?"

There's silence in the room, I think everyone is excited and are already thinking about projects.

Dr. Kennedy continues, "Right, well, I am sure there will be plenty of questions soon, therefore a discussion board has been set up on the Virtual Learning Centre where you may ask any general questions. Think about it carefully. Best wishes. Have a productive summer," he finishes.

He really emphasized the *think about it* bit, it's like he only wants a few people to do this. The teachers leave smiling confidently. The students seem anxious but eager. It is such a great opportunity! This message is going to spread like wild fire. Everyone is going to try it, I just know it. It's NASA! Even the people who don't really want to become astronauts or a space scientists will try their luck. People begin to leave, the room is loud with chatter. I look at Rio who looks at me unsure about the whole thing.

"Hmm, good, but not for me, I'm a car guy. You?" Rio says leaving his chair.

"I have other passions to pursue," I say smiling wide.

Rio shakes his head subtly and presses his lips together thinking about what I'm thinking.

"Oh come on! This is the opportunity she's been waiting for!" I say.

"Yeah, but Kye, look at how many restrictions there are! How is she going to get a supervisor and equipment? What if she can't come up with a decent idea?" Rio asks, waiting for me to pack up.

"We'll figure it out. Trust me! And don't worry about ideas," I leave my seat too. "Ahh! I can't wait to tell her!" I run in front of him. I'm so excited I literally can't keep it in.

"Hey! Don't you think we should read the brief first?" he calls from behind.

We run home. This is made for Jen. Everything happens for a reason. She wanted to go to NASA, but NASA has come to her. *Thanks God!*

***

"Jen!" I shriek running up the four flights of stairs.

Rio runs two steps at a time almost over taking me.

"Jennifer!" I shout again reaching the top, completely out of breath.

Jen casually comes out of our apartment eating an apple, ready in her gym wear. We planned to have a work out session after exams since we had put it on hold whilst examinations took place. Lia follows her also dressed in gym wear and the boys come out of their apartments looking sleepy.

"What?" she asks.

I ran so fast that now I need a moment to catch my breath. Meanwhile Rio runs up to her and hugs her.

"Jen! *I* have got some fricking awesome news for you!" he says letting go and winking at me.

Jen frowns and then walks into our apartment biting the apple, "What's the news?"

We all follow her into the living room.

"Well, what is it?" Brian reinforces the question.

Jen sits on the high stool in the kitchen, Lia sinks into the sofa with Deq, Marcus also sits on the sofa and Brian sits on the other high stool.

"I mean, I personally think it is a bit of a challenge, you know it's…it's tough. But if you want it then, yeah, you should go for it," Rio doesn't make things any clearer as he leans on the kitchen bar speaking to Jen. "It's wicked," he whispers intensely.

"What's wicked?" Deq says making a jumbled face at Rio.

I dump my bag on the floor, sigh hard so that I can be heard and then accompany it with a fake cough, "Jen, what Rio is trying to say is that we have just found you your way to space!" I speak dramatically with enthusiasm.

"Space?" Marcus says intrigued.

"Space." Rio replies.

"Guys, can you cut the suspense please?" Lia says.

"Yeah, and if this is like a stupid prank, then I'm going to slap you both and Kye…" she pauses to eye me. "We are wasting gym time!" she harshly takes a bite from the apple and crunches on it loudly.

I quickly get to the point. "That lecture we just went to, was hosted by Dr. Nigel Hadfield."

Jen freezes. The crunching stops. I thought she might know who he is. She knows every single person, monkey, animal that has been to space, past and present.

"Dr. who?" Deq says making the boys laugh.

"Nigel Hadfield?" Jen whispers.

I nod.

"The astronaut Nigel Hadfield?" she stares in astonishment.

I nod again. She looks at me, gets up from her chair and holds my shoulders.

"Nigel Hadfield was on campus today and I didn't know!" she yells shaking my body. "Oh my God, is he still here?"

I shake my head, "No."

"Nah, he left like half way through, but you know who he is Jen?" Rio asks surprised.

Jen lets go of my shoulders and now walks up to Rio, "Of course I know who he is. He's the guy who went to space a few years ago, he was commander of the undersea mission NEEMO 12, remember Brian, I was watching interviews of him on YouTube and he was talking about that mission, he's done so much and has had many different roles at NASA and…" she stops. "Wait a second… he came from NASA? What was he doing here?" she finally asks the right question.

Rio looks at me with an impressed expression.

"He came to tell us about an internship opportunity NASA are offering fifty final year science students, two each from twenty five selected universities," I explain.

"Internships!" Jen smiles, her mouth wide open, "No fricking way!"

"Yes fricking way! You heard right, NASA have chosen our university to select two *exceptional* in Dr. Kennedy's words - students to join the Young Astronauts and Scientists Training Program also known as YAAST Program for a yearlong internship," Rio describes, "And it's paid!" he adds.

"Yes, and there's an opportunity to secure a full time position with NASA," I explain further.

"And you can chose which department you'd like to train in if you get selected," Rio adds.

"But, the application is tough Jen," I move in closer.

"How tough?" Lia asks.

"Very tough," Rio keeps everyone intrigued.

Jen sits back on her chair, listening intently and taking in all the bits of information Rio and I are giving.

"Tough? Like is there an assessment? An essay? Exam?" Marcus asks.

Rio laughs dramatically, "Yeah all that and more."

"What more, idiot?" Deq asks.

"Yeah, what is it man? Cut the suspense! Do you have to build a rocket? Jeez." Brian yells.

"Pretty much. You have to design and build a prototype piece of equipment that can be used in space," I reveal.

They all shut up.

"But not just any old piece of equipment and not just a drawing or something made from a cardboard box. This has to be innovative, real, practical, sensible, and useful-"

"And it has to work," Rio cuts me off but makes a good point.

"Shiiiiiiit!" Deq says thrilled.

I look at Jen who has her thinking face on, "Tell me more," she says.

I take out my notebook and we go through everything bit by bit, we tell her everything Dr. Kennedy said and everything Dr. Hadfield said. From the project requirements and what the internship will offer, to the presentation, final assessment and equipment policies. Everyone seems to take an interest into this, I mean I don't blame them, this is NASA. I even get my laptop out and all seven of us sit in the living room surrounding the laptop which displays the project brief. We go through it line by line.

Afternoon turns to evening, we cancel our gym plans and order in food. The project brief is extremely long, it has sixteen pages of health and safety conditions alone that the prototype has to comply with. There is a checklist and all of the assessment information as well as some useful resources such as books and websites. Jen doesn't speak much, instead she just takes in all of the information and writes things down as we go along. She seems happy at times and then a little tense at other times. I put my all into throwing in persuasive comments while we speak, I really want to make sure she is motivated to do this. We finally finish reading through the brief.

"Wow," Jen sits back and ties her hair up.

"That's a long brief," sighs Lia.

"That's a big project Jen, are you up for it?" Brian asks her.

The question we've all been waiting for. There's silence as Jen is put in the spotlight, but it doesn't take long for her answer.

Jen straightens her back sitting on the floor leaning against the sofa, "Yes. Yes, I am," she says, nodding gently looking at each of us in turn.

I smile lengthens. We all smile. My girl. I knew she would do it. She looks at me last and I nod back at her with determination.

"Do you have any ideas?" Lia asks fascinated.

"Well, yeah I think so, not like fully developed concepts, I couldn't explain them right now, I need to think about it more, but yeah I think I have a few possible suggestions," she responds positively.

"Damn, she's already on it," Deq laughs.

"That's great Jen, we're all with you, but you do know there's a lot of shit in that brief that you're going to struggle with," Marcus points out.

If Jen is going to do this we need to identify what's going to hold her back.

"Marcus' right. For example, how are you going to get a supervisor?" Brian asks. "I mean you hide from all the science teachers as it is."

Jen thinks about the issues. That is an important point. She needs a supervisor to check that her project is going well. There's stillness already, we can't even get passed the first hurdle.

"Look, at first I didn't think this was a very good idea to be honest with you," Rio speaks. "However, Jen, after talking through it, you seem like you can handle it and you've done two years of this subject *undercover* plus literature and so far – fingers crossed for the results – it's gone well. So maybe you don't need a supervisor. You don't have to have one."

"I don't?" Jen asks.

"Well...you know... nah! They're only there to make sure you're doing stuff correctly. As long as you know what you're doing and it's good, then you can just present it," Rio responds.

"Yes, and if you need any help we can ask together or I'll ask for you," I say.

"Yeah okay," Jen looks like she has the passion to overcome these little issues. Her confidence is strong when it comes to astrophysics. It's just the stupid ways that this world works that's makes her nervous.

"Don't worry Jen, we've got this," Brian reassures her.

"Okay, no supervisor. Cool. Any other issues?" Lia asks.

I can't think of any at the moment and nor can anyone else. Getting a supervisor is the only major problem and so what if we have to break a few rules. Who hasn't? Everything else is fine.

"I don't think so, you just need to design it, we've got paper and pens and the internet and then you just need to build," Deq says.

"Yes, trust me Jen, this is what you've always wanted, this is your opportunity and it has come right to your doorstep. As long as you have a good idea, you can make something wicked. I know you can, we know you can and you know you can. " Brian hugs her.

Jen smiles with determination in her eyes. The sound of a lucky charm rings in the air. We all pause anxiously listening to the magical sound at this magical moment in time.

"Oh the pizza's downstairs. I'll go and get it," Marcus says looking at the message he receives on his phone.

"You better get designing Jen. Bring those ideas out!" Rio says, opening the fridge to get some drinks.

"Cheers to that!" Deq says getting off the couch to help him. "Get a lemonade for Kye."

We embrace the happy moment. For once something has come to us. The dream has come to the dreamer. Things happen when you least expect them, that's true. I just hope this goes well. Jen's determined and we all know she can do this. Time for dreams to come true.

CHAPTER SIXTEEN

JENNIFER

Books are heavy.

 I carry four thick, hardback books covering the topics of Astronomical Equipment, Planetary Rovers, Space Technology and Astrobotany from the library back to our apartment on a quiet afternoon as most people have returned home for the summer. I have quite a few project ideas and have produced a brief design of each one. The first one is a hubble telescope with a feature that excels the current maximum magnification, the second is an enhancement of the space suit and the last idea is a similar design to a rover but with a feature that allows it to plant plants and monitor their growth or a rover that can actually return to earth. All are challenging my mind very much, but I like it, because this is what I think and daydream about anyway. After a brief design of each, the telescope seems a little futuristic and not possible for me to actually build and for the second I would need space suit. So at the moment it looks like I'll be building a rover prototype that can return to earth or that can actually attempt to assess the growth of simple plant life on Mars for example.

 I reach the crossing on a small road that leads to the back

entrance of our apartment and lean my head over the books to look both ways. Clear. I begin to cross as I hear someone's heels click-clocking behind me.

"Hey Jennifer!"

I know that annoying voice. It's Betty… Blondie. I get to the other side and stop just before heading inside and attempting the climb.

"Betty! Hi," I say more enthusiastically that I intended to.

"Oh I'm good. How are you?" she peers at my books. "Are those science books? Don't you study literature?"

My eyes widen for a moment as I try and think of a lie to tell. "Oh… yeah, no, haha, these… are for Kye, you know she's always… err…reading… stuff."

"Kye? Really?" she larks.

Damn. I should've said Rio.

"So do you two just stay here all summer? Not planning on leaving anytime soon huh? I mean, you know, leaving to go home, for the summer?" Betty says, but before I could even answer she continues, "I'm going home tomorrow, the second year drama performance just finished last week, oh you already know that, so I'm still packing and I thought I'd spend a few more days here with Nick. But, anyway it's about time Kyara started concentrating on science stuff. She's always, you know, getting in my way," she jests sarcastically.

I don't know what she's trying to do, she never really talks to me and she doesn't even like me. I'm just concentrating on holding these books at the moment. I nod along.

"You know what she did," she begins to gossip. "She was like totally talking to my girl Abbey about me."

"Really," I respond not caring much. It's like she's trying to befriend me, she's trying to be nice I guess by gossiping and telling me something that she thinks I don't know already. Or is she trying get information out of me about Kye? Whatever she's playing at, it's a little creepy.

"Yeah, she's been talking to Abbey like a whole lot these days. They're both getting along really well. Abbey wants to join the dance team next year and not the drama society. I think Kye has something to do with that stupid decision of hers."

I already know that, we do tell each other everything, maybe it's not like that for Blondie and her girls.

"Oh, well, you know maybe that's a good thing. I mean you'll have one less person to compete against," I say.

"Compete?" Betty laughs out loud. "Abbey is no competition for me," she gets a little defensive.

"Hmm," I don't really know what to say next without completely obliterating her high self-esteem. "Whoosh! These books are heavy, Kye's waiting," I indicate my leave from this awkward situation.

"Oh yeah sure. You should try the gym, weight training is good for girls too you know. You could work on those arms a little," she calls as I enter the building.

Work my arms? Try the gym? Seriously! I'm in the gym five days a week! I train with two extremely motivated girls and four tremendously fit guys. My arms are cut, carved and toned, and this little shrimp thinks I need to *try* the gym! Asshole!

I reach the living room and drop the books down on the table stretching my arms out immediately. Kye sits on the couch typing away. She's editing her book. As I take some deep breaths so that I can begin my gossip, Deq walks in with Lia behind him.

"Alright I'll see you guys in two weeks," he calls walking into the living room.

"Aww, why do you boys go home more than us girls?" Kye stands up making a sad face and giving him a tight hug.

"Because you girls complicate things and like to make your own lives inconveniently busy," he replies sarcastically.

"Have a good break Deq, see you soon," I hug him.

"Thanks, you too, take care," he says as he walks out with Lia.

We hear them kiss and then Deq makes his way down the stairs. We wait for Lia to come back in. She does slowly with an exaggerated sad face and falls onto the couch next to Kye hugging her.

"Ah, I know, it sucks doesn't it," I say. "It's only been a week since Brian went home. It feels like a year." I know exactly how she feels, I hate being away from Brian for so long but I suppose that's something I need to get used to.

Kye's face saddens, "Aww, can someone please find me a guy! Why doesn't anyone like me?"

"It's not that no one likes you, it's that you are too fussy," I tell her.

"All I want is like a Chris Hemsworth or a Chadwick Boseman," Kye replies.

Lia and I make a face at Kye. She only chose like the two hottest guys on the planet right now.

"How long will Deq be gone for?" I ask.

"Two weeks," Lia replies.

"Brian will be back next week, I was video calling him this morning, he said Rio will be back the week after and Marcus is on an internship so he'll be away all summer," I inform them.

"Well, at least we get some girl time, where we can actually do girly stuff without being interrupted or bullied with sexist comments," Lia makes a good point.

"Speaking of that, guess what just happened?" I recall the Betty incident that occurred a few minutes ago. I spill on everything that just happened in frustration. Kye and Lia giggle uncontrollably.

"It's not funny guys!" I throw my bag at them.

"Ouch! What? She's like that!" Kye replies still laughing.

"Does it not look like I go to the gym? I'm pretty fit and toned right? You can see it," I say looking at myself in the reflection of the balcony doors.

"Now you sound like her," Kye giggles back.

"What is she still doing here anyway?" Lia asks.

"She said she was hanging out with Nick before they go home for a few weeks," I say understandably.

"Oh, I see," Lia also considers Betty's feelings genuinely.

"Argh! Oh will you two stop or wait for me at least!" Kye yells making Lia and I chuckle.

"She still peed me off though, like she was really trying to get on my good side. And how! Just how? Can she tell me that I need to work out?" I shriek.

"You need to get over it," says Lia.

Kye adds, "Yeah, forget about it, look I need some help."

I take a deep breath and then flop onto the couch next to Kye and look at her screen because that's obviously what she means by, she needs help.

"What?" I ask.

She hands me her laptop and stands up to stretch, "I've got like a motivational speech bit that I need to put in this highlighted section, but I can't figure out how to word it."

Kye walks over to the kitchen and pours herself a glass of water. I look at the screen with Lia, there are a few blank lines highlighted in yellow. I read a few lines before to gain an understanding of what is going on. What I gather from it, is that the character is going to explain why dreams are important and why we should support them, to an audience who doesn't really agree with the whole idea. Yep. I'm pretty sure that's real.

Kye walks out of the room and then walks back in with a box of nail kits so that we can do our nails, something girly. Kye likes her nails and hairstyles and she's drawn me and Lia in too.

"Right. Any ideas?" she sits down looking through the box of colors.

Lia also scurries through the box and then finds me a nude color that I quite like.

"Hmm, I'm not too sure," I say still thinking and beginning to paint at the same time.

"How long do you want this part to be?" Lia asks.

"As long as it needs to be. This is like the main part of the story. The turning point or the eye opener, if you know what I mean. So it really needs to be good and it needs to hit the audience."

"Yeah, the part where you get that enlightening music in the background and people begin to feel sorry for their sad lives?" I say looking interested.

"Yes exactly," Kye replies.

"And then they get really inspired to do something they really want to do and then they just go and do it, with extra exaggeration?" Lia adds on.

Kye nods.

"The kind that last for like five minutes before you give up again because life is just that damn hard?" I imagine it as I speak.

"Yes. However, in the book it lasts a lot longer and actually gets the character to where she wants to be." Kye comes back.

"Alright, I think you should say it out loud. Perform it to us." Lia has a good idea.

"But I haven't got anything written down yet."

I like Lia's idea, "Just improvise for now Kye, see what comes out when you're acting. The feelings and emotions will help you come up with the speech. We'll write stuff down if it's good," I nod at Lia. "It's best to just go with the flow. Ready?"

Kye stands up startled, "Err, wait," she fixes her hair and takes the center of the room. "Okay, so, err…dreams… dreams are…" she pauses trying to think of something. "A dream… is… a wish that your heart makes," she bursts out laughing and so do we.

"Is this character Cinderella?" Lia jokes.

"Nope," Kye replies holding her head trying to come up with something original.

"It's a great line and it is true," I turn my head to tell Lia and then look back at Kye, "But it's taken. Be you Kye. You're always giving us motivational speeches. What would you say?"

"What would I say?" Kye asks herself in thought. "I would say…dreams are there for a reason… dreams give us a reason to live, they are what drives us to continue into our future."

Kye looks at us and we stop to look at each other for a brief moment. She's getting it out. Lia waves her hand indicating Kye to continue and I start typing.

"We all have dreams, some seem bigger than others, but for a person their dream is theirs and to them, it's a big deal. For some it can be to get married, or to have children, or simply to wake up every morning in good health. For others it's a profession or an achievement like becoming a Lawyer or going to university, winning a medal in the Olympics or even just to taking part in the Olympics. They are our goals in life. We only have one life..."

Kye's emotions come through. It's hard to tell if she's acting or just being her but I know Kye, this is her when she talks about dreams. There's a soft tone in her voice, like the one she had when we first met and spoke about our dreams on the balcony. I can almost hear that motivational music in the background of my imagination. The atmosphere changes as she speaks, the sharp evening sunshine hits the wall behind her, the sound of trees softly rustling and the tweets of the birds outside gently flow inside the room, accompanied by my typing, which is ignorable. We listen intently.

"...One life, to make our dreams come true. You know, it's funny because whether you admit it or not you all have a dream, or have had a dream. Especially when you're young and you really want something in life or you want your life to go a certain way, but then life itself gets in the way; our families, friends, relationships… money. Then, we forget we even had dreams. But who are we to get in the way of dreams? I ask you, think back to when you were young, what was your dream?" she pauses. "Has it come true?" Another pause. "I didn't think so. Why didn't it come true?" Pause. "Because you didn't have the guts to pursue it."

Woah. I look at what I'm typing on the screen. I feel emotional.

"How often do you meet a person who's living their dream? Anyone you ask will say 'oh I wanted to be this, but then I ended up doing this' why? Because they didn't have the determination to pursue it or because their parents told them something else. Everybody has the right to live their dream. Dreams give us freedom, they lead us on the right path. They give us an aspiration in life. Without dreams we wouldn't look forward to the future. And you know what's crazy? Everybody has them; the rich and the poor. You know, some people say money makes the world go around, yeah maybe," she laughs gently. "Most will say that love makes the world go around, also quite true. But I say that hope makes the world go around because hope gives us faith in life and with faith dreams come true."

I finish typing as she finishes talking. Lia sits in awe and I sit feeling a little bit sad but enlightened and motivated. There's still silence. Kye waits for a response from us. She looks down at us waiting.

"Well?" she finally says.

"Wow." Lia's still in admiration.

"Yeah," I breathe out. "That was it." I'm still in the moment too.

"Did you get it all down?" Kye asks.

"Yes I did." I snap out of my trance, "Sorry, wow Kye, that was really good."

"Did you seriously make all that up?" Lia asks.

Kye nods, "I think so. It was a bit too much wasn't it."

"No, no, I thought it was really good. It was really inspirational actually," Lia states.

"Thanks guys!" Kye says as she sits in front of us on the table.

"This book is definitely going places!" I say, handing her the laptop so that she can have a look.

"I really hope you two get what you want," Lia begins in a similar tone to Kye's speech tone. "You guys are so optimistic and I love that. I hope you become a Hollywood actress Kye, and Jen, I hope you become an astronaut. You guys really deserve it. And hopefully I will be a good lawyer and I hope I can actually help people. We're all going to do great things," she finishes.

We feel a rush of happiness and squeal as we form a tight hug.

"See how many times you said *hope* then?" Kye giggles as we hold on to each other in a hug.

We embrace the moment as we embrace each other. These are my girls and I love them. I hope they get everything they want in life. The moment is interrupted by Lia's phone which buzzes. We untangle ourselves.

"It's Deq, he's on the train and wants to video chat," Lia says looking at her phone. "I'll talk to him on the way home, I better go now."

"You're not stopping over?" I ask.

"No, my mom's taking me out for dinner tonight, remember?" she replies.

"Oh yeah. Well, enjoy!" Kye says hugging as she makes her way to the front door.

I follow them into the hallway and also see Lia off, "Talk to you later Li."

She leaves and we stand in the empty hallway with the sunset gleaming right through the big window on top of the stairs. It feels so lonely without the boys here, I don't know how we're all going to split up after this final year. It's going to be heart breaking.

"You want to call Brian now, don't you?" says Kye, cheering me up as I lead the way back into the living room.

"Yep, exactly what I was going to do. What are we eating tonight?"

"I made pasta earlier."

"I love you Kye!" I yell.

"Hey, what do you think we should call the book? I still haven't come up with a title," Kye asks. "And still haven't painted my nails!" she sits down again and looks through the box.

We haven't really thought much about the title, so that's an interesting question. I find the pasta in the kitchen and then pull out two plates from the cabinet.

"I think we should keep it simple. By the way, it's very well written thanks to me, you know because of my literature skills," I boast.

"You only like it because it's about you," Kye quickly responds.

"Hey!"

"It has to be eye-catching and unique," Kye adds.

"How about... *My Friend's Dream*?" I say.

Kye stops in the midst of opening a nail polish bottle that she finally chooses. She turns her head toward me and gives me a very peculiar look, "*My Friend's Dream*? Seriously!"

"Yeah! It's simple and to the point," I reply quite certain

about my choice of title.

"It's stupid," Kye responds. "It's too simple. *My Friends Dream*," she says it out loud again to me, making a silly face. "Yep. It's stupid. It should be something like…*Dreams…Destiny*, yeah *Dreams Destiny*," she waves her polished hands around in front of her, picturing it.

"What? Now that's stupid. It's the person's destiny to fulfil the dream not the dream's," I say irritated, making a good point and carrying our pasta plates to the living room table.

"Okay, what about…*A Dream*…" she pauses to think, "… *A Dream within the Stars*," she winks at me. "Do you get it? Now that's clever and unique."

I give her a plate and a fork, thinking about that one. It does make sense but dreams and stars in general are always grouped together so the whole astronomy thing might lose its value here, or maybe that would be the whole point. For the first time ever I'm actually using the analytical technique we're taught in literature.

"Hmm, maybe," I say not too keen on it, "I still like *My Friend's Dream* better," I take a mouthful of food.

"Okay, *A Dream within the Stars*, it is," Kye blows on her nails and then quickly types the title on the laptop before clicking the save button and shutting it down.

CHAPTER SEVENTEEN

KYARA

Final year.

     Honestly, it has come so fast that I didn't see it coming. I always thought that I would get cast in a major movie during my time here and then would have to leave my studies to go and fulfil my dreams. That's how I imagined I would become an actress. Yet here I am, in my final year of education with no real opportunity or likelihood of becoming an actress before we graduate and leave. Then again, *anything is possible*; I've lived my life so far by that phrase, though nothing much has happened. *God, what are you planning dude?*

     Classes are getting harder and everything in this final year is so much more intense than I expected. Jen is all over the place too with the NASA project almost coming to a finalized design and her astrophysics course becoming busier with exams, class tests and final year assignments. Plus, she has a huge literature thesis to write on the one and only Shakespeare, which is the final assignment for English literature. I've completed the first draft of my book and I'm half way through the second edit, which has been delayed thanks to my parents, who forced me to stay an extra week at home due to a cousins wedding. Physics is becoming tougher to study and to top everything off, I've started writing a screenplay which is about an actress, *obviously*, and a group of aspiring dancers, so it's a dance movie like no other! All of this has meant that Jen and I have had to resign from working at The Mirage, because everything is just getting too much to handle. Brian has begun his master's and it actually seems easier than the bachelors! He's in class only one day a week, although he does have quite a few assignments to do and it is research based so I suppose he has a lot of work to be getting on with. Marcus still has this year followed by another to go before he graduates as a doctor, however he is now in practice as a student doctor at the local surgery twice a week. Lia and Deq are just getting through their final year like me, though they argue a lot these days. Which makes things a little awkward for us because we don't know what to say or do when they argue. I mean, Lia's our girl, we take her side most of the times, but Deq's our guy and he pretty much lives with us. It's crazy how we won't be living together this time next year. Everybody will have jobs, except for Marcus and we'll all be going our own ways, different ways. I don't have a clue what I'll be doing. Hopefully, I'll be on a set shooting scenes for the next blockbuster. Argh! I can't imagine myself in an office, working nine till five. *What am I going to do?* This scares me. Like seriously after this year, I have no plan. Education has been my excuse to stay out of work, out of a job and out of a career that I don't want to follow. It's my excuse because I know students get more free time which allows me to write and audition, nine to five won't give me time for that! So when education is over, my excuses will be over. I don't know what I'm going to do. *Maybe I'll do a master's, that'll give me an extra year of excuse?*

"Hey," Jen comes in, interrupting my stressful thoughts about my life after this year.

"Hey, how was your day?" I ask putting my pen down, tired from holding it while procrastinating.

"Usual, literature is just so long, I sit in class just thinking, *why am I here*," she heads to the kitchen to find lunch.

"Yeah?" I question for more detail.

"Yeah. At least the final year teacher is nice. We've never had her before."

The boys come in together, also as usual, at the usual lunch time to take a break and gossip.

"Dr. Kennedy?" Brian asks leading the way.

Jen nods.

"She only teaches final years. She's nice. Not my type, but nice," he jokes.

"Ew. She's like fifty," Jen reminds him in sarcasm as the boys chuckle.

"Well, not like our Dr. Kennedy then," I say.

"Hell no! She's the complete opposite, really helpful, caring and approachable," Jen warms some snacks up in the microwave.

It is winter, cold and frosty outside. It is forecasted to snow soon and we still need to put up some Christmas decorations.

"Anyway, I need to go and work on my design. I aim to complete it before we start the final semester after Christmas."

"Speaking of Christmas, this will be our last one together," Marcus says with some emotion.

"Yeah, so I expect good presents!" Rio laughs.

"Like what?" I ask.

Rio places his hand on his chin, "I would like…"

"…And no we can't afford to get you a GTR," Jen interrupts him.

"Forget it then," Rio shrugs his shoulders and then cheekily smiles, "I don't need anything, as long as no one goes home for Christmas and we all celebrate it together here, I'm happy with that."

Jen and I let out a girly, "Awwwww!" at Rio's heart-melting comment.

"That's touching dude," Brian says.

"I think we can give you that," Deq says slowly.

We didn't even see Deq sitting there. He and Lia have been having some relationship trouble, over very minor things. Well, they are minor to me, but I guess if I was in their shoes it would be major.

"What do you want bae?" Brian asks Jen.

"Hmmm, I think I'd like that too, just everyone here for Christmas, together," she replies, "And some new gym shoes would be great."

"What are you going to get Lia, Deq?" Brian accidentally asks.

Deq purses his lips, "Hmm, I don't know."

"Sorry dude, I forgot," Brian says.

"It's okay, I mean she's okay with me for now. You know, it's the festive season, I'll make it up to her."

"That's my boy," Rio hugs him sarcastically.

"What about you Kye?" Marcus asks.

Me. I want something that's easy to say but hard to achieve. It's simple but complicated at the same time. I've wanted it always, but still haven't got it. I've asked for it every Christmas, birthday, religious festival and still have not got it. Now, I want other things too, but that's still my top wish. We are merely human, we will always ask for more.

"I want to be blessed with my dream of acting turned into reality," I press my lips together. "Can you get that for me please?" I giggle, but it hurts my heart.

They sadly laugh too.

"Ah, if only," Jen replies. "We should probably put some decorations up."

"Yes please!" I close my books quickly. I've been sitting in front of them for like three hours and haven't written or learnt a single thing.

We munch the warm food down and shove our books out of the way. The Christmas decorations are stored neatly – by me – in one of the kitchen cabinets - ours and the boys'. We have three small Christmas trees, one for each apartment and then we usually put all the gifts under the one in our living room (because it is slightly bigger but also because we don't trust the boys with presents). We'd usually open them a few days before Christmas as everyone goes home, but this year we'll open them on the Christmas day, together. Lia joins us soon after. As normal, we girls are the neat decorators and the boys just make a mess with all the decorations in all three apartments. We have music playing out loud in the background and we sing along whilst putting up Christmas lights. This is the last time we'll be doing this and I can feel the emotions in my body but I don't let them out. Instead, I capture everyone's beautiful expressions and joyful faces that will remain with me forever because I don't know where we'll be next year.

We complete our and Brian and Marcus' apartments and are putting up lights in Rio's and Deq's when I feel a vibration from my phone. I stop reaching for the lights as Rio takes over from where I hold them in position and take out my phone from my pocket. It's an email. I unlock it and then click on the email. At first, all I see are the words 'Casting Audition'. It's probably a newsletter from one of the many casting networks I have joined and am paying for monthly to receive casting notifications. But the email address has an actual name rather than a 'noreply'. I scroll down, frowning. My heart begins to beat faster. *Could it be? God?* I begin to read.

> Dear Kyara,
>
> We attended your School's performance last summer and found your acting skills to be exceptional. We thoroughly enjoyed watching your performance.
>
> We are currently casting roles for an upcoming film by MSR Productions and would like to consider you for casting.
>
> If you are interested, please send us a self-tape of the sides (selected part of the script) attached by January 12th.
>
> We look forward to hearing from you.
>
> Best wishes,
>
> Angela Weir
>
> Casting Director
>
> Angela Weir Casting Ltd.

I stand in shock. Staring at my phone, which I hold out in front of me. Rio switches the music off and they all stop to look at me.

"Kye?" Lia says.

I'm unable to speak. If this is a joke, it's disgusting. If it is not, then... I scowl and sit down on whatever is behind me, which luckily is the arm of the couch. I read it again in my head but this time I mime bits of it, not making a sound. I check the email address. It is certainly from Angela Weir. No pranks. No junk mail.

"Kye!" Rio shouts.

I look up at them with my mouth open. Brian takes the phone from my hand and reads the email as I freeze.

"Kye!" he shrieks. "You got an audition!"

"What!" Jen yells taking the phone from Brian, reading the email out loud with Lia looking over her shoulder.

"No fricking way!" Deq says in surprise.

"Kye, this is what you wished for, kind of," Marcus says putting his arm around me.

"Damn! I should've wished for that GTR!" Rio yells looking up to find God.

"Oh my God! Kye, it's an actual movie! An actual Hollywood movie!" Lia yells, shaking me.

"We better get started on that self-tape! Kye!" Jen wakes me up from my shock.

Oh my God, I have never received an email like this, asking me to audition, usually I'm the one asking to audition. "I can't believe it, there were casting directors watching our plays!" I say in disbelief.

"Yeah, what's Blondie going to say to that, huh?" Jen says out loud.

"Kye you got an audition. That's something. I told you, you were going to be an actress. I knew someone would pick you," Rio embraces me. "Now you better hire that bodyguard," he winks.

"Shh, guys, I haven't been picked yet," I say. I'm nervous already. "Auditions are a long process, this is just a self-tape, after this there's so much more to do and they might just call it quits after watching the tape."

"Well, girl at least you got an audition, that's an achievement in itself!" Lia shakes my arms.

I feel a smile coming along. I have waited so long for this! It is a step forward, whether I get it or not. "I got an audition!" I let out my excitement holding whoever sits nearest to me.

"Angela Weir," Marcus reads from my phone.

"Yeah, I know her, well, I don't know her but I've heard of her, she's casted so many top movies in Hollywood." I have done my research and I do know who she is, that's why this is a big thing.

"Whoop! Kye's going places!" Brian says in delight.

"Okay guys, lets' not get our hopes up, because well, I only have a teeny tiny chance. You know it's going to be tough. I'm sure I'm not the only one auditioning for this. I could be, but we don't know that," I try and settle myself. "I know what this industry is like, I've been rejected many times before."

"Yeah but this time, they emailed you and it's not advertised all over the internet for publicity purposes like the other ones with a one-off random email address," Jen talks sense, that's what they usually are. "This has been sent personally to you, by a top casting director who has already seen you act!"

"Hey, don't stress Kye. We'll keep it cool, no pressure," Deq reassures me.

"And we are going to get this self-tape done as perfectly as possible," Lia adds.

"One hundred percent. There's plenty of time and we are all here to help," says Marcus.

"I'm reading lines!" Rio announces.

"No! You put me off!" I yell.

"What? Nooooo, I bring the best out of you. I'm telling you, you need me," Rio expresses.

"What if it's a girl, dumbass?" Jen talks to Rio.

"Then…I'll put a voice on. I'm good at that."

"You're right, you are good at that," Brian jokes as Rio punches his shoulder.

"Alright, it's good news. Now let's finish the decorations and tidy up, then we'll take a look at the sides and Jen, you better get working on that project," I say getting up and carefully saving the email before putting my phone away.

"Jen, you really need to start building that thing," Brian says.

"I know. I know. I just want to make sure that the design is perfect because I don't want to mess the construction up, if the design is near enough perfect it'll be easier to build."
`We all get back to work and finish the decorations quickly and quietly. Much quicker than before. Everyone is eager to read the sides, so not time to delay.

After we finish decorating and tidying the mess the boys had created, we sit down to read the sides. They aren't long, only a page and a half. It is a strong piece with a feisty feel, or at least the girl seems feisty from what I can tell from the short sides I received. And the other character is in reality a guy – a bad guy from what the script reads – so Rio takes the first bid on reading for the tape - not that it matters anyway. I still can't believe I got an email! *Thank you God!*

* * *

"Merry Christmas!" Jen runs into my room and jumps into my bed waking me up. I've noticed when she is excited about something, that's the only time she'll get up early.

"Merry Christmas Jen," I greet her hugging her back. "Is it snowing?" I ask.

We get up, Jen lifts the blind on my window letting in a strong shine of brightness. It's not snowing now but it had snowed all night and it has set well. It looks beautiful. We take our morning coffees over to the balcony and enjoy the scenic view of the university grounds. It's quiet on campus but still festive, Christmas trees are up in places all around the gardens and the colorful lights had already been turned on today. They can be seen clearly against the glistening snow. We turn our lights on too.

"This is nice," I say enjoying the warmth of the coffee, watching the cold outside.

"Hmm," Jen makes a sound wandering off into the wonderland.

We hear Shakin Steven's 'Merry Christmas Everyone' being played on a speaker getting louder as the boys and Lia join us, Deq places the speaker on our TV stand.

"Merry Christmas Everyone!" Rio exclaims with joy in time with the song.

We run into the living room and everyone wishes each other a Happy Christmas, then we get the breakfast going. Jen, Marcus and I had prepared Christmas Dinner last night, so all we need to do is stick everything in the oven and get on with the prezzies!

That was probably one of my best Christmases. Even though we got each other crazily stupid presents like a pack of funky pens from Deq and a small flashlight that in tiny writing says 'To Light up the Path that Leads to Your Dream' from Rio and a keyring to go with it from Brian; the presents where keepsake and special because they are from friends. Jen got her gym shoes and a phone case with the solar system on it, with the planets in order. Her project had been finalized, by, well... us; and she started creating the materials list. The longest part is now over, we just hope the design doesn't have any flaws that might cause her problems when actually building the thing.

The New Year is on its way and I want to get the self-tape done and sent before then. We'd already recorded the intro or as they call it the *Slate;* which basically is my name, height, where I'm from etcetera and we are half way through filming the audition in the kitchen against the plain wall, which is proving difficult with Rio reading lines. Although, we can't blame him alone, we've done it plenty of times before and it is always difficult, only this time I have a better chance of actually getting the role, so it needs to be perfect.

"What do you mean you don't know?" Rio shouts in an interesting accent from behind the camera that Deq holds.

"I don't know! And don't ask me again or-" I act sharply toward the camera.

"Or what!?" Rio cuts me off in good timing reading from the script.

"Or I swear, I will knock you out and leave you here," I reply quickly. I imagine my character to be confident, quick and unafraid, so I don't think she'd stutter here. That's my take on it.

"Huh," Rio shrugs awkwardly still trying to stay in character.

"Keep up!" I shout at Rio's character after some stage directions, keeping well in character.

"What the hell was that dude?" Marcus blurts out laughing at Rio.

"Cut!" Jen yells as if we're on a real set.

"Ahh guys!" I cry taking a deep breath and then using the opportunity to quickly look at the script.

"Huh," Brian imitates Rio's shrug laughing at him.

"What! That was good!" Rio defends.

"That was actually a good run," Lia says looking back at the recording next to Deq.

"It's okay, I'll edit it all together. Let's just get it all filmed," I say quickly remembering the last few lines.

"Was that not good?" Rio asks.

"Actually, it was," I say impressed.

"See!" Rio yells.

"Can you imagine Rio on the screen?" Brian whispers to the other boys.

"Hell no!" Deq whispers back.

I put the papers down and position myself back to where I was to avoid the shots jumping when I edit the tape.

"Okay, last little bit guys," I call.

"Yeah, don't mess it up, we've been doing this all day. I'm hungry," Jen reinforces to the boys.

"Ready?" Deq asks.

I nod.

"Action!" Jen unnecessarily shouts.

We finally finish filming. After so many takes, it comes to a point where I kind of just have to be satisfied with at least one of them. Marcus and Rio go and take a break outside playing some basketball. Brian helps Lia and Jen cook dinner while Deq and I sit down to put together the several takes as best as we possibly can to make the final self-tape. After a few hours of fidgeting with the takes and asking everyone what they thought about each one before selecting the right one to go into the tape, we finally complete the self-tape. We show it to everyone and I watch it multiple times to ensure it's the best it can be. Honestly, I always feel like it can be better, but you get to a point where you just have to go with it. Also, I have a tiny feeling that this self-tape isn't that great, but I always have that feeling. Now, the problem is time. It is twelve thirty two a.m. if I send the email now, it'll look stupid. I know people don't usually check what time an email was sent but this might put them off. It's unprofessional sending an email late at night. What if it's on their phone and it bleeps while they sleep? I'll have to send it first thing tomorrow morning. I make a note in my diary and highlight it in bright orange.

Ten a.m. I'm up and already checking the tape once again, reading through my reply email a million times and just waiting to hit the send button. I don't want to do it too early, I think around about now…is a good time. I can imagine the casting director settled into their office, with some coffee, checking through their emails and then they'll receive mine, it'll be fresh and right in front of their eyes. Send! I press the button, breathe and look up. *God, I have faith.*

"Sent it yet?" Jen comes out of the bathroom drying her hair with a towel.

"Yes, just now," I reply.

She touches my shoulder as she walks into the kitchen.

"It never happens but worth a try right? At least I won't regret not taking the opportunity," I mentally prepare myself for rejection as I shut down my laptop.

Jen smiles at me, "Just forget about it now. You've done your bit. Let's see what *he or destiny* does," she points up and then changes the subject, "It is freezing!"

"You're going to get pneumonia, you better go and dry your hair!" I shout like a mother.

Jen frowns at the myth.

"This will keep you warm." Brian flirts as he enters with the boys and hugs Jen tightly wearing a warm knitted Christmas sweater.

"Get a room," Marcus comes in with a plate of breakfast.

"Sent it Kye?" Deq asks.

I nod.

"Have you guys heard about the Final Spring Fling Ball?" Rio questions looking at his phone.

"Oh that email we got a few weeks ago…" I begin, not really interested in the ball and thinking no one else is either.

"Oh yeah, we're all going," Jen says pretty assured that she is going.

"Well, my final year is next year, so I'm not invited," Marcus sits down with his breakfast.

"Lia and I have booked tickets too," Deq adds.

"What?" I ask very confused at the moment. "So everyone's going?"

"Yes," Brian responds.

"And you didn't tell me?"

"We thought you knew! We…we discussed this…didn't we?" Jen asks trying to remember and leaving me confused.

Rio interrupts with a yell, "Nope! No you didn't, because I didn't know! Someone just posted it in the mechanical engineering group chat, that's how I found out. It's on the 1st February for all final years," he reads from his phone. "I'm going. You coming Kye?"

"Err, nah, I don't think so…" I say.

"What! Why not?" Jen's quick to respond.

"Well, I'm not going to have anyone to hang out with," I make my point.

"You've got us," Brian says.

"No. You've got each other. You've got Jen, Deq and Lia will be together-"

"You got me!" Rio winks at me.

"Yeah, you'll go off with a million other girls that you either already know or will meet."

"That's not true," Rio pretends to be defensive.

"That's so true," Marcus buts in.

"I'm a very *loyal* person. To the one girl I'll call 'Wifey', one day," Rio says quite nicely.

"Have you been watching Love Island?" Jen asks him ironically.

"Kye, we won't leave you and you'll have your class mates there too. Mingle in! You're an actress, you need to get used to it," Brian speaks the truth.

"Yeah but my class mates are you know… stereotypically unsociable."

"Hey come on! I won't wonder off, it'll be fun!" Rio's excited.

"Yeah, you know we're still going to sit together anyway and I won't leave you, sisters before misters," Jen says high fiving me.

Brian wears a dumped look on his face, "Yeah okay, bros before…" he whispers the last bit to his pals and then fist bumps them.

We're going to the ball.

CHAPTER EIGHTEEN

KYARA

"I'm here ladies!" Lia yells coming in through the hallway and into Jen's room carrying a large bag where Jen and I get ready.

"There you are! You better hurry!" Jen tells Lia.

We are getting ready for the ball and need to leave in fifteen minutes. Jen and I have done our makeup. I have done my hair in a braided up do and have almost finished Jen's. Lia was supposed to arrive an hour ago to get ready with us.

"Don't worry, I've done my makeup and I've sorted my hair now Kye, I just need you to pin it back a little please, then I'll put my dress on and I'm done."

"Cool, I'm almost done with Jen's," I mumble as clearly as possible biting a hair grip.

I finish Jen's elegant up-do hairstyle and quickly move on to pinning Lia's hair back. We hear a few of the boys walk into our living room, calling us to hurry up as the taxi is on its way.

"Alright! Who called it so early?" Jen shouts back at them.

"Is that okay?" I ask Lia finishing and looking at her hairstyle through the mirror.

"Yep! Thank you!"

"Cool," I swivel her chair around. "How does my face look?"

"Gorgeous! Although, your makeup is quite light. I mean it suits you, but it's not that heavy," she replies looking at me thoroughly.

"I told you its light," Jen says undressing and rushing. "Girls at the ball are going to be drenched in makeup."

"Yeah, but what more can I do?" I say looking in the mirror. "I don't like wearing too much, I mean to me, I'm wearing a lot! I just like looking like the same person when I take it off. "

"Yeah, you're right and you don't need it to be honest. You look beautifully elegant," Lia says getting her dress out of a bag.

"Okay, you're making me feel bad about my fake lashes, but I need them, I'm blonde," Jen jokes.

"Stop being racist to blondes," I laugh.

"I can, I'm blonde," she jokes.

We all put on our dresses, mine is a long, dark blue, halter neck, slim, sequined dress, and one that I had worn for a beauty pageant I got scouted for quite a few years ago. I didn't win the main title but I won the eco round, because I'm so eco-friendly... I think. It is comfortable to walk in and my figure looks good in it, plus it is quite elegant with sparkly. I match it with some simple silver earrings, a silver watch on one wrist, a silver bracelet on the other, matched with a pair of silver heels. For Jen and Lia's dresses we had gone shopping about a week ago. Jen's dress is red with no straps, it is long and flowy with a slit down one side. It's quite simple and chic with some intricate gold embroidery around the top half. She matches red heels with it, a small black sparkly choker necklace, earrings and red and gold bracelets on both wrists. Lia's dress is a short, baby pink, shift dress, it has long sleeves that are embroidered throughout, with some pink embroidery on the neck and back, the rest of it is plain in a lovely, velvety material. She coordinates her dress with black heels and heavy black earrings. The three of us stand looking through the narrow mirror at how we look. We do look stunning! Makeup's match, hair matches, yeah, I like it. I love dressing up for events and parties, back at home weddings are my favorite! I can't wait to dress up for red carpet events soon. *Hopefully.*

"Yep!" Jen says breaking the silence but still looking through the mirror. "We look fire!"

We agree nodding and still posing.

"Guys!" Brian's call breaks our modelling.

"Coming!" Jen shouts back.

We get our fancy clutch bags, fill them with essentials and then walk out into the living room. The chatter from the boys stops and they stare as we walk in. Brian's eyebrows are raised. Deq pouts and Rio's jaw drops open.

"Woah!" Marcus's surprised voice from behind us reaches our ears.

"Yeah. Woah!" Rio adds.

"Yes. Woah!" I yell looking at how handsome they all look. "You all look dashing!"

"Thanks, you guys look stunning too," Brian says.

"We know." All three of us say spontaneously at the same time, quite confidently.

The boys exchange scared looks.

"And you," Brian continues, "You look beautiful," he tells Jen.

"I know," she responds with complete confidence towards him but blushing as her eyes find us.

Lia coughs.

"Sweet!" Deq says nodding his head at Lia. "What about me?" he asks.

"You look gorgeous Dequan," Lia compliments.

"Can you stop, I'm here in my pajamas and you guys are telling each other how good you all look!" Marcus cries, carefully pushing past us. "Argh! I wish I was going!"

"Don't worry bro, we'll snap you, it'll be like you're there," Rio slaps him on the back.

"Oh great. Thanks."

"Taxi's here," Deq yells after receiving a text on his phone.

"Woohoo! Let's partaaayyyy!" Jen yells heading towards

the door.

"See you later Bro!" Brian says to Marcus.

"Bye. Have a good time," Marcus mumbles.

"Marcus, I left some chicken curry for you in the fridge, okay," I say pecking his cheek.

"Thanks Kye, at least someone cares."

Outside, there are people all over the place in their ball gowns and tuxedos, waiting for taxis, laughing, drinking and fixing makeup. There are people I know, people from my classes looking different but good. Jen, Lia and I went to the Women in Industry ball last year but it wasn't like this, this is so much busier and there are cute guys everywhere! *I might meet someone!* I calm my thoughts down, that's a long shot with all these girls around wearing cleavage-full and back-less dresses. *My time will come.* We load into the taxi and we're off to the ball.

***

The ball is buzzing. I'm actually enjoying it. The DJ is wicked, the setting is glamourous and the food is okay. We leave the dance floor after a good but stiff dance thanks to our dresses. Rio wonders off chatting up some girls and Deq and Brian find their respective class mates. We girls make our way over to our table. Surprisingly many people greet me from the drama society and from my classes. I suppose people do know who I am. *I do know lots of people.*

"Kye!" someone calls my name. It's Sheera! She graduated last year and is now a representative of the Drama Society, she runs it alongside the drama teachers.

"Sheera! Hey! How are you?" I give her a hug.

"I'm good, thanks. You?"

"I'm good too. This is Jen and Lia, my room mates."

"Hi, I'm Sheera," they shake hands. "Kye, congratulations on receiving an invitation to audition for that new film," she hugs me again. "With… what's her name? Oh yes, Angela Weir."

I had forgotten about that for a little while, "Thanks! But how do you know?" I ask.

"Well, Angela watched our show last year and then this

year I got a call from her, she wanted a reference for you. So I gave a good one."

"Did you give a good one for me?" Betty Blondie's voice enters my ears.

She stands behind Sheera, the disco lights light up her made up, pretty face. She steps forward and I feel a lump in my throat. *She got an email too? Oh my god!* I feel even more nervous now. Her followers linger behind her. She wears a plunging dark red dress and obviously looks like the show stopper. Maya wears something over the top, Ellen wears a nice short dress and Abbey wears a jumpsuit.

"Oh hey Betty!" Sheera greets her. "Yes of course I did! Congrats to you too!"

I greet Abbey with a hug as Sheera and Betty embrace. I catch Jen and Lia's faces with stern expressions, I use my eyes to try and tell them to soften up. They can't believe she got an email either.

"Oh thanks," Betty replies loudly, confidently and like she knew it was coming.

"So, have you guys heard back?" Sheera asks. "I mean, they can take a while so don't worry if-"

"Err obviously!" Maya – Betty's loudest side kick interrupts.

"What!" Sheera says happily.

What! I think. I see Jen's eyes grow bigger.

"Yeah, I got an email today actually," Betty begins.

"She sure did!" Ellen yells in the background.

"Angela's invited me for a live audition in two weeks!" Betty shows off.

My ears go numb for a moment. All I can hear is the vibration of the music beating through my body. All I see is red and green flashing lights from the dance floor and within that Betty hugging Sheera and her girls. *I haven't heard.* I knew I wasn't going to get an audition anyway, but the fact that Betty did is like putting salt on my wounds. I feel my little makeup beginning to sweat off as my ears find the music again and my eyes focus.

"That's... that's really great," I force words to Betty.

"Ha! Thanks. I assume… that you haven't heard?" Betty slyly asks.

"No… I haven't-"

"Well, actually she hasn't checked yet," Lia cuts me off and takes a few steps forward confronting Betty's overconfidence.

"Aww, don't worry Kye, sometimes they just take time to respond, just hang in there," Sheera comforts me. "Anyway, I'll see you guys around," she leaves as she sees some friends.

"Yeah, see you around," Betty repeats staring down at me before spinning around and leaving.

I quietly take a seat at our table, in utter disappointment.

"Hey, come on Kye, don't let this ruin your night," Jen says sitting next to me.

"You took the opportunity, you tried and we're proud of you," Lia says sitting on my other side.

I don't know what to say. I feel hurt. I know I tried not to get my hopes up for this but this time they approached me! So somewhere deep down inside my hopes were high.

"It's alright Kye, I honestly believe you'll get there one day," Jen says.

"I just felt like this was my closest chance, you know. And I'm not even that upset about not getting it, I'm just shocked that I was competing against Betty. Maybe that's what they were looking for? Fair play to her for getting it," I speak with a headache.

"But, she didn't get it. It's just an audition yet. She just got an email for an audition not the part," Lia tells me.

Lia's right, it is only an audition and an email. I pull my phone out of my bag and unlock it. I hesitate before clicking. I select the email icon and then click on sync. I watch the loading curser spin round and round. Lia and Jen watch over my shoulder but struggle to see. New emails load and I begin to scroll through the pointless newsletters from shops, jobsites and casting sites. I'm looking for an email. I briefly see an 'A' and a 'W' but I'm scrolling too fast, I pull the screen back down. Slowly this time. I squint. There it is. An email from Angela Weir. I sit up from my slouching position and open the email.

I skim read it and then read it out loud and fast; "Dear Kyara, after thorough consideration we are pleased to invite you to a live audition on February 17th…"

"Ahhhhhhh!" Lia screams hugging me.

"Oh my God! I knew it Kye!" Jen yells, yanking the phone from my hand.

"Ahhhhh *God!*" I laugh out loud listening to Jen mumble through the rest of the details such as the time, location and the attachment of sides. "Are you sure they've invited me?" I ask.

"Yes, yes February 17th!" Jen shrieks, reading it out again.

"I can't believe it! This is the first time I'll be going to an actual audition in front of a casting director, live, in front of real people!" My hands shake a little as I reach for my glass of water and take a sip to calm down.

"Why are you shaking girl?" Lia yells.

"I don't know!" I laugh. "I'm going to have to remember lines properly!" I scream excitedly over the loud music

We see the boys approaching the table.

"What happened?" Brian asks.

"Why are you all screaming?" Deq adds.

"Kye got called for another audition for that film! They loved the self-tape!" Jen shouts.

The boys jump for joy and congratulate me as my nerves settle down.

"Kye! That's awesome!" Rio yells. "Now it's a party people!"

We all raise our glasses in celebration, a toast to my call back. Then we're back on the dance floor. The night goes by quickly and I enjoyed it so much more after reading that email. We snap Marcus who snaps us back eating my curry by himself. I mingle in with my class mates too and make new friends from other courses. And we don't leave until the DJ announces 'last song'. I still can't believe I got an audition! And I don't even know if Betty overheard or not. *Anyway, what will happen is in your hands, God. I have faith in you.*

CHAPTER NINETEEN

KYARA

This is like the twentieth time I've changed position but I still can't sleep. The audition is tomorrow. I'm nervous about everything! My clothes, my hair, getting to the place, meeting the people, auditioning…everything! I go through my lines in my head with actions and expressions, I feel my cheeks change shape on my pillow and yes, I do know my lines. Too much practice isn't good either, but I just can't sleep! I reach for my watch on my side table. It's one thirty seven a.m. and I still have about seven hours until my alarm goes off. My hand finds my glasses and before I know it, I'm up and on my way to the kitchen to make some warm milk. In the hallway, I notice that our front door is a little open and light leaks in from the landing, but then again, we don't really lock it. I ignore it and walk to the living room but stop as I enter under the arch trying to find the lights in the darkness. All of a sudden, I hear some ruffling. I freeze in the darkness. *It's just me.* I reassure myself. Then I slowly move my hands on the wall finding the light switch. As I switch it on, bringing light into the living room and blurring my own vision, I see a large man like figure rising quickly from the couch and leaping towards me. Uncontrollably, squinting, I feel my arms go for a scrappy punch and then I inhale to exhale a loud scream when a hand covers my mouth.

"It's me! It's me!" My brain registers Rio's quiet but rushed voice as I feel his arm holding my arms down and his hand over my mouth. "Kye, it's me!

I exhale and the scream dissolves and my eyes adjust to the light clearing my vision.

"Rio!" I shout in a whisper. "What the heck are you doing? You scared the shit out of me!"

Rio now places his hand on his nose where I accidently punched him, "Damn! You have a hard punch Kye!"

"Sorry, but you freaked me out!"

"Is my nose still straight? It's not bent is it? Does it still look good?"

"Yes, your nose is fine."

I switch on the kitchen light and then notice that Rio's actually sleeping on our couch. He has a pillow and blankets and his phone is on charge on the floor. He sits back into his pillow and readjusts the blanket.

"What are you doing here?" I ask.

"Well, Deq and Lia had a fight," he explains, yawning.

"Oh?" I'm not too surprised, they're always arguing like parents. "Like a proper one?"

"Hmm," he thinks. "Nah, just you know over stupid stuff, in fact I don't even know how it started, but anyway they were arguing and Lia said she was going home, but it was really late and there were no trains, so I told her to stay until morning. By this time Deq had stormed off into his room, so I let Lia sleep in my bed and then I moved onto our couch which is too small, and yours is bigger, so I came here."

"Aww, they're like a married couple," I say finding utensils in the kitchen.

"Yeah, that's exactly what I was thinking. They argue like my mom and dad. They'll be back together by tomorrow. Deq will call her." Rio laughs.

I giggle, "Haha, yeah, bless them. Milk?" I offer, holding up a pot.

"Well now that you woke me up and gave me a broken

nose, yes please! Anyway, what's your story? Why are you up? Worried about the big audition tomorrow?"

"Yeah, I'm so nervous. I know my lines and everything, I've just never been into someone's office to audition for a movie role. I think that's what's freaking me out and I can't sleep." I wait for the milk to warm up.

"I understand, but honestly, just be you. That's who they want to meet, they want to meet you, Kyara. Even if that means you're a little nervous, like you say, some nerves are good. Then when you begin auditioning switch into character, take your time, make sure you're fully that character before starting. Do you know what I mean?" he advises me.

"Yeah, thanks Rio," I smile.

I am a little calmer now. I just need to be me, then switch. Nerves are good. It's okay. I pour the warm milk into mugs. We hear deep voices coming from the landing and give each other confused looks. I put the mugs down on the coffee table and walk into the hallway to find half-drunk Brian and Marcus coming to check why our lights are on. They went out with some of their friends tonight.

"Hey Kye!" Brian yells.

"Kye!" Marcus shouts with his arms open.

"Shhhh! Jen's asleep!" I whisper.

"Oh shit! Jen's asleep. Shut up Bro," Brian tells Marcus.

They follow me into the living room.

"Yoooo!" Rio hisses. "How was it?"

"It was sick bro," Marcus says.

"Yeah *tings* everywhere!" Brian adds wide eyed.

"*Tings*?" I ask for clarification.

"Girls. Damn I should've gone!" Rio responds taking a sip of milk.

"I see what you're drinking nowadays," Marcus chuckles uncontrollably.

"Shut up. Kye woke me up."

We hear a loud bang of a door closing. Jen's sleep is disturbed.

"Argh! What are you guys doing!" she shouts irritated, walking into the living room. "Is that milk?" she points at Rio's and suddenly has a mood change.

We nod.

"Do we have cookies?" she yawns.

I nod and get the cookies.

"So babe, did you have a nice time?" she asks Brian squishing next to him on the armchair.

"Yes it was decent. Just a nice lad's night out, that's it, just lads." He replies cuddling Jen who giggles looking at me.

"Why are you guys up so late?" Marcus asks.

I sigh and flop onto the couch, "I can't sleep because of my audition tomorrow and Rio gave his bed to Lia."

They all exchange weird looks.

"It's a long story between Deq and Lia, I'll tell you guys tomorrow," Rio says getting his mug back from Jen.

"So are you guys planning to stay up for long?" Jen asks yawning again bringing water to her eyes, "Because I'm a little tired."

"Well, go to sleep babe," Brian says kissing her head.

"But then I don't want to miss out on the fun," she wines.

Marcus and Brian begin to tell stories of their night out and then I get some last minute advice for the audition tomorrow. I try not to think about it too much, but some simple advice is good. With the midnight gossip taking my mind off the big day, the warm milk calming me down and the soothing advice building my confidence, I think I'm ready for tomorrow. I'm ready to get it over with.

I arrive at the address after a nervous train journey and a long sweaty walk to where the auditions are being held. The building is very modern for a theatre and towers high up into the sky with offices located on the top floors. I breathe gently to assist my heart rate so it returns to normal before entering the building. I'm just glad I made it without getting lost! I am early, but that gives me time to cool down. I enter the building and right in front of me is a signpost directing me to the 'Angela Weir Auditions'. Before I follow the directions I take a trip to the bathroom to freshen up, cool down and check my face and hair. Then I take a lift to the eighth floor and find another signpost directing me left down a long hallway, then I see an open door with a poster on it that reads, 'Waiting Room'. A young woman appears in front of the door, she's dressed professionally in office wear with a ponytail. She holds a folder and a pen in her hand and seems friendly, so I decide to ask her if I'm at the right place.

"Excuse me..." I say as she approaches me with a helpful smile, "I'm here for the audition with Angela Weir, do you know-"

"Oh hi!" she says enthusiastically. "Yes! Oh my, you're a little early, but no worries. I'm Donna, Angela's Assistant."

She shakes my hand and I try be as polite as possible. If she's Angela's assistant then she needs to like me too.

"I'm Kyara Averoni."

She finds my name, ticks me off a list she holds and leads me into the waiting room, "We're just preparing the audition room. You can wait here and practice lines or something."

I take a seat slowly, "Thanks."

"How are you feeling?" Donna asks.

"Err, I'm a little nervous, I've never auditioned before."

"Really?" she's surprised.

"Oh no, I mean, I have auditioned before, but like online, not *online*, I mean like a self-tape, this is my first time actually auditioning in front of a casting director...for a movie...I have done live auditions for theatre...before," I speak very quickly and then laugh it off. *What was that God? Was I supposed to say that? Is it bad that I've never done this before? Now they're going to think I'm inexperienced! Oh Kye!*

"Oh, don't be nervous, it'll be fine. Angela's really nice! To be honest with you, I'm a little nervous too, this is my first time casting with her and in fact this is my first time casting a movie. We started casting two days ago, forty five girls were selected so we had to split you up over three days. It's a great experience, everyone is different and wonderful in their own ways. So I'm excited for today but also still quite nervous, haha!" She comes to the end of that sentence as if she wasn't supposed to say that in front of me.

We both giggle our silly mistakes off. We all make mistakes. Up until now I didn't realize that casting is also a job, a career that some people want to take. I'm glad I met Donna, I feel more at ease now.

"Okay Kyara, the rest of the girls should be arriving soon, so if they ask, then this is the waiting room. I'll call you in when we're ready," Donna says as she leaves the room. "Oh and don't be nervous."

She leaves and I'm left alone in a large room, waiting. In the quietness, I realize what Donna was saying and I realize how many chairs there are. There are fifteen chairs! There are forty five girls I'm competing against! And they've already seen thirty girls which means that I'm *really* going to have to stand out! I know I'm different, we all are, I know I have potential, but…I don't think I have a chance, I have no real movie experience or an agent or anything! As I panic, a few girls walk through the door. They seem like they know each other as they talk amongst themselves. I smile and they smile back and then continue talking. I take the script sides out of my bag and recap my lines. Then I notice that they are talking about school. They're from the same school. Angela must have watched plays from lots of different drama schools and then she must have selected potential actresses. A few more girls walk in and Donna comes in to take names. She tells us to wait for a few more minutes when Betty walks in. I forgot about her.

"Hi! What's your name please?" Donna asks.

"I'm Betty Johnson," she says politely, almost too politely.

"Thanks Betty, take a seat," Donna leaves.

Betty has her back to me and looks for a seat. It's weird seeing Betty alone, without her followers or her boyfriend. I've never seen her nervous either. She actually looks anxious until she takes a seat and her eyes meet mine. Her expression is priceless! It actually makes me choke a little. She is totally shocked to see me here. She looks confused, lost and angry.

"Hey…Kye…what are you doing here?" she asks

defensively.

"Hey, I got invited for an audition too, I checked my email after you told me, and yeah, I had one. Thanks," I say.

"Oh…well, good for you," the diva inside returns.

I lower my gaze and concentrate on my lines, I'm already nervous and with Betty here everything could go wrong. She too finds her script and quietly reads. Half of the seats are full and Donna comes to count and announce.

"Okay, thank you for coming everyone. I will take you in one at a time for a very quick chat with Angela, myself and Rob the casting associate and then of course you'll audition. Don't be nervous, we're all very nice. Just a few tips; leave anything you don't need in here please, such as bags, phones etcetera and walk into the casting room prepared. You may take your sides if you need them but it's not recommended. You'll be in the room for no longer than fifteen minutes each. The room is not very big and I know this scene involves some action and the character is very energetic so please be careful and be aware of the space, basically don't hurt yourselves. Once you've auditioned I'll escort you back to this room, you may leave the building to go and get some lunch or fresh air, but we ask you to be back in this room by three p.m. as we will be announcing call backs at three p.m."

There's a scatter of surprise amongst the room. My heart just drops.

Donna continues, "I know it's exciting! It is a bit of a wait but please do bear with us, the movie is scheduled to shoot very very soon, so we are in a rush for casting actors, but I'm sure you won't mind. Toilets are down the hall to the right. There will be some more girls joining us during the afternoon, so if you could tell them to wait here if I'm not around then that would be great! Top tip: Be yourself! We want to know you as a person first and then watch you act, so just be you in the chat. Okay. Any questions?"

I don't have any questions and nor does anyone else.

"Okay great. Good Luck! First up is… Natasha Wright."

A very nervous girl who seems to be by herself follows Donna, the other girls whisper 'Good Luck' as do I, everyone does, except Betty. I don't even know when it's my turn. What if it's last or next? I don't like waiting long, I just get more nervous. I'd rather get it over and done with, but I'd like to know who I'm after. I try not to think about it too much, even reading too much of my lines is making me uncomfortable. I close my eyes for a while pretending to memorize lines while I actually pray and have a moment with God. *God, I am really nervous. Whatever you do, I have faith in you. I really want this, but I only want it, if it's right for me and only you know that. Please make sure I don't mess up and embarrass myself. Argh God! I'm scared. Make everything go well please! Love you!* My chat with God comes to an end and so does Natasha's audition. A girl asks Natasha how it went. She doesn't give much away except that it went okay. She looks a little disappointed, which freaks me out. She gets her bag and leaves. She probably wants to get some air, she does have a long wait ahead of her. I try not to think about her. They take a good ten minutes before calling in the next candidate, Betty. She follows Donna, pretending to be confident in front of the other girls, but I know her, that's not her confidence, she's nervous.

Fifteen minutes later, Betty's back, her face is gleaming, she looks awfully happy. I can't tell if she's acting to throw us off or whether she's actually that happy. She doesn't say anything to anyone and no one asks, maybe they're too afraid. Betty smiles to herself, collects her bag and leaves looking down at me as she walks past. Another ten minutes pass by.

"Kyara Averoni," Donna calls standing in the doorway.

Oh shoot! God, this is it! I take a deep breath, tuck my bag under my chair, smile at Donna and follow her as I hear whispers of 'Good Luck' towards me. This is not going to go well after Betty's huge smile. Now they've got her great audition and her pretty face in their minds. I've got no chance. The audition room is a few turns away from the waiting room.

Donna stops outside the room, "Okay, are you ready Kyara?"

I nod.

"You'll be great! Take a deep breath. Remember to shake hands and all that. Shall we?"

"Yes please," I reply. *This is it.*

Donna opens the door and leads me in. The room is small and painted all white with dark laminate flooring, there's a long desk at the back of the room, with three seats. Donna takes the seat on the end. In those seats sit the three judges, with mugs, water bottles, papers and pens. An empty seat is placed opposite theirs.

"Kyara Averoni?" Angela says standing from her seat with her hand out.

This is my time, "Hi, yes, I'm Kyara," I shake her hand confidently, only my inner me knows how nervous I actually am. I've never shook hands with a casting director before. This is special.

"Nice to meet you Kyara, I'm Angela, this is Rob, our casting associate," she gestures to her left.

"Hello Kyara," he says shaking my hand as I greet him with a 'hi' and a smile.

"And you've already met Donna our casting assistant."

"Yes, we have," I say shaking Donna's hand again and then thinking that was stupid, because we already did that.

"Please have a seat," Angela says putting on her glasses and looking at some papers.

"Thank you," I mumble.

"So, how are you feeling today?" Angela asks.

"I'm well, thank you. A little nervous, but I'm okay," I speak in a polite and open manner. *I mean, if they like me, they like me, if they don't they don't.* I tell myself.

"Ah yes, we understand. You'll be fine," Angela responds to my answer. "So, tell me about what you currently do? You are a university student right? Do you study Drama or Theatre studies or…?"

"Oh… err… no, I actually study Physics," I swallow hard. I bet that's a shock.

"Oh wow! That's a tough one…" Angela is shocked, in fact she doesn't really know what to say next. "Err…how…what made you want to join the drama society?" she takes off her glasses, stops looking at the papers and now looks at me.

Donna seems very impressed and starts writing stuff, Rob on the other hand sits in silence with no expression whatsoever, he just stares.

"Well…" I pause, I need to get my words out right. "Acting is my aspiration and always has been, I've always joined my school's drama clubs from a young age. I love it. It's my goal…to become an actress. So I joined the university drama society."

"But, then why did you chose Physics?" Angela is quick to ask the question. The question I dread!

I don't know how to answer that. Any answer is going to go against me not choosing a Drama related subject. I try to say something, "If I'm honest, I don't really know. My academic path has always been scientific and somehow it lead me to study Physics. I didn't really know what subject to choose so I just chose one I was good at. I suppose I chose it for my parents, being the oldest in my family and the only one who's been to university." I spill half of the truth, the other half is that I personally don't feel the need to have a degree in drama or theatre to become an actress, that's luck and also physics is a good back-up, but I can't tell them that.

"Alright. Okay. That's fair enough," Angela seems quite genuine with those words and as if she's empathizing. "Okay so tell me a little bit about your creative side. Have you been in anything recently?"

"I did some amateur theatre work a few years ago, I also created my own short student film, I wrote the screenplay, directed it, acted in it and edited it." I giggle in memory.

"Really! That must have been fun. Was this for a competition or something?" she questions.

"It was for a college project, my teacher told me it was a bad idea and that I shouldn't make a film and that I should write an essay instead. However, I was really determined, so I did it anyway and got an A," I boast shyly.

"Haha! Oh my! I like that!" Angela laughs. Her personality is bubbly and loud.

"Yes, it was worth it," I fake laugh back as naturally as

possible.

"Sure it was! I'm going to have to watch it. Is it on YouTube?"

"Oh dear," I say blushing. "It is now." After Jen made me upload it when I showed it to her.

"What's it called?"

"Err… Lost Diamonds," I say getting really worried, what if she watches it and doesn't like my acting. *What the heck am I getting myself into?*

Angela writes 'Lost Diamonds' down on her sheet of paper, still chuckling, at my teacher I suppose.

"Oh I also write screenplays and I'm currently writing a novel, I just love getting my ideas down on paper." I had to get that out there but I also try changing the subject.

Donna notes down everything as quickly as she can, while Rob still glares at me.

"Great! You seem very enthusiastic. I like that," Angela finishes her questioning. "Right, now if you'd like to stand up, take the center of the room, I know it's a little small. Take your time and when you're ready, you may begin your audition. Donna will read lines with you. So be sure to make eye contact with her as and when you want to. Alright?"

I stand up, tuck my chair under the table and find the center of the room. Their eyes' are fixed on me and I see Rob taking down notes as I just stand there getting into character. I try to avoid eye contact with Angela and Rob and look down at the floor as I take deep breaths to switch into character. *Okay God, let's do this.* I begin.

I finish with a sharp emotional stare at Donna's eyes. They don't applaud or say anything. Rob still takes notes, Donna smiles to indicate that we've finished and Angela whispers something in her ear before thanking me and then asking me to sit back down. I sit in the chair again, relieved that it is over, for now, but unsure as to whether I've done well or not.

"Thanks again, Kyara," is all Angela says but she smiles widely with her teeth. "Now, I just need to ask you a few admin questions; are you available on April 22nd, if selected for a callback?"

I have no clue what I'm doing on 22nd April. I don't have my diary or my phone calendar with me to check, "Yes, I should be." *Obviously.*

"Okay and I know you're studying but what about from May 28thth to July 1st and onwards? They are the initial scheduled shoot dates and obviously if selected you would be required for a few days before that and then many days after that, but there's an important action sequence being filmed during that time."

"Yes, that's fine. I'm available," I smile. Honestly, that goes over exam period but if I get the role then I won't need to attend my exams, believe me!

"Brilliant! So we shall let you know of our decision for callbacks later today. Do get some fresh air while you wait. Thank you very much for joining us today," Angela shakes my hand again.

"Thank you very much for the opportunity," I say gratefully, getting out of my chair. I begin to leave following Donna.

"I'll be sure to watch that short film of yours!" Angela calls as I walk.

Shit. I turn around and smile back. She is not letting that go anytime soon. Donna walks me to the hallway where the waiting room is. I make my own way back from there as she goes back to the audition room, probably to discuss my audition. I am relived, but I'm also scared. Angela seemed quite positive towards the end when she was asking for my availability. Nevertheless, I've heard stories where the casting directors give you that trusting handshake or that wink that makes you think you've nailed the part and then they go and break your heart. For now, the hard part is over, I've done what I could, now it's a matter of time. I find a few new faces have turned up in the waiting room, I scan the room for potential threats. To be honest, they are all a threat, they're all unique. I get my bag and leave the room for some air and to call my girls and fill them in. *It is literally in your hands now, God.*

After talking to Jen and Lia, forcing myself to eat some

lunch on an uncomfortable stomach, walking around the theatre twice and checking my phone a million times in the waiting room, three p.m. finally arrives. In fact, it's gone a few minutes over three p.m. and we still have no news. Every seat has been taken up in the room now, all fifteen of us wait eagerly and anxiously for the results. There is some quiet chatter amongst those who are from the same schools, Betty talks quietly on the phone to someone and a few other girls just sit staring down at their phones.

"Hi girls, thank you very much for waiting," Donna enters.

There's silence, phones are put away and everyone's attention is on Donna. The room is so tense that you could virtually hear everyone's racing heartbeats. It is strange how we're all here waiting for the same thing, with the same hopes and the same dreams but only a few of us will succeed, it's even crazier that in the end, it may be that none of us succeed.

"Okay, Kyara Averoni…" Donna reads from a list. My senses come to life. I look up in anticipation holding my breath, but she continues to read names, "…Jude Hayworth, Ashley Miller, Saskia Bridges and Betty Johnson," she looks to locate us. "Please make your way to the audition room. You may take your belongings with you," she gestures to the door with her hand.

I quickly gather my bag and dump my phone inside it. My palms are sweaty and my cheeks are hot. Betty leads through the door followed by the three other girls and then me. We all exchange worried looks as we walk out. *Maybe they didn't like ours or maybe they want to see them again! Please don't make me do it again!* We walk to the end of the hallway and then hear some chatter behind us, I turn for a quick look, the rest of the girls are walking in the opposite direction as Donna catches up with us. *What the heck is going on?*

"This way girls," she says with no smile, no emotion, nothing to give anything away.

We quietly follow. Donna knocks and then opens the door leading us into the audition room where we naturally stand in a horizontal line facing the casting directors. Angela and Rob are mumbling between themselves pointing at papers as Donna takes a seat. They stop the mumbling and Angela takes off her glasses.

She smiles broadly looking at each of us in turn. I smile back politely.

"Welcome back girls," Angela starts, "I hope we didn't keep you waiting too long. It has been a very tough decision. Everybody is hugely talented and as casting directors we try to understand each and every one of you."

My heart thumps in my chest. It's extremely warm in here and Angela's dragging on is making it worse. I feel like I'm going to faint or cry. I think I need to sit down.

"So, with a lot of discussion between the three of us and after being entertained by your auditions…"

Hurry up Angela! My knees shake.

"…We are delighted to invite you five from today's session, for a call back on the 22nd April," she ends with another stretching smile, showing her coffee stained teeth.

We gasp and look at each other in surprise, happiness and most of all relief. My hands make their way to my mouth and nose covering them. Betty let's out a small shriek on the other side of the line and one of the other girls takes a mini leap in the air. I am in amazement, this is really happening. I just got a call back. I blink the water away from my eyes and move my shaking hands down. *You did it God! Thank you so much!*

"Well done. Donna will send you an email with some new sides along with some further information regarding a screen test and a fitness test which will be held on the same day. Don't worry too much about the fitness test, we'll just make you jump over a few obstacles like a pillow and make you do a few sit ups just to assist the screen test, however don't ignore it as it is important for the role. Also, the producer will be accompanying us in the next audition, no pressure. You have all really impressed us and you are making this very hard for us, this will be the final callback due to a tight schedule so practice well. Thank you very much for coming." She stands up to shake our hands.

Donna also stands up and makes her way to the door so that we can follow her. Betty is first to shake hands, Angela greets everyone with their names as if she's remembering them.

When it's my turn she says, "Kyara. The physics girl. I'll be sure to watch your film."

And then… she does the typical casting directors wink or at least that's how I imagined it. I freeze. I don't really know how to react! I feel a beam of potential success entering my heart. I express my gratitude sincerely and follow the girls out, of whom I find Betty standing directly behind me, eavesdropping. She looks worried and is noticeably unhappy that I got a call back too, I ignore her and make my way out. I do have a thought for all those other girls though, I wonder what Donna said to them. This is savage. But the world is a selfish place and sometimes it is good to be a tiny bit selfish and this is the furthest I have ever been with my acting career, so I should be happy, I too have received so many rejections in the past. Today I got a call back!

CHAPTER TWENTY

JENNIFER

Save. Save. Save. I click multiple times on the save button on my screen and then take a look at all of my mechanical drawings laid out on the living room floor and the final edited designs on the three laptops I have in front of me. Yes. That's right. I have officially finished my design! It has taken a long time and I've checked over it a million times with Kye and Rio. I've edited and edited and then checked and checked and I think now it's time to just get on with the build.

"Hey, all done?" Kye asks walking in with lunch. She's just finished the quantum physics class that I missed.

I exhale, "Yes, I think so." It's weird because I feel nervous but more excited that I have actually designed a piece of space discovery equipment all by myself! "I can't find anything else to change or edit, I think it's ready. What did I miss anyway? Did you bring me notes?"

"Yes I did. You didn't miss much, you can catch up easily, but Dr. Kennedy was looking at me as if he was trying to say 'where's your friend'," she chuckles and then looks at my screens. "Damn, that's a lot of work Jen! I think it is ready. You need to move on now."

She's right, I need to move on now. Timing is good, I have plenty of time to build and if any surprises come along the way then I'll have time to fix them.

"Why didn't you come to class anyway?" Kye asks.

"Well, I went to my Space Dynamics class this morning, then thought I had miscalculated something in my design and ended up missing my literature class and quantum physics to come back and check. It actually turns out that I had done it correctly in the first place, so yeah, I'm going to have to do a bit of catching up." I stand up with one of the laptops, "Okay, I'm going to print some final stuff at the library, make sure this..." I point to the floor, "...stays in order, exactly where it is. Please."

"I got it. Don't worry, I won't let the boys in," Kye responds as I leave the apartment.

I make my way to the library. This is it, the last time I'll be printing out my designs, God knows how many trees I have had cut down from the amount of printing I have done for this. I don't even know what other people's designs look like, or what they're designing. Theirs have been checked by supervisors too. I bet they're all way better than mine! *Ah what are you doing Jen?* I reach the printer, there's no cue and the library is quiet. It is Friday, most people usually take a trip home on Friday when there's no major nightlife events and it is the middle of the semester so everything is quite quiet and calm. In other words, party season is over. I connect my laptop and print. Then I shut the laptop and adjust the large printed diagrams and the equipment list making them easier to carry and so that they don't blow away outside. As I walk, ruffling the papers and laptop in my hand, my shoulder collides against someone. My instincts save the laptop. Some of my sheets crumple between my legs and the rest fall to the ground as I unflatteringly try to hold onto them. My diagrams spread all over the floor.

"I'm so sorry!" I hear a familiar voice bending down to help pick the papers off the floor.

The idiot is no other than Blondie, Betty Blondie and her

annoying friend Maya. I swear, I could swear at her right now. I calm myself.

"Betty!" I smile gritting my teeth, "No worries, it's okay." I bend down and collect my papers.

"Oh Jennifer! Hi! I'm so sorry, I didn't see..." she stops and holds a diagram in her hands. She looks at it upside down (which I won't hold against her because they are hard for a non-scientific person to understand). "Are these yours? I thought you study English or something?" She's confused.

"Yes!" I'm too quick to answer, I snatch the paper from her hand, "I mean no! No, no, these are... not mine. No. This is actually Kye's stuff. I was meant to say 'yes' to the... err... fact that I do study English, yes...I study Literature." I clear my throat.

I just confused her even more from that look on her face, "Oh." She shakes her head and then strokes my arm. "Oh poor you. Kye makes you do everything for her. Last time you were carrying her books and now she's making you print. I feel terrible."

Her sympathetic acting is beyond me. I don't even know what to say right now, so I play along, with a sad, victimized, sorrowful look in my eyes, that I guarantee I am not doing right at all and I'm pretending to act in front of an actress.

"I know right. We feel so sorry for you. I mean you shouldn't take it from her," says Maya. "You should tell her to do her own stuff."

"Yes of course," Betty agrees. "You know what Jen, is it okay if I call you Jen?"

I nod.

"That Kyara is jealous of you. She is jealous. You're pretty, tall, intelligent, I mean you even understand all this diagram stuff, right," she points at my papers. "She probably doesn't like that at all. She wants to be good at everything and can't stand it when someone takes over her. Like me! For example, she's totally jealous of me too and Abbey and now you."

I don't like the fact that she's dissing my girl. I feel like slapping her right now, but my hands are full and I have secrets she can't know. "Oh no, I don't think so, Kye is Kye, you know," I say as nicely as possible on the outside, but inside I want to pull her hair out and her stupid friend's. I know my facial expression has changed and she can sense my anger, but she just won't stop and to top it off, Maya is nodding and shaking her head at every sentence Betty unsympathetically blurts out.

"Obviously you'd say that, you're her friend," she rolls her eyes and Maya does the same. "Look, I'm just saying, be aware of her. Watch your back. You never know when she might betray you."

"Hmm," I grumble. She's making me sick.

"And let her do her own stuff," she begins to walk away followed by Maya.

"Yeah, thanks for the advice guys, I really appreciate it," I lie.

"Anytime!" Maya waves at me.

Idiots! Next time she says something about Kye I will whoop her ass! I felt like telling Maya to watch her back with Betty lurking around, but I haven't got time for bitching. They totally ruined my mood. My drawings almost got ruined. *Thank God they're okay!* I kiss my papers as another figure approaches me.

"Jen! What *are* you doing?" It's Deq with a weird expression.

"Ah, nothing. I just saved them from getting ripped."

"Oo...kay..., I just had to pay my fricking library debt. Thieves I tell you!"

"That's typical of you."

"Save it till later. I'm having a bad day," he sighs looking upset. "Do you need a hand?"

"Yes please," I give him the laptop and the A4 sheets. "Spill."

We take a stroll back to our apartment. He tells me what's been happening with him and Lia, and most of it we already know because, we girls talk a lot. They've been on and off quite a lot over stupid things, like him playing video games all the time and when he's free Lia's got reading to do and vice versa. Lia wants him to meet her mom but he's too scared and that's annoying her. He is genuinely upset and really wants to be with her and make her happy. We already know how Lia feels, she adores the guy! It's like a silly Ross and Rachael thing. He continues to express his feelings as we enter our apartment. Kye joins in the conversation. He finishes spilling on the balcony. We comfort him standing either side of him. Kye's hand is on top of his as he holds the balcony rail and both my hands hold his shoulder. We give our opinions and our advice, which are mostly one sided towards pleasing Lia since we've heard her side too. We tell him to be more considerate towards her feelings and that playing video games is definitely not the priority. He seems to be absorbing our advice. We tell him that if she is *the one* – which we definitely think is the case, because they argue like husband and wife and then are fine the minute afterwards – then meeting her family is the next step. As we talk, I realize that my feelings for Brian have grown. Kye always talks about marriage and how it is so important in life to settle down with someone who is yours and you are their's forever. She says that each person is half a soul and half a body, then your partner – life partner – is the other half of your soul and body, that's why we *connect*, when we *connect* we become one and complete. I've never thought about this until now, but I do feel like Brian makes my life complete. I don't know what I'd do without him. I definitely wouldn't be where I *am* without him. *Kye's God, do I love Brian?*

"Yo yo!" My Brian walks in attractive as ever, followed by Rio and Marcus.

"Yo! Guys!" Deq makes a quick and nervous escape from our girly conversation to greet them with their manly handshakes, he then gently nods his head towards us in appreciation for the advice.

"Have you finished the design Jen?" Marcus asks.

"Yes I have," I feel excitement and a small hint of pride as I look at my designs and drawing neatly laid out.

"About time," Rio jokes as he receives a smack from Jen.

"So what now?" Brian sits down to study them.

What now? Oh my God, what now? Now, I need to turn these designs into the real thing. But how am I going to do that? I need equipment and materials. What I need is extremely expensive to buy, I can't afford that. I don't know how I'm supposed to get materials from the school labs, I don't have an ID card, there's staff patrolling the labs during the day watching who's taking what and we have to record what we've taken out or used. I explain the situation to the guys, we all sit and think of a solution. I need to start building ASAP. Rio or Kye could to get the equipment since they have access cards, but then they would have to sign out any material and equipment under their names, which wouldn't work because the staff will check my name against the equipment lists on the day of presentations. I don't want them to get in trouble for this. Marcus suggests coming out clean and telling the teachers that I've been secretly studying astrophysics and now I need the equipment for my design for this NASA competition. However, that is risky. If they don't agree and find out what I've been up to, they could suspend me, tear my designs to shreds or worse. Argh! I don't know what to do! *Help me God.*

"Don't worry Jen, we'll think of something eventually," Brian reassures her.

"But I need to start building now! It's taken me ages to perfect my design and I might find more problems when I build," I stress out.

"Haha! Oh dear God," Kye giggles to herself. We look at her waiting for an explanation. "I'm sure we'll think of something Jen, don't worry. But I just thought of the craziest movie idea, if this was scripted, I imagine something super cool, like a mission… impossible. The characters would wait until the staff are off duty, late at night, maybe midnight, then the I.T. guy – Deq…" she gestures, "…would hack into the watchful security cameras underground and in the labs and he'd open the door without the need of an ID card. Then we sneak in from the outdoor underground entrance where the delivery trucks enter the labs. We get in, do our stuff and get out!" Her eyes are wide as she tells her fictional, made-up on the spot story. "Pretty cool right? I think I'm going to write that. Maybe a short story or a short film? You know what, I think we should do that," she finishes sarcastically.

She jokes, but I like the idea, "Yes," I say enthusiastically.

"Ha! Yeah!" Kye still jokes.

"Yes!" I yell with excitement, nodding at her.

"Yes?" Kye squints her eyes.

"Yes!"

"No!" she realizes that I genuinely like the idea. "Jen, I was kidding. That's crazy!"

"Yeah, well, it'll work. I know it will, it's the only way!"

"Woah woah woah, Jen, that's scripted stuff, we can't pull that off in real life. That is stealing! And Deq can't hack into the security system."

Pause. We all look at Deq, who wears a smug face, "Actually, I can." He's confident.

Kye's mouth drops open.

"See!" I make my point.

"I like it!" Rio expresses his view. "Staff usually leave at around seven p.m., and the nerdy research students leave at around ten p.m. unless they want to work all night but I doubt that, campus is usually dead by midnight on a weekday, so there's a chance that no one will be around to see us."

"Hmm, we'll make it really quick, if all of us go, we can carry everything in one go," Brian adds.

"Deq, can you seriously hack into the system bro?" Marcus asks.

"Well, the ID entry is the easy bit, someone will have to swipe for the doors to open but then I'll wipe the entry data off the system for that time. The cameras' however, aren't so easy but it's not impossible, it depends on the kind of security camera, I should be able to do something, for example I could redirect them, pause them or cause interference. I know that doesn't sound too promising but what I can definitely do is access them, so I can get the live footage up on my laptop screen."

"So we won't get caught?" Rio asks.

"Well, it depends on if I can control them, but I'll only find that out when I hack the system."

"So there's a chance we will get caught?" Rio persists.

"Dude, there's always a chance you'll get caught, but I doubt that will happen because I'll find a way," Deq replies.

"Alright done!" I say.

"What! No! Guys, are you hearing yourselves? We are planning to break into our own school labs and steal very expensive stuff!" Kye moans.

"That's why we're stealing it, because it's expensive," Rio replies.

"But it's a crazy, stupid idea!" she yells.

"Kye, we've done a lot of crazy stuff already, I am so far now, I might as well finish it off with crazy." I am serious about this. I see no other way and I need to start building right away. "Please," I hold her shoulders and look into her eyes.

She looks into mine and sighs, "Alright-"

"Yes!" I jump into the air. The boys also get excited for this so called mission.

"I can't believe this is my idea," Kye puts her head in her hands.

"So when are we doing this?" Brian asks.

"A quiet day would be good," says Marcus.

"Tomorrow." I make the decision.

"Tomorrow?" Kye yells.

"I need that stuff Kye. Besides, it's Tuesday tomorrow, quietest day ever."

"Yep tomorrow's good, get your backpacks ready!" Rio hoots.

"I'm going to need a car," Deq says to himself.

We spend the rest of the afternoon planning the big mission. The more we plan, the crazier the whole idea becomes, nevertheless I need to do this. This is my final year here and this is the biggest project of my life. I'm not stealing from somebody specifically or for bad reasons, I'm doing it for a good cause, for my dream. Sometimes we have to make those tough, bizarre decisions, the risky decisions and in the end I'm sure it'll all be worth it. I'm more worried for my friends who are endangering their place here for me. They're all excited for this mission even Kye, her concern is the whole stealing thing, but like I said it's for a good cause, at least that's what I'm telling myself.

* * *

"The coast seems clear team." Rio whispers as he stands outside the apartment building looking around corners for by passers. "Roll out!"

It's two o'clock in the morning, dark and a little cold. Kye, Marcus, Brian, Rio and I leave the building with a large backpack each and a few carrier bags for the equipment. It is eerily quiet on campus, most people are busy with dissertations so lucky for us, nights out are on hold. Our faces are disguised with bandanas and caps, just to be on the safe side. We scurry through the night and head down the side roads to reach the School of Engineering and Applied Sciences. As we arrive, we spot a black car parked up in one of the side roads near the underground lab entrance. A guy waves through the windscreen. It's Deq. We shuffle through the road to get to him.

"You guys look like a bunch of idiots," he laughs quietly rolling the window down.

"Deq, where the heck did you get the car from man?" Rio asks.

"Better still, whose car did you hijack?" Brian questions.

"It's Lia's mom's," Deq looks at me and Kye. "I went to sort things out last night which we did and then I met her mom and luckily she has two cars so I charmingly borrowed one. Don't ask how, it's a long story."

"Sweet! I'm going to want to know all the details later," Rio fist bumps Deq.

I look through the window to find two laptops and a tablet. One laptop displays four camera screens and the other reads 'loading'. There's a bunch of wires connected to each of the laptops. It looks very sophisticated and complicated, I can't believe we're doing this. My nerves kick in.

"Looks good right?" Deq asks. "Brian I'm going to call you now, stay on the phone, that's our mode of communication. I will warn you of any night patrollers or any cameras that I can't control and so on. I'll be keeping a sharp watch on whatever I can inside and outside from here. If we lose connection because you're underground, then… use your instincts."

Kye's eyes widen at me. Now that we're here, this actually seems like a bad idea.

"Cool, you better have our backs on this, you geek," Brian answers his phone and begins to lead us down the road and down the ramp towards the underground entrance.

"Good luck!" Deq whispers. He rolls the window back up.

We follow Brian. I genuinely feel uneasy but at the same time, I can't wait to get my hands on the equipment. The boys whisper through the phone to Deq as we walk through a large tunnel, wide and long enough for a supplies truck to fit through. There are cameras in the tunnel which Deq tells us he's hacked and frozen. As we venture further into the tunnel, the light from the streets outside fade. Marcus and Kye turn on their flashlights to light the way. All we see now are our shadows on the walls of the creepy tunnel. I look back at the start of the tunnel, but I can no longer see it. I feel scared but I don't know if it's because of what we're doing, the dark or some kind of supernatural powers that may live underground. I hold onto Kye and she holds onto me. We don't trust the boys in this situation, they're already making spooky sounds in front of us scaring each other and us. I hear Deq making most of the sounds through the phone.

"Stop that!" Kye hisses at all of the boys. "This is serious stuff!"

They stop the sounds with a chuckle. I see two large double doors a head of us. That's the entrance into the lab.

"Guys, I'm causing some interference in the entrance camera so you're good to go, however there seems to be cameras in the hallway past the entrance doors which I can't get into. Are there any?" Deq questions.

"Yes, there are two I think straight after the door," Kye replies.

"Okay well, I can't get into them so cover up," Deq orders.

"Shit!" I whisper, I didn't expect us to actually be caught by the cameras.

"What! What do you mean cover up?" Marcus quietly yells.

"You mean they're going to see us now?" Brian asks worried.

"No you idiots. No one's watching, it's a school not a police station!" We hear Deq through the phone. "I don't think they watch the recording all the time, only if there's an incident they'll play it back. But you're not going to let an incident happen, are you? We're keeping this clean! Okay?" Deq's voice sounds like an annoyed parent.

"Alright, alright," I say.

We reach the doors, Marcus shines a light on the ID scanner. Rio pulls out his card and is about to swipe us in when Kye reaches it first with her card, gently pushing his hand out of the way.

"Just in case, it was *my* idea," she says to Rio. She swipes, the red light turns green on the scanner and the doors open sliding each way.

Everyone holds their heads down avoiding the two cameras. They are located right in front of the door and if we hadn't known they probably would have picked up our faces. We crouch past them and into the long, dark hallway. On each side of the long hallway are further hallways which lead to locker rooms and labs of all kinds. We need to find the physics and engineering labs and workshops, the ones I saw on our first day. Luckily for me, Kye and Rio have a pretty good idea of where they are.

"Erased," we hear Deq though the phone. "The entry details have been successfully erased from the system."

We hear some clicking and popping through the phone.

Brian pulls a face, "Is that-"

"Beer?" Rio finishes Brian's sentence.

We hear a slurp, "Ahhhh, yep! Cheers guys!"

"Deq! Seriously!" Marcus says.

"Drinking in a car, on the job!" I yell at him.

Deq continues to sip and laugh through the phone, then he yells in a whisper, "Everybody stop!"

We freeze. My heart thumps.

"Deq?" Rio whispers for a response.

"Don't move," he says.

"Who is it? Night patrollers?" I whisper, regretting this whole idea.

"There's something there!" Deq's voice echo's through the phone, Brian reduces the volume.

"Don't do this man!" Marcus gets scared.

"Some…*thing*. Not some *body*?" Kye questions not so scared.

"It's…it's coming toward to guys!"

Marcus squeals and jumps behind Rio. I'm frightened in the moment, but at the same time I wonder why Deq's voice has increased in volume.

"Ohhh! Oh my God! Guys! It's…. it's a…CAT!" Deq shrieks through the phone.

My fear vanishes and now I get angry, "DEQ! How can a cat get inside the lab you idiot!"

"Haha! Lol! I was just kidding. You guys are wimps!" he hoots.

"So there's nothing there?" Marcus asks gathering himself together and letting go of the tight hold he has on Rio. We didn't expect that from big man Marcus if I'm honest.

"No, you wimp! I was just having a little fun. Hey Marcus, I didn't expect that from you bro," Deq teases. "Carry on, make it quick!"

"Make it quick…" Brian imitates him. "I'm telling Lia what you're up to, jackass, hacking into the system, assisting a crime, and breaking the law."

"Oh shit, yeah about that guys, I haven't told her about this mission thing and if you want to keep on living then don't tell her, or at least not until she's…drunk or something."

That's actually true, Kye and I haven't told her either. She's very serious about the law and crimes and I don't think she'll like what we're are doing, albeit for a good reason. We can't hide it from her for too long, she'll find out somehow, so we will tell her, just not yet, maybe when she is drunk.

    Rio and Kye lead us left through another long hallway. The hallways are all wide, I guess they have to be for the ease of moving large equipment. They are very tidy from what I can see in the dark and smell exceptionally fresh, like a dental practice. We must be near the chemical engineering labs. Deq keeps us informed of which cameras he can control and those which we should hide from. He warns us of another one coming up straight ahead that he has no control over. Before I can even find it through my squinted eyes, I hear a loud yelp.

    "Marcus!" Kye yells.

    Marcus misses the tall block of stairs descending in front of us. He falls a few steps before being rescued by Rio who bravely pulls Marcus back. Kye swings her bag up in front of her and on top of the stairs knocking a camera so that it now faces the wall and away from us.

    "What the heck happened? You jolted that camera's direction towards the wall," Deq tells us.

    "Are you okay Marcus?" Rio asks, flashing a light down the staircase.

    He nods. Catching his breath. He seemed quite uneasy after Deq's ghostly cat prank.

    "That was quick Kye, very quick," Brian compliments her quick thinking.

    "Thanks, I practice these things in the mirror straight after watching action movies."

    Brian yells at Deq for not warning us about the stairs and the camera. In his defense he did warn us about the camera and I don't think he can see the stairs. Marcus shakes out of the incident and lectures us on his hard work at medical school, he has been here the longest and still has longer to go until he graduates.

    "…I do not want to get kicked out now, so can we just hurry up, get the stuff and get out of here! How far is it?" he finishes.

    "Down the stairs and on the left," Kye replies leading the way.

    We take one step at a time. The hallway changes

downstairs, it's concrete and smells of wood works, like a garage. There seems to be a securely chain locked garage door at the end of the hallway, it probably leads to another underground exit tunnel. We follow Kye.

"Deq, do you have control over the lab's cameras?" Brian asks.

"Bri…Bri…ca…" Deq's voice struggles to make it through, there's harsh crackling as Brian tries to get an answer to the important question but then, the call ends. We lose connection.

"Well, there go our eyes," Brian puts his phone away. "Just keep covered up and away from any cameras."

Kye leads us to another set of large glass double doors. She reaches for her ID card but Rio swipes his this time.

"It was everyone's idea to go ahead with this," he says softly.

The red light turns green again and Rio pushes the handle down opening the door. The lab looks huge from what we can see with our flashlights. The smell of metal and wood lingers in the air. The first thing we all look for are cameras and together we point out seven of them. I ruffle through my bag and find the long equipment and material list and hand a copy to each person along with a pen. As soon as they locate the item and gain the correct quantity, they are to say it out loud so that we all tick it off and move on to finding the next item. We split and search. There are work benches located all over the room and there's lots of free space for building. There are cabinets under each bench with all kinds of equipment and material. I would have loved to have been able to actually build my project in here! I let my imagination of me working in here sink in, who knows when I'll see it next, if I'll ever see it. Rio kicks off the search by finding wire connectors and from then on we move quickly to find most of the smaller material and equipment. I'm glad I showed pictures of everything to everyone and that we planned this bit well with a rehearsal from Kye. However, the bigger stuff is hiding elsewhere.

"Where's the storage room?" Rio asks Kye.

Kye points to a door at the other end of the room, "I think

it's there."

They make their way to the door and I follow them. The door has another ID card scanner but it looks a little different to the others. There's a screen on this one, where we need to place an ID card instead of swiping it.

"My turn," Kye says.

She places her card on the scanner and waits for a green light. The red light flashes twice and a small beep sound is heard. Rio pushes the door. It's still locked. Rio and Kye exchange confused looks. I get worried. She tries again. No green light. The red light flashes again. The beep again. The door is still locked.

"Damn it! How are we going to get the electrical base and the cutting equipment?" I freak out. I need that stuff. That's the expensive stuff!

Kye tries a third time but the door remains closed, "What is going on? Do you think they've blocked my card? Oh no! What if they've found out?" she's anxious. "I hope Deq is erasing all of this!"

"Let me try," Rio moves her out of the way and places his card on the scanner.

Click… click… click! The sound of heavy unlocking is music to our ears and a green light shines from the ID scanner screen.

"Viola!" Rio opens the door for us.

"What!" Kye walks passed him, offended by the door.

"I'm the man!" he says confidently, following us inside. "I hope Deq erased that," he mumbles.

Dim blue lights light up the room, it is cold in here. There are shelves on each of the walls, rows upon rows of them and on top of them lie the expensive, good sized for modeling, equipment. I love it! I can't control my smile. I recognize instantly what I need and other objects catch my eyes too. To me, this is like Disneyland to an eight year old and Hollywood to Kye. Some things look dangerous and delicate, no wonder they are locked away in a separate room. I gather what I need, carefully. Rio finds a large tray in which I can carry the bulky, heavy things.

"Woah!" Brian stands in the doorway. "That's a lot of fancy

stuff. More than tweezers and scissors, right Marcus?" he hits Marcus on the back who also looks astonished.

"Okay, I think that's everything," I read from my list making sure everything is ticked off. Then I compare my list to everyone else's. I do not want to be coming down here like this again. Kye reads everything out loud once more as we all check our bags as best as we can in the dark with our flashlights to make sure we have everything and some extras, just in case. With the final count complete, we pack everything away, shut all the cabinets and head back out the way we came. I pick up the tray full of expensive material.

Then, we hear something smash on the concrete floor beneath us, "Shit!" I yell in a whisper. Something slips from me, "Guys, I dropped something! What did I drop?" I cry, not being able to search very well with the tray in my hands.

Brian crouches down along with Marcus. He finds my phone with the screen noticeably cracked and my new solar system phone case split into pieces, now only showing the sun to mars.

"Argh no! Not my phone! I loved that case!" I'm disheartened, that was the best thing anyone had ever bought me and my first Christmas gift from Brian.

Marcus still searches for the other piece of my phone case, he doesn't find that, but what he does see is a glint of light coming from the hallway. He pops his head through the double doors and looks down the hall. We follow him. There's light coming from beneath that garage door.

"Is that daylight?" Marcus questions.

"I think so," Kye awkwardly checks her watch without dropping anything from the pile she carries. "It's five twenty one!"

"We've been here for like three hours! We better get out of here!" Brian says leading us through the double doors.

"Wait! What if I dropped something else too?" I call.

"Don't worry Jen, we've got extras of everything," Rio reassures me. "We need to go."

I take another look around me to check, the others begin to leave the lab. *What if I dropped something else too? What if we didn't get enough extras?* I question myself, unwilling to leave without a good look around but being unable to with everything I am holding.

"Jen! Leave it. Come on!" Brian yells, holding the door open for me.

I have no choice but to leave. We'll find out if I dropped anything else when we get back to the apartment. We exit the building much faster and more swiftly than we had entered. It is still dark in the hallways but as we reach the top, daylight floods through the tunnel. Deq is back on a phone call with Brian. He tells us that he has successfully erased all of our entry and attempted entry data from the system even from the storage room. He also states us that he actually was able to freeze the cameras inside the main lab, so we were all worrying about hiding our faces for no reason. We arrive outside to find Deq opening all of the car's doors. The sun is beginning to rise and we run as quickly but as safely as possible to the car and place everything anywhere we can, where things won't break. In fact, the car is so full of equipment, that there are no seats empty for us to sit on.

"Take off your goon costumes. I'll meet you at the apartment," Deq turns on the engine as we take off our hats, scarves and bandannas and throw them into the car.

"Deq, slowly please, everything is fragile," I tell him.

"Don't worry," Deq reassures me. He very sensibly takes off and drives into the side road, taking the long way back.

We see a few morning joggers out around the campus.

"Well, I'm going to go this way folks. I'm just doing a short jog today," Rio talks loudly, smirking as he begins to jog the short way back home, hinting that we should split up.

"Yeah me too!" I say, already jogging behind Rio, I just want to go and see my equipment.

"And me-"

"No you're not Marcus, you're coming with us, you need some practice with looking at where you're going," I hear Brian tease him in the distance with Kye pulling him along.

They take a different route. I can't believe we pulled that off!

I just can't wait to get home and see my equipment safe and sound. I hope Deq has arrived with my equipment safely. I actually feel like I've accomplished something. I don't feel nervous or afraid. I did what I needed to, no one got hurt and I didn't bring anyone any harm. I'm just chasing my dream, and now, I'm another step closer.

"I hope you got everything Jen because I am not doing that again," Rio runs smoothly.

"Why would you even say that?" I shake my head laughing and keeping up with his stamina quite well. "You don't have the guts to do that again?"

"I don't know about me. I'm not going to lie, I didn't think you had the guts to do that... until now."

"To be honest, me neither. It's surprising what you can do for your dreams, or what they make you do. The closer you get, they crazier they get."

CHAPTER TWENTY ONE

KYARA

Fifty eight, fifty nine, sixty! I mime out of breath, as I finish my daily sit ups and exercise in preparation for the final audition. I have already learnt my script sides and have practiced my lines in many different characters just in case they ask me to redo it differently. I have read it in front of mirrors, in front of the sofa and in front of the guys and girls. I've even been to see Sheera and Dwaine for some advice. I really want this role. I really, really do. It's only been two days since we accomplished our so called *mission* and Jen has already built the main frame of her design. It is looking very complicated and highly detailed already. She had come across a few issues yesterday which she solved quickly and efficiently as I expected from her. She's taken up most of the space on the back wall in the living room for her project and there are delicate wires and attachments loose on the floor so we have to be extra cautious when maneuvering around the living room and kitchen.

    I hydrate and start to pick up the pillows and a chair I had placed as an obstacle course in the hallway for practice.

    "Guys!" Brian and the guys run in through the hallway tripping over my obstacle course.

"We are screwed!" Marcus cries.

Jen and I are startled at their truly terrified faces.

"What happened?" Jen asks moving away from the build so that no one steps on anything.

"Have you not checked your email today?" Rio asks.

We shake our heads. Jen has been busy building and I've been busy rehearsing for my audition.

"We are all so dead, man!" Deq yells leaning on the kitchen counter with his head in his hands.

"Tell us what happened!" I shout.

Brian shoves his phone in our faces, "Your Dr. Kennedy sent out an email to everyone, to the entire university this morning, saying that the engineering and science labs and workshops have been broken into on the early hours of Wednesday morning. He's written that some equipment has been taken without records and that technically there has been a theft! He's called an emergency meeting today at one o'clock in the Great Hall."

"Oh. My. God." Jen sits down in shock.

"What are we going to do?" I shriek. I fear getting caught and kicked out, losing my audition place, Jen losing her opportunity, the guys losing their careers, their degrees. I am actually scared. I feel sick. *What if he already knows that we did this? What if he wants to humiliate us in front of the entire university! God help us!*

"How hidden were our faces Deq?" Marcus asks.

"They were hidden quite well if I'm honest. I couldn't tell who was who," he replies.

"And you definitely erased all the ID card data stuff?" Rio asks.

"Every single bit, I'm sure."

"And what about your hacking stuff. You left no traces?" I asks.

"Yes, I'm sure. I used tech that can't be tracked. I made sure of it. I was sure to save my own back guys, come on!"

"Well, then we just won't go," Jen suggests. "The entire university isn't going to turn up. We'll just be like those people, we'll pretend we had no idea of what's gone on."

I wouldn't mind totally avoiding the situation, but at the same time, if we don't go, I won't stop thinking about it.

"Wait, I think we should go, especially you two," Brian points at me and Jen, "And Rio, because he recognizes you guys and you guys study the subjects. If you guys go, it'll be less suspicious. If you don't go, he might wonder why you're not there."

That makes sense, I nod along, "Yeah, I agree with Brian."

"Listen, I don't mind going too, we're all in this together," Deq adds.

"Yes, we'll just sit separately," says Marcus.

We agree on all going to the meeting, Jen and I will sit together because that's how Dr. Kennedy usually sees us. This news has ruined my whole day. I'm anxious and don't want to confront anyone, but at the same time I really want to get this humiliation over and done with. Jen has been extremely quiet since the boys came in with the distressing news. We're literally watching the clock tick until it's time to go down to the Great Hall. She feels awful, fearful and guilty. I tell her not to be, if any one of us goes down, then we're all going down together. At one point she even tells me that we should start packing our bags and get ready to leave; which kind of made me laugh in pity. She's already done so much with the material in just two days, she's a genius and we're not going to let this hard work slip out of our hands so easily. I know I won't. I'm staying positive.

The afternoon arrives and we arrive inside the Great Hall. It's packed out! Way more than I imagined. People are standing along the sides, at the front and along the back. Dr. Kennedy stands at the front, in the middle of the staging area telling people that we won't be long so standing is fine. He is joined by the vice Chancellor and a few other professors. Jen and I come to a halt between people standing in the doorway. I gesture at Jen to stay here, we don't want to be right in front of his eyes. My eyes find the boys; Deq and Marcus stand on one side of the top balcony with Rio and Brian on the other side. I also see Lia with her law friends, seated in one of the rows, we still haven't told her about this situation. Then, Dr. Kennedy's eyes find us. *Of course they would. They're Dr. Kennedy's eyes, he doesn't miss a thing, even without his glasses on.* I remove my sarcastic thoughts from my head and feel the embarrassment and guilt in my skin.

"He's looking at us," Jen mutters in my ear.

"Shhh," I mumble back.

Dr. Kennedy puts on his glasses and then fiddles with something in this hand. I can't see properly with all these heads in front of me. He looks down for a moment and then taps the microphone to begin our doom.

"We appreciate your attendance," he starts the meeting in an uncomfortably serious manner. "In the early hours of Wednesday morning, the School of Engineering and Applied Sciences Laboratories were broken into via the underground entrance. The CCTV cameras caught five hooded bodies moving through the hallway. When our staff arrived in the laboratories in the morning, they found that equipment had been taken from the Mechanical and Astronomical Laboratory without any record or sign out information on these pieces of equipment. Hence, the equipment has been stolen. This is an extremely serious incident that has occurred on our university grounds and it is currently under investigation. We have been inclined to suspect that students of our own may have been involved in this hideous crime."

I stop breathing, literally. Jen grasps my arm. We wait for our names to be called out.

"Unfortunately, no identification entry was to be found on our systems and the five thieves have not yet been identified."

I find my breath again. Jen let's go of my arm.

"This is a revolting incident! I can only hope that none of you would even think about doing such a thing let alone have been involved in this organized crime. However, if you have had any involvement whatsoever, I would encourage you to come forward and see me or any of us in our offices immediately. That way we shall come to a solution quicker. If you do not come forward but are found to be guilty there will be severe consequences. This incident has truly upset our university's honor and we hope that no student of ours is involved to protect us from being completely dishonored. For security reasons, anybody taking part in the NASA competition please see your respective supervisors immediately after this meeting for a count of equipment. "Exceptionally expensive and important equipment has been stole and not only is this material expensive but it can also be very dangerous and must be handled with care, therefore if you find anything on campus please alert a member of staff immediately. Finally, if anybody has witnessed anything or has any suspicions, speak to any one of us straightaway. We would like to get to the bottom of this as quickly as possible and your assistance in doing so would be greatly appreciated," he pauses looking down at his hands again, "Thank you for your attendance," he finishes bluntly.

    Dr. Kennedy leaves followed by the vice Chancellor and the other staff. The silent room heaves into shock, chatter and conversation. I can't feel my legs as people push and shove past me to get out of the hall and I don't think Jen can either as she just stands still with a pale face. I see the boys leaving and Lia seems like she's already on the case asking questions to random people and investigating the situation. I can't even look at her right now. She wants to be a lawyer not a detective!

    I finally move my neck to face Jen with a very ill look, "We need to tell Lia."

* * *

"Can you believe that?" Lia walks up the four flights of stairs with the six of us following her feeling very sickly. We exchange woeful looks behind her as she speaks with excitement about what she has just heard. "I mean it must have been a well-planned crime, no entry data, some CCTV footage was missing..." she continues.

    In our minds the *well-planned* crime originated from a very stupid movie idea and took only a day to plan with one voice acted rehearsal of selecting equipment, which the boys didn't take seriously anyway.

    "...and in our own university too! No trails left... nothing-

"

"Lia," Deq cuts her off. "Can we talk for a second please? In my room."

Lia gives Deq a muddled look as we reach the top of the stairs, "Sure! Is everything okay babe?"

"I feel bad, so I just need to tell you something. Come on," Deq takes her hand and gives us an, *I've got this,* look.

I feel bad for letting Deq do the exposing, however it makes sense for him to tell Lia his story first. We're going to back him up and we're going to have to persuade Lia that this is a good idea, or *was* until now. Knowing her, she won't tell on us, but I'm not sure how she'll take the whole idea, the crime and the fact that we didn't tell her. The rest of us wait in our kitchen with the door wide open, waiting for them to come back in. We hear a few 'What!' and 'OMG's before Lia comes storming into the kitchen. It's weird because her facial expression is more of astonishment and amusement rather than anger and disappointment. Deq comes in laughing behind her. I guess she took it well.

"I can't believe it was you guys!" she shrieks, her eyes and mouth wide.

"Shhh!" Rio sniggers with his finger over his lips.

"I can't believe it was you guys!" she repeats in a whisper.

I hear Brian whispering to Deq asking him if he gave her anything because this is not the reaction we expected, but he shakes his head proudly.

"Why didn't you tell me?" Lia cries looking at us, still grinning. "It's stealing! This is wrong…" she stops and notices the equipment and Jen's project in its build stages, "…Oh my God, you stole *all* of this!"

Jen decides to take lead on this, "Yes, we did Lia, but look…" she gestures, "…Look what I needed it for, I couldn't have gotten *all* this any other way. You know how much this means to me."

Lia thinks for a second, "It is good, whatever it is. But why didn't anyone tell me?"

I explain, "Because, well, you weren't there when I came up

with the stupid idea and then…Lia, we love that fact that you love Law, you are so passionate about the law that you would've persuaded us to not do this and we respect that."

"And that's why Deq told you pretty much right away. We trust that you won't tell anyone," Brian says.

"I still can't believe it!" she chuckles. "Deq, you hacked into the system? Man, you are good."

"Ha, I know," he grins.

"Lia, don't mention this to anybody, please. I have never done anything like this before and I need to finish med school. I want to help people. Just like you. More than you," Marcus grins with a cheesy smile.

"Don't worry, your secret is safe with me. I actually wanted to investigate this and be the first law student to solve the mystery and take it to the Chancellor," she laughs. "You have a lot of law students on this case by the way. I'll redirect them, don't worry."

"I imagined a very different reaction to this," Rio blurts out.

"I'm surprised myself, I don't know why I'm not angry. I just can't believe you guys pulled this off in two days! How long has it been since I last came here?"

With Lia now a part of our secret, we move on to thinking about the meeting. My heart feels a lot lighter after knowing that Lia is okay with everything. I don't feel as sick anymore. Telling her the truth has somehow calmed my nerves.

"Anyway, I'm just glad that we didn't get humiliated or suspended," Deq says.

"I know. Dr. Kennedy even gave us a mean stare when we walked in," Jen tells them.

"But what are we going to do now? What if they find out eventually?" I ask.

"Then they find out eventually. No one says anything, we carry on like normal," Brian hatches a plan. "Jen you continue working on your project, everyone else do what you would usually do. If we go and confess we'll all be kicked out. We won't stand a chance, especially not against that asshole of a teacher you guys have. I don't know how you've coped with him. Just forget that this ever happened. Forget that we ever did this. Okay?"

No one has a better idea so we nod in agreement.

Rio finishes the plan, "They won't get to us so easily. We left no clues! Just let them do their work and we'll do ours. If we ever get caught, we'll deal with that when and if we ever have to cross that bridge. Which hopefully will be once we've all graduated and all have our certificates in our hands."

We leave it at that and vow not to speak of the *mission* again.

CHAPTER TWENTY TWO

KYARA

We are in hiding.

I'm just kidding.

We arrive back at the apartment after a class with Dr. Kennedy, I think he's developed some sort of anxiety because he's always fiddling with something in his hand nowadays, maybe it helps him to concentrate. We have all forgotten about our crime and to be honest I think the university has too. *Thank God.* Jen was right about the design part being the hardest and the longest because she has almost finished constructing her project. She's already started the accompanying essay and is just adding the last few touches, perfecting the model and making sure it works. She's done so well in this short amount of time and now she has a decent amount of time left to perfect it and finish that essay. I'm proud of her. We're all proud of her. To top it off, she is still doing alright in literature though she has dropped from excellent to just above average. She doesn't care much, her focus is the project, that's where her heart and soul is. It worries me a little – what if she doesn't get selected? What if they find out about her and things don't go the way we planned? She would be heart broken. I would be heart broken. I don't want her to put all her hopes into this project, I don't want her hopes to be broken. Nevertheless Jen seems to have a lot of faith and so do I. I suppose studying literature and doing the project at the same time is a good example of multi-tasking, which is a requirement of an astronaut.

Jen takes her laptop out and continues the essay. I pick up a printed copy of my short film screenplay that I have finished from my desk. I flick through the papers. This is my own work. I stare at it for a few more minutes.

"Feels good doesn't it? That's exactly how I feel, when I look at that," Jen points to her beautiful project.

I smile, "Yes, yes it does. I just can't wait to finish my book. That will be so much longer and heavier," I dream.

"Soon," she says. "Are you going down to show it to Sheera?"

"Yes. I hope she likes it. I hope she gives me some constructive feedback."

"If she doesn't, then that's because it's already awesome."

"Ha, thanks, I'll be back in a bit. Then we seriously need to start studying for exams! I need some books from the library."

Jen stops typing and looks up at me, "I think we need a break. We'll start studying tomorrow for sure, but today I think we just need a reboot. In fact, I'll stop writing as soon as you get back, we'll get the guys and go watch a movie or something. Or you, me and Lia could just go for a quick spa day. It's only eleven a.m. we have the whole day."

I like the idea, I do need a break even for a few hours just to refresh my mind and soul. "Okay, but before we head out I want to show you my obstacle course thing for the audition, then we'll go."

"Cool. See you soon." Jen waves.

I leave to see Sheera, with my pride in my hands.

Sheera stands in the audience seating watching the stage change color and giving directions to the lighting team. I'm not in this year's play because of the auditions and my writing work, I decided not to take part. I see Abbey on stage helping out. She joined the dance society this year but still helps Sheera choreograph some of the drama performances. Sheera notices me walk in and waves. I wave back.

"What do you think Abbey?" Sheera calls.

"Yeah, I think that's good," Abbey calls back. "Hey Kye," she waves from the stage.

"Okay great, we'll go with that, thanks guys, take five." Sheera walks to the end of the row and greets me with a hug.

I hear the back door swing open and turn to look, *she has such great timing doesn't she?* It's Betty and her two remaining friends. She stops as she spots me and Sheera talking, frowns and then changes her facial expression to a happier one.

"Sheera! Hey!" she runs down the steps. "Can I borrow you for a moment? I would like to read my lines to you, just once more."

"Sure Betty, but I'm just going through something with Kye and then we'll go through your audition. Cool?"

I did email Sheera to arrange some time to go through my screenplay and talk about my audition, Betty could have at least had the courtesy to email her as well and arrange and appointment that doesn't clash with mine. I'm quite surprised that she's come here for help, I thought she was so stuck up her own ass that she wouldn't ask for anybody's advice. Sheera and I sit down and begin reading my short screenplay. Betty waves cunningly at Abbey as the girls walk down to the stage. However, Betty walks very slowly and then stops to place her bag on a seat just a few rows in front of us. Eavesdropping.

"This is wicked Kyara! I don't even know what I can criticize."

"Thanks," I humbly respond. "I'm not sure what to do next, or how to... you know, get it out there."

"Hmm, to be honest I'm not so sure either, but I would try and publish it on this website I've heard about. If someone comes across it and they like it and want to produce it or whatever, they can contact you. I'll email you the web address."

"That would be really great, thank you."

She continues to flip back and forth through the screenplay, "You know what? I think this could be done on stage too. How would you feel about us putting this on as a short production, say next year?"

"Really?" I'm stunned! Is it that good that Sheera wants to test it out on the school stage?

"Yeah, really! It's good! Although, it will need a few changes. If you could change it from a screenplay to a script for stage and send it to me, I'll try putting it up for a short play. By the way, what are you doing next year? Are you still here?" she asks a question I have barely thought about.

I don't know what I'll be doing next year. *Oh dear! This is my last year. No! These are my last few months here at university, what the heck am I going to do after I graduate?* I suddenly feel fear. I've been so busy with writing and my studies I forgot about the part after the studying. I'm not an actress yet, I don't have a contract in place and I don't even have a small role anywhere. I need to sustain myself. *Oh God, am I going to have to get an office job?* My mind crashes at her question. All sorts of things fill my head. I don't want a job. I HATE working, especially in an office! Everyday. Knowing that for the rest of your life you will spend most of your time in an office, staring at a screen doing almost the same thing every…single…day. The thought of it kills me! Education has been my excuse not to fall into an actual career path other than acting for my entire life. Education has given me time to at least try and pursue my acting career. Now, I'll be in a full time job, no time for acting! This pause is taking way too long. Unless…I stay in education? I have thought about enrolling straight onto the master's course, yes. I'll still be here, with Marcus. I'll still be here to watch my play come to life on this stage. I'll have an extra year to sort out my acting life and if I still haven't reached my dream, I'll do a PhD to buy me more time. I create a plan on the spot. The first thing I need to do when I get back is send an email to admissions to have me enrolled onto the master's course.

"Kyara?" Sheers nudges me.

I snap out of my rather long thoughts, "Huh, yes sorry, I am planning on doing a master's degree, so I should still be here.

"Great! Oh you're so determined! Well, if you are, then you

can help direct it or be in it. It is your play, you can do what you want with it. How's that?"

"I'd like that very much. Thank you Sheera, I really appreciate your help."

"No problemo, that's what I'm here for. Okay, audition call back, are you ready for it?"

"I think so, I hope so," I say a little nervously as it is getting closer.

"Don't worry! You'll be fine. Between you and me, they really like you," she lowers her voice.

My face brightens up. I look at her frowning with a smile.

"Yes, they called for another reference for you and Betty, but they really like you. So smash it up girl!"

We smile with joy between us. I don't know if that has eased the pressure off or added more on, nevertheless at least I have a chance now. *God, I hope this is the one for me.* My eyes catch Betty's and she quickly blinks away and begins walking down the steps and onto the stage. I stand on the stairway and audition one last time for Sheera's advice.

When I return, Jen stops typing and I perform my obstacle course to make sure I can flatteringly jump over things for the screen test. According to Jen, I look like Lara Croft! I love Lara Croft! We all head out for a movie and then we laze around for the whole night. I fill everyone in on my future plan about the master's and possibly a PhD, everyone is supportive. Jen doesn't really know what she's doing either, at the moment her attention is on the internship. Marcus will still be here for another year and a half until he graduates. Rio has already secured a graduate engineering role so he'll be moving straight into work. Lia plans to go back to her internship place and work for them for a while, she's training to become a barrister. Brian says he will start job searching when he graduates and Deq knows he'll find a technological job quite easily, so he's cool about everything. The night goes by with bitter sweet chatter as our final few months together begin. Hopefully the best months. The successful internship, successful casting, successful graduations and most of all the three years of successful friendship that we have all endured.

* * *

The next evening, I collect some books from the library. Rain pours mistily outside, in the dark. Spits of it hits the library windows. I hope it doesn't get any heavier, I have to walk it all the way back. My phone buzzes in my pocket but my hands are too full of books to attend to it right now. I place the books on the counter in the library for the librarian to scan. While she scans them I find my phone. It was Jen. I call her back and wait for her to pick up. The librarian gives me the go ahead to take the books. I unzip my raincoat, neaten the sides of the pile of books so that they are neatly stacked up and then I hold them in one arm, covered by one side of my coat as much as possible and make a quick exit before the rain gets any heavier. The roads are quiet. I hear the rain drops hitting the floor and my coat, and then I hear the sound of ringing in my ear.

"Hello, Kye! Where are you?" Jen picks up and immediately questions me like a mother.

"I'm just walking back now. I'll be there in like three minutes," I say walking as fast as I can.

"Okay hurry up its raining and it's late and I have food on the cooker. You need to get here before the boys find out and eat it all! I will not cook again!" she yells through the phone.

"Haha! I'm coming!" I yell back trying to overpower the sound of rain.

"Did you get all of what you needed?" she asks.

"Yep I got everything."

"Where are you now?"

I stand opposite the back entrance of our building, at the crossing. I briefly look left and right and then continue my speedy walk, "I'm opposite, just crossing the-"

* * *

JENNIFER

A loud bang pierces my ears followed by some crackling.

"Kye? Hello. Kye? Can you hear me?" I increase the volume on my phone, "Kye?" I stand still for a split second. Then my hands begin to tremble and my heart thumping is the only sound I can hear. "Kye?" My voice shakes. No reply. The line cuts off. I drop my phone. I run to the window above the stairs in the hallway. I see papers, white papers in the darkness of the night. Books thrown, covering the width of the road and…*No! Is it?* I blink fast. *It can't be!* I run down the four flights of stairs as fast as my legs can move. I burst through the back door and run out into the rain, my socks soak up the cold water beneath me. I see a body amongst the books in the middle of the road and disappearing car lights in the distance.

"Kye!" I scream from the top of my throat.

She lies on the wet, cold ground in the rain. Her hands scraped, her body messy and her leg! Her leg torn with blood dripping and diluting into the rainwater. I feel shock coming over me but I prevent myself from going into that state. I have to be strong right now.

"Kye! Kye! Hey look at me!" I tap her face and nudge her shoulders. "Look at me, Kye!" My voice gets more aggressive as I fear the worst. "God! Please! Please God!" I shriek. "Kye!"

Her forehead crinkles and she squints her closed eyes.

I breathe a sigh of relief and my heart begins to beat faster, "Kye! Oh God! Are you okay? Can you hear me?"

She slightly opens her eyes, squinting from the raindrops hitting her. Her face is pale and her lips are blue. She's in pain, so much pain! She tries to lift her head to reach for where the pain is utmost… her leg. She groans and then drops her head back. I think she's losing consciousness again. I need to stop the bleeding right now. I take off my cardigan and wrap it as tight as I can around her leg. The position is so uncomfortable that I don't know how to tie it without hurting her. She groans louder, unable to move. I tie it as best as I can with my hands shaking.

"Marcus!" I think out loud. Tears drip from my eyes as I look for my phone in my pockets. I left it upstairs! I look for Kye's but hers is in pieces all over the road. "Kye, stay with me okay. Keep your eyes open. I'll be right back," I run inside and up the stairs. "Marcus! Marcus!" I scream. My neck stretches as I look upwards calling him with all my might.

The boys come out of their apartments startled.

"What? What happened?" Marcus asks.

"Oh my God, Jen are you okay?" Brian sees blood on my hands and on my wet clothes.

"It's...it's Kye!" I can't speak properly, I'm scared and out of breath. Tears roll from my eyes.

"What happened to her?" Rio asks.

"She's been hit by a car just outside!" I point to the window. "She's... she's by herself."

Rio and Deq run to the window.

"Oh Shit!" Deq yells.

Rio and Deq sprint down the stairs. I begin to follow but Marcus calls me.

"Jen wait, where is she bleeding? Is something broken?" he asks very seriously.

"I... I... think so," I cry. "Her leg is like cut open. I wrapped my cardigan around it..." I speak really fast.

"It's okay Jen, pull yourself together. She'll be fine," Marcus brings out what looks like a first aid kit from his room. "Brian get some towels or a blanket or something, quickly! Is she conscious?"

"I don't know," I follow him down the stairs.

Brian catches up quickly. Marcus asks Rio if she's still conscious as we run outside. Thankfully she is. Rio places his knees on the ground and lifts Kye's head on to them. Her hair is soaking wet. Her eyes are tired and teary. I sit next to hear and hold her hand tight, I don't want to let go. I hear Deq calling the ambulance and police behind me. Marcus attends to her leg with Brian's help.

"Kye, are you okay?" Marcus makes conversation.

Kye doesn't say anything back, she squints in pain.

"You're okay Kye, you're okay," he speaks loudly and very clearly. "Good job Jen, though it needs to be tighter," he says to me looking at her bleeding leg.

He takes off his belt from around his waist. We all look at him. He nods at us to indicate that this will not be easy.

"This might hurt a little Kye, stay strong," Marcus warns us all.

He takes her leg and wraps the belt around it. Tight.

Kye growls, gritting her teeth, her hands tightens around mine. Her other hand finds Rio's shirt, she grips it to release pain.

We all comfort her as much as we can, but the pain is too much to bear, she stops screeching, her breathing slows down. I look at Brian and he looks at me. We fear the worst.

"Kye!" Rio shouts at her.

"Her breathing has slowed down," Brian tells Marcus who seems to be disinfecting her leg with something.

"Hey, Kye!" I talk to her.

Marcus checks her heart beat via her neck, "She's losing consciousness because of the pain."

She blinks softly and looks up into the sky. The motion around me seems to have slowed down, everybody moves in slow motion. My heart is afraid. We are all afraid. I hear the sirens of an ambulance and a police car getting louder. Deq waves his hand in the air. The ambulance stops, I see the reflection of the siren lights in the puddled rainwater on the ground. I see shadows of people coming out of the ambulance. A few people come outside of the buildings around us, a crowd forms. Others can be seen looking through their windows. Someone helps me up from the ground. I don't know who it is, my mind is too slow for me to notice. I just hold onto Kye. My hope lies in God's hands now, Kye's God. *She has so much faith in you! So much! Let nothing happen to her, God, please!*

CHAPTER TWENTY THREE

KYARA

"Mom. Mom, will you please stop crying. I am fine! Look at me. I'm fine," I talk to my family through a video call.

"No. We're flying over right now," My mom sobs on the screen with a tissue in her hands. Her face is red and teary.

"Mom, please don't do that. You don't need to do that. Will you calm down please? I am absolutely fine," I plead, but she still cries. "Mom. Stop crying mom. Can you stop. Mom stop. Can you please put Dad back on?" I get frustrated. "Dad, I am fine," I tell my Dad, who is concerned but so much calmer.

"Are you sure you are okay? Because if you want, we can come right now?" he says.

"I am really really okay, please don't cancel anything and come here. I will come home in the summer anyway. You can come and get me yourself. I have a lot of studying and stuff to do right now. There's just a few weeks to go. Okay?"

"Okay. But if you need anything, you call me straight away. Do you hear me? Straight away. I know your friends are taking good care of you."

"Yes they are," I look at them all lined around the room.

"Take care. Love you."

"Love you too. Love you Mom," I say before ending the call. I let out a sigh and point at Jen, "You told my parents!"

"Well, they had to know," she defends herself. "Are you okay Kye?" she sits next to me.

I reflect on what has happened, "I actually am, I feel fine, I'm a little shocked at being here but I'm fine, honestly guys don't worry. I'm glad to be alive put it that way. Everything was just a blur. I saw a flash of lights and then that's it, I was out. Oh but I do remember pain!"

"Sorry," Marcus says giggles.

"Kye, do you know who did this?" Brian asks.

I think hard, "No, I have no idea. It just went so fast."

"Don't strain yourself, it'll come to you. Anyway, I bought you your favorite flowers," Lia points at the colorful bunch of gerberas on the side table. "I couldn't find anything acting related."

"Thanks Li, now you've got the investigation you always wanted."

"The university and the police are investigating, we've all spoken to them, and they'll speak to you soon. A case has already been opened," Rio explains. "We're just glad you're okay."

"Yeah Kye, we're happy you're back. Now you have another story to write," Deq grins.

I laugh too and shake my head at the poor humor. The doctor walks in with a few papers in his hand.

"Kyara, I'm Dr. Singh. How are you feeling?"

"A lot better, thanks," I reply.

"Good. It's all thanks to your friends, Dr. Marcus in particular for his quick thinking. He saved you a lot of blood loss and ultimately your leg."

Marcus as humble as ever, "Nah, Jen stopped the bleeding first. I was just doing my duty Doc."

I am so grateful for the people around me right now. I love each and every one. If it wasn't for them I may not even be here right now. *God, thank you for such loving friendships.* Dr. Singh tells me a bit about my injuries and wounds. I have scratches and cuts on my hands and arms and a bruise on my jaw. Then a nurse walks in interrupting him, she holds two crutches and smiles at me. My body turns cold. *Are they for me?* Now I feel ill. Since I regained consciousness I didn't realize that my right leg had been raised beneath the covers. Now I am aware that I can't move it, I actually can't even feel it! I slowly move my hand discretely under the blanket to check if it's there. *Thank God, it is.* I probably just need some support for a few days. I calm myself and wait for the doctor to explain, I still don't know what is actually wrong with my leg.

"Further to those minor injuries you have suffered an open fracture to your leg, Kyara. This means that at the time of your bone breaking, it protruded through the skin slightly, which is why there was a lot of bleeding," he looks at Marcus and then back at me. "You are very lucky Kyara, these type of fractures are usually more complicated but in your case we have managed to successfully realign the bone and it will fully recover."

I take a deep sigh of relief and nod at Dr. Singh. It still hasn't hit me yet that I was involved in a car accident and that I have broken my leg. I am pleased that it will recover, but I'm still scared for some reason. I'm anxious. I've never been in a hospital before, not for myself.

"You will need the assistance of crutches to walk…"

I saw that coming.

"…As your leg is currently in a cast…"

Oddly, I didn't see that coming. My heart rate increases.

"…The recovery time is expected to be around eight to ten weeks and you will need the crutches for approximately four to six weeks-"

"What?" I interrupt him. That, I definitely did not see coming. "Four to six weeks!" My thoughts switch from my present situation to the future. I panic and sit up straight. There's only one thing on my mind right now - my call back audition. My lips begin to tremble as I try to get some words out but I don't know what to say. My hands quiver as I reach for the sheet that covers me, I take it off and see my leg wrapped in a white cast. I take my left leg off the bed and then I try to move my right. It's heavy and numb. Dr.

Singh is confused by my actions as is everyone in the room. He steadies me. Tears fill my entire head and face, I try to hold them back. I angrily lift my right leg with all the power I have in both my hands and shove it off the bed in grief. "No no no, I need to walk," I speak in a state of confusion and disbelief as I urge myself to stand up on both feet, but my leg gives way, it's so numb, that it's painful. I collapse into the doctor's and nurse's arms. Brian is nearest to the bed, he leaps next to me and holds my hands back. I can't bear to look at anyone, I feel them close by and worried.

"Kye. What are you doing?" Brian asks as he helps me sit down.

"I need to walk," I reply holding back my waterworks, looking down at the ground. I don't know how to tell the doctor, they never take acting seriously and I am not in any mood right now to hear that it is not important. I've worked so hard to get to this stage of the audition.

Dr. Singh tries to reassure me, "Kyara, are you okay?" He pauses. "Look, I understand this is a lot to take-"

"Eight to ten weeks?" I question, my voice is low from the lump of sorrow at the back of my throat.

Dr. Singh looks at me and I look at my friends, who all know exactly what I am thinking about.

"I can't...I can't wait that long," I tell him with my voice trembling. "You have to do something please."

"Kyara, your leg will fully recover. Don't worry about it. It'll just take time," Dr. Singh tries to uplift me, but he's missing the point.

"No, you don't understand. I...I have an audition, a callback for a big movie in two weeks and I need to be able to move well for it. Please," I beg, my bottom lip trembles.

Dr. Singh, takes a moment, he is sympathetic and looks directly into my eyes, "Recovery time can vary hugely. It might be that you recover much quicker than we anticipate. This depends on your body. However, I have to be honest with you, Kyara, I doubt it will fully recover in two weeks. You may be off the crutches but it's unlikely that you'll be able to walk normally in just two weeks.

I am very sorry. Try and get it postponed or tell them it will take time. I would be more than happy to provide you with a doctor's note with all the necessary details. If there's anything I can do to help, then I will, okay?"

I swallow hard and force a nod because words are not coming out of my mouth.

"I'll leave you to rest now. Just try not to stress about it. I'll see you later," he places his hand on my shoulder and leaves.

The nurse comes my way to settle me back down in the hospital bed but Marcus politely tells her that he'll manage. We wait until she leaves the room and the door closes. I feel everyone coming closer. They're all silent. I can't open my mouth because if I do, I'll cry. I can feel my eyes heavy with tears, red and watery. I see Jen, she feels my pain so much, that she is just as lost for words as I am. Brian wraps his arm around me and Rio sits beside me. He takes my hand.

"Kye-" he begins.

"It's okay," I quickly say, I don't want them to feel bad or sympathetic. I act strong, "I mean, it can't happen now, it's no one's fault." I find myself smiling out of pity, I laugh a little too in the midst of my sorrow, but I'm not acting. I'm lying. "It's just meant to be…I'm okay…" Tears drip from my eyes, as much as I try, this is something I can't act or lie about. "I'm okay…" I squeeze out of my throat before covering my face with both my hands and wiping my tears as they uncontrollably pour from my eyes. "Sorry," I whisper crying, shake my head in my hands hiding my wet, red, veiny face, apologizing for nothing.

"Oh Kye," Jen kneels in front of me with tears rolling down her face too, "It'll be fine. You can still go to the callback."

I shake my head still weeping as quietly as possible in my hands. I inhale with shuddering breaths. "They won't take me."

"You don't know that," Lia joins Rio's side.

I wipe more tears from my face and try to speak, but if I open my mouth I'll choke on my words. My tears won't stop, not today.

Rio places his hand on my back, "Let it out Kye. Let it out."

* * *

I'm discharged a few days later. It feels good to be back at home although the stairs are a killer! The accommodation staff offered me a place on the ground floor but I wouldn't be with the guys and Jen, and I need them more than ever right now. My eyes are still swollen from crying, I don't think I've ever cried so much in my life but I'm happy to be back and I'm grateful for my life even though I've questioned it. After much discussion with Jen, Lia and the boys, I have decided that I will go to the callback and I will try everything I possibly can. I pray to recover sooner. Who knows, they might still like me. They liked me before, what difference is a broken leg for a few weeks going to make? I even got the wink!

The past week has been busy with the lawyers, police and Lia all trying to find out who hit me with the car. All I can remember is that the car was white and it may have been really far from me when I thought it was safe to cross. It was my right of way anyway. So the police think it was a hit and run or worse… an attempted murder. I, on the other hand really wish it was just an accident. Lia has her own investigations going on. She already has a suspect – Betty Johnson. And as much as I hate to admit it, she has been acting very strange lately. She's avoiding me and where she would usually say something to me or at least confront me, now she acts like I'm not even there. Knowing her and her followers, Maya and Ellen, they would definitely have something to say about my crutches but none of them have. What makes it even stranger is that Abbey was acting really weird when she asked me what happened to my leg. She made it super quick and then disappeared. After all this and Lia constantly suspecting Betty and her friends I seem to have remembered something from the accident. When I was hit, I didn't pass out right away. I seem to remember seeing a blonde girl driving and an even brighter blonde in the back window. I also seem to remember the car awkwardly breaking, jerking and swerving after it hit me. However, this could all just be in my imagination. With everything going on, I can't distinguish whether this is what I really saw on the night or whether my brain is just making it all up, I mean I did have concussion. The one thing I don't remember is the registration which would be the biggest help. Honestly though, I don't think Betty could do such a thing. Yes, she's mean, jealous, big headed and just an idiot but she's not criminal minded.

"Hey, how are you doing Kye?" Lia enters the living room in a hurry.

"I'm good," I say sitting with my colorfully signed casted leg raised on the table, studying for examinations.

"I've been speaking to your lawyers – thanks for appointing me by the way this is really going to help my profile – apparently the police are suspecting Betty too! She is acting very peculiar from gossip around campus and she has a white car, which, seems to have disappeared for the past week and Maya apparently is ill and has gone home!"

"How do you know all this stuff?" Jen asks.

"I know a lot of people from different courses and word gets around quick," she replies.

"The police are suspecting Betty?" I ask. I am worried, I really don't want it to be her, I can't imagine it being her, *or can I?* But everything is leading towards her and no matter how much I wish that she didn't do it, even *I* am beginning to think that she might have.

"Yep. They are going to interrogate her soon I think." Lia nods.

"I still can't believe this has happened," Jen articulates.

"Me neither, but it'll all be fine Kye, you just recover soon. Leave the criminal catching to me," she winks. "Anyway, I have to go to Deq's quickly and then I have a lot of reading to do, so I'll see you tomorrow."

Lia leaves and Jen sits on the floor with her goggles on, testing something from her project, "I never imagined Betty would stoop so low. I know I shouldn't say anything yet, because we don't know for sure, but if she did this, then…then I have no words. I mean, is it because of the audition? Or that she just doesn't like you? Like how? How can you hit someone with a car?"

"I don't know, but if it was her, I'm sure she was not thinking right. She was probably having a bad day," I say.

"A bad day? A bad day, Kye!" Jen stops, takes off her goggles and looks at me. "Why are you always thinking about other people's thoughts and feelings and their reasons for when and why they do stuff? Especially bad stuff!"

"You know what I mean. She couldn't have done it for fun," I respond.

"I don't care what her stupid reason could have been. Running someone over is unacceptable no matter how someone is feeling. I swear if it is her, I will…" she mumbles the rest in anger and then puts her goggles back on and carries on working.

I stay silent. She is right. It is unacceptable. And if it is her or whoever it is, I know I'll feel angry. I'll be hurt to find out that someone did this on purpose. This might cost me my audition and that's what would upset me the most.

Jen turns back to face me after noticing that I haven't spoken, she takes off her goggles again and leans on the table, "Are you okay, Kye?"

I smile at her and nod, "Yes. You know what Jen, this whole thing has given me a little bit of a new perspective. I don't know if my perspective is better or worse but I think I've moved on from the whole accident thing. I just feel calmer, like what is going to happen in life, is going to happen in life. However, at the same time I want to recover quickly, prove that I am still suitable for that film and basically move on with my life. I want to move forward, be happy and achieve my goals. If I'm alive right now then I'm sure this whole thing happened for a reason, whatever that may be. I don't know but God does. I just have a lot of faith and I hope God keeps it."

"He will. He has to!" she says enthusiastically. "You are recovering quite quickly. You might even make it to the callback next week without any supports."

"I'm just a little gutted that I can't practice the physical stuff, I have to rely on the dialogue now, but yeah you're right, all thanks to Dr. Marcus and you guys."

It's true, I am grateful to have them and we all help each other somehow; Jen and Rio are helping me with my exam studies, Brian is helping Jen with literature, Lia is solving a mystery, Deq is assisting her and Marcus is doing everything he can to help everyone including helping me recover quickly. I don't know what we would do without each other. My health is improving quicker than I thought, I try to walk without the crutches as much as possible and I can (holding on to the walls or at least using one crutch). Marcus says it's partially in my own hands. He says that I need to rest my leg and give it recovery time but also I must exercise it to strengthen the muscles.

"Alright, that is enough for today," Jen puts down her tools. "Watch. That. Wire." She points very specifically at a looped wire on the floor near the breakfast bar. "I can't tuck it in anywhere because, well, I just can't at the moment. It is connected to a lot of things. So watch it and tell the boys too." She stands back and admires her work.

"Looks good," I compliment.

"Damn right it looks good," she smirks. "That is a lot of hard work right there."

"Yes it is and I'm witness to the hard work. I'm really proud of you Jen."

"I'm just glad it works! I hope it works on the presentation day too," she crosses her fingers. "Right I'll carry on tomorrow."

* * *

It's early in the morning. Jen is at Brian and Marcus' asking Brian for some literature help. I stand at the breakfast bar it the kitchen crunching on a bowl of cereal. It just makes it easier because I don't have to get up off the couch again when I'm done. I finish and wash up maneuvering around the kitchen holding onto the drawers and surfaces. There's a knock at the door, which is weird because no one ever knocks, they just barge in.

"Come in!" I call waiting for a fresh face to appear as I find one of my crutches to help me to the edge of couch.

As I pass the archway, I see a familiar face, nervous and

frightened. It's Betty. I stop and stand still surprised by her appearance. This is strange. *Why is she here?* She also freezes when she sees me. In her hands she holds some fresh flowers. Her face is pale and looks smaller, she isn't wearing any makeup. She actually is pretty, prettier without it. She wears a long, sad and slightly swollen face and is if her bad attitude that she carries is not with her today.

"Hey..." she forces a smile and then tries to find words, "...These are for you."

I still stand motionless and anxious. She has never been to our apartment. *How did she find out where I live?* I say hi and then take an awkward step back letting her into the living room.

"I'll just leave these here," she places the flowers on the breakfast bar and then looks around. She fiddles with her hands awkwardly, "How are you, Kye?"

This is very strange. Her voice is soft and meaningful, there's no sarcasm or bitchiness at all.

"I'm... okay. Thanks," I respond trying to take a seat on the arm of the couch. My crutch falls on the floor.

"I'll get it," she bends down and picks it up, then unsure where to put it she leans it against the breakfast bar. Her mind is elsewhere.

I finally sit, "Betty, what are you doing here?" I ask trying to get rid of her quickly.

She sighs deeply and leans back against the bar. She huffs and puffs and then places her hands over her head in irritation, grief and anger. Her forehead wrinkles up and her eyes show...guilt.

"Kye I..." she starts to sob, "I...I'm so sorry. I didn't do it on purpose. You know I would never even dream of doing..." Betty's words come out faster than I can hear them. Her voice crackles from her crying and her cheeks flush red.

My eyes open wide. She did it! It was her! All kinds of emotions and questions take over me. *Why did she do it? Why is she crying? Why is she telling me? Should I trust her being alone with her right now? She doesn't seem like she's come to harm me?* I really was hoping she had nothing to do with this. I feel slightly scared but more annoyed, "What? Betty, *you* were driving the car?" I ask to clarify.

"Kye, I can't believe that I... I don't know what came over me," she weeps at her own actions. I see signs of anger in her. She's angry at herself, "You don't understand! I can't believe that I did something so stupid! With my own hands. These hands!" Her muscles are tense as she looks at her hands in shock and grits her teeth as she speaks. "I feel sick at my own actions, Kye! I'm…I'm sorry. I'm glad that you are okay. If something more happened, I wouldn't be able to live with myself."

I hear her guilt and the realism in her voice but what if something did happen? I wouldn't be here. She attempted to – I can't even say it.

"Why? Why!" I ask in anger raising my voice.

"I don't know! I was intoxicated! I don't know why!" she answers with tears rolling down her face. "I am a terrible person, I know." She calms down and begins to explain, "All I ever wanted was to become a Hollywood actress. I studied it since school. I took part in every single play they put on. It was my career, my goal. And I was good at it. I was better than everyone else and I knew it. I never had any competition. In all my life, all that time that I have been working towards my dream, I never had any competitors. Then you came, a mere physics student who joined the drama society. The people like you, Sheera likes you, even my own friends like you. When I got that big audition I was so happy, Kye. I really felt like that was my time, but even the casting directors liked you better!" She is opening up and sharing her truth, her feelings. I've never seen that in Betty before, so I listen quietly. "I don't understand Kye? Why do you study Physics? All I've ever worked for is acting and drama, my entire life. I want it so bad, Kye. So bad! I guess you know that feeling. And yes you are good. It's not just that you're good at acting and that people like you, it's everything about you; your tanned skin, your long hair, your intelligence, you're different, not the typical blonde girl," she pauses and shakes her head sniffing her tears back. "I guess… that's what came over me. I am so sorry Kye. I never meant to hurt anyone by my actions. Believe me, I hate myself for what I've done. I'm not here to ask for you to forgive me, because what I did is not forgivable, I know. And I'm not here to ask you to drop the case – I've already had a phone call from the police and I should suffer the consequences. I just came here to tell you the truth - it was me and I just had to tell you myself." Betty pulls herself together and wipes her face ready to leave, "I really hope you get the role, Kye. I'm not going to the callback. Not after what I've done. I hope you recover quickly. And I hope your dreams do come true. You deserve it. Maybe we can be friends, when you're in Hollywood and after I've done my time. " she finishes with a wry but genuine expression and walks past me and into the hallway, I mildly laugh at her last sentence, it could partly be true.

"Betty," I call her.

She stops still facing the other way.

"Go to the callback."

She turns around and shakes her head in guilt and grief.

I reinforce my words, "Go for me. I need some competition. Please."

She thinks for a moment and then gives me a sad smile, "I'll see." She walks out.

I take a deep loud breath and wipe my hands over my eyes. That was intense. My mind is muddled. It was Betty. Lia was right. It was Betty! She is such a complicated person under the thick coat of makeup. She's similar to me – although I don't think I could run someone over not matter how sad or intoxicated I was. However, when you're upset sometimes your actions are wrong and crazy. That's why people say, never take action when you're upset because most of the time you end up doing the wrong thing and then you regret it. Betty expressed herself and opened up, she showed a different side, a side I never thought existed, a side that was covered up by her dream, the same as mine. After hearing her, I feel sorry for her. I am sorry that I took her limelight. That wasn't my intention, I just wanted to fulfil my own dreams and I have been working towards acting since I was a child too, but she's right, she has worked harder than me I suppose and more consistently. So understandably it would hurt her if someone takes over. I know Betty's acting, she was all real there... that was her. She does feel guilty, she feels terrible, and I saw it in her eyes and heard it in her voice. The fact that she pleaded guilty herself and feels remorseful is good enough for me. Feeling true guilt is the biggest punishment of all. *God, I don't know what you're planning up there, but at the end of the day all I came out with is a broken yet recoverable leg. If you can forgive, then who am I not to?* I don't agree with her running someone over, but I understand her pain and guilt. Somewhere in my heart I forgive her. People are not bad, it's their circumstances that make them do bad things. I hope that one day we *both* become friends in Hollywood. She deserves a chance. I'll drop the case.

With my thoughts coming to a close and my decisions made, I make an effort to get going and do some studying in my room. I look around for my crutches, the nearest one leans on the breakfast bar. I hop, holding on to the walls to get to it. My hand slides through the ring and I hold onto the handle. I lift the crutch to begin walking, but I hear a loud clang behind me. The crutch pulls back and crashes out of my hand. I hear loud clattering behind me. The project! I lose my balance as the crutch falls to the floor. My foot slips! I'm down on the ground with a clang. Pain shoots up my leg, through my spine and straight to my head. I let out a groan but the pain quickly vanishes when I see half of Jen's project, smashed on the ground next to me. I hold my breath.

"What happened?" I hear Rio's voice coming from the landing.

"Kye are you okay?" Jen runs in from the hallway followed by the boys.

Jen and Rio help me up.

Jen giggles at my clumsiness, "Kye, you need to be more -" she sees the disaster I caused behind me.

Jen lets go of my arm. Deq replaces her and slides a crutch under my arm. They all then stand back and gasp at the catastrophe. Jen's face turns red, her veins can be seen in her forehead. She stares at the mess, breathing heavily.

Brian places his hand on her shoulder, "Jen-"

"No!" she shoves him off, still staring. Her eyes turn red and watery.

"Jen, I'm sorry, I just fell-"

"Don't!" she shouts at me pointing her finger in my face. Her face rages with anger like I've never seen before. "Didn't I tell you to watch the wire, Kye? You've ruined everything!" Tears drip from her fuming face.

My heart races. She is furious. She has put her heart and soul into this. She has worked day and night on this project and I have just gone and ruined half of it in seconds. It's due in a few weeks! I feel sick. I feel like crying. *How did this happen? How could I do this to Jen?* I feel her wrath and this time she's not joking, it's not the funny kind of anger. This is serious.

"I didn't mean to-"

"No no no Kye! Stop with the bullshit! Are you hurt?" she asks in fury.

"No...no I'm not," I answer confused by the question.

"No? Then why did you do it, Kye? You could have fallen anywhere, anywhere!" she screams.

"Jen calm down," Brian interrupts her sternly.

"No Brian! Kye, you know how much this means to me, how could you do this? It's due in a few weeks! You smashed the whole damn thing!"

"Jen, it was an accident!" I shout back.

Cold, angry laughter emerges from her, "No! No, it wasn't an accident. You did this Kye, I told you very clearly about that wire!" she sobs in anger. "Why did you go near it? Huh Kye? Why? When have I not supported you?"

"What?" I say defensively.

"Is that what this is Kye? Is it that *I'm* doing this project and you're not? Can you not take it that I've made this?"

My brain freezes. *Is this Jen? My Jen? What is happening right now?*

"What are you saying Jen? It's okay we'll fix it," Rio says in a calming tone.

"Fix it? Fix it?" she reaches for a piece of metal on the floor, "This took me weeks!" she chucks it back down. "*She* did this!" her fingers point at me. "People were right, you are jealous of me! You can't take it that I'm actually succeeding with my dream and you're struggling with yours! You can't take it that I'm doing well in astrophysics! You can't take it that I'm doing two subjects! I am really really sorry, Kye. I am sorry about your accident and your audition, but that wasn't my fault! I supported you in everything! And this is what you do to me? In my final few weeks!" she shouts and cries as she speaks in frustration.

The whole world around me has turned. My body and mind is numb. I don't know if this is really happening or if it's a dream. If it is a dream, it's a nightmare. *How can Jen possibly even think like this?* I don't know what to say. I don't know how to defend myself, its Jen, I never thought I would have to.

She wipes her tears and catches her breath, "I can't believe you. This is despicable. Three years of friendship, dreams and having each others' backs and this is how it ends?" Her voice softens but her tears are still hard. "I feel really betrayed Kye. You ruined everything. No callback, no project, no NASA! All of this was a mistake! This is over… it's over," she pushes past me nudging my shoulder.

Brian squeezes my hand quickly and then runs after Jen. I stand with my head spinning, holding back my tears of embarrassment. My cheeks shake and I purse my lips. Rio, Deq and Marcus slowly empty the room, leaving me to my disbelief. I'm wounded by what Jen has said. I thought she understood me. I thought I understood her. *What is happening, God!?*

CHAPTER TWENTY FOUR

JENNIFER

I lie on the couch under a blanket staring at my broken project. It's been a few days since Kyara cracked it to pieces and shattered my dreams. Rio and Deq tidied up around it and then made efforts to put it back together but I stopped them. It won't work and I've given up hope. My eyes are still sore from my tear ducts over working. I feel ill. Heartbroken. All this time I actually thought I would become an astronaut. All this time I had so much faith in my dream, in my education and in my friendship. I was living in a dream. I've wasted my time. I don't know why we even thought of this whole dream chasing thing in the first place. I was ready to forget my dream when I started university. I was prepared to let it go, I was prepared to embrace English literature for the rest of my life, but then I found a new hope, a new way with Kyara. I achieved so much in three years and everything was going to plan, opportunities came my way, I was believing in dreams. I got so attached, that now seeing my final project broken, seeing my last hurdle impossible to overcome has destroyed me. It all gets worse when I think that my own friend, my sister, the one I trusted more than myself broke that trust. I hate Betty for what she did to Kyara, but Betty was right all along, Kye is jealous, she's an actress, she needed my help to get her writing going. Argh! I hate saying stuff like that about Kye. I know her, but then why did she ruin my project and pretend it was an accident? I don't know what to believe anymore. My hope is lost. I'm just going to concentrate on literature now, graduate and get out of here. No more astrophysics, no more astronaut shit, no more dreams.

Kye walks into the kitchen. I haven't spoken to her since the incident. I don't want to be around her. It hurts me when I see her. She hasn't even tried to speak to me, *why is she in a mood with me?* She's the one crushing dreams. I understand she's been through a lot. I get that and I feel for her, but that does not mean she can get angry over her own life and ruin mine. I kind of wish I never met her. I get up and leave before awkward eye contact is made. I find Brian playing on the PlayStation in their living room. Marcus seems to have gone out. As soon as he sees me, he switches off the game. It's odd, because of this situation, even the boys have gone quiet. It's uncomfortable and I don't like it, but every time I see my project, it just reminds me of my unworthy journey. Brian still talks to Kyara, I'm not the kind of girl who will stop her boyfriend from talking to other people. That's his choice and I respect it.

"You okay?" Brian asks, making space on the couch.

I join him, "Yes I am."

He sighs and moves my knees towards him, so that we're almost face to face, "Why are you doing this Jen? You are only hurting yourself."

"What? What do you mean, *what am I doing*? Brian, I am hurt. Everything that I worked my ass off for has been destroyed by my best friend." I keep my cool and explain softly trying not to yell or go moody.

"I know you've worked hard but you can still rebuild it and I know you are hurt, but doesn't a little part of you think that Kye didn't do this on purpose? That maybe it was an accident?"

"It wasn't an accident. I told her very clearly to watch that wire. It took me weeks to build Brian. I can't rebuild it now, I have no time and no material," I stick with my decision.

"I don't want to argue with you but I'm going to tell you my opinion – I think it *was* an accident. It's Kye, Jen. Our Kye. She would never think of tarnishing your project, she is the one who brought the project to you. She is the one who told you about it, for heaven sake she is the one who came up with the crazy idea of stealing the equipment!" his voice slightly increases in tone. "And you still think that she did this on purpose, she fell in her crutches with a broken leg on purpose?"

What he's saying makes sense, but my mind is not ready to accept it. Since she got back from the hospital she's been getting around fine with the crutches, she hasn't once fallen over. So why did she fall on my project, especially when no one was in the room? "People change Brian. Their circumstances change them."

"Yeah, people do change," he says, coldly.

I feel a negative vibe from him and I'm annoyed by his statement. I wonder if that was meant for me. *Is he trying to say I've changed?* I feel my heart beating faster. I want to question him on what he meant, but I really don't have the energy to argue.

Before I can think of something to say, he holds my hands and looks at me again, "I just think it's unfair that you are not talking to her. You two have shared dreams together. In just a few days of meeting each other you guys bonded like... like covalent bonds," he tries to make me laugh and I do. "You've lived together for just three years but it feels like much longer. You guys fight and argue and then happily gossip and do girly stuff all the time, but this, this you're taking way too far. It has been blown way out of proportion. You two have something so special and do you know what that is, Jen?"

I wait for the answer.

"Friendship. True friendship. Friendship is the strongest relationship anyone can ever have. It can be with anyone; mom, dad, brother, sister, cousin, uncle, boyfriend anybody because it is made by you, but the most precious friendships are those who aren't related by blood or attraction. Those that form from nothing. Those that are genuine. Those that are solely linked by one another and those that don't have another name except for friendship. That's what you and Kye have. You are lucky to have that."

I look down thinking about the deep, meaningful things he is saying.

"Do you wish she hadn't recovered from that accident? Do

you wish... it was worse?"

My heart jumps and I respond quickly, "What! How can you say that?"

He smirks, "I thought so. So how can you think she wanted to hurt you?"

I close my eyes and sulk. Brian wraps his arm around me and pulls me close to his chest. I absorb his comfort. His sweet scent and his soft hoodie fill my senses and relax me. I sob but I don't know if it is for my project or for... Kyara.

Brian's words have been wandering around my head for the past couple of days. I'm so lost in my own thoughts that I'm having trouble sleeping. It is Kye – Kyara's call back today, I left for my literature class (that I didn't really need to attend) and Lia's there helping her prepare. That would usually be me. She did look at me before I left. Her eyes were sorrowful but I left anyway. Thinking about it, I now feel bad, I don't know what I am supposed to do with my life. I hold tightly onto my books in my hand as I make my way to my last literature class ever through a dull, windy day.

Dr. Kennedy – the literature one - explains some final tips for the essay, she points at the board using a laser light. I take a picture of the board with my phone just in case she changes the slide and then I write everything down, taking in all the advice. My focus is on my notebook, for the first time ever in a literature class I'm not thinking about astrophysics. I'm actually concentrating, a little late but nevertheless. My attention is on my notes when I notice a figure walking in from my peripheral vision.

"Julie, sorry to interrupt might I... have... a.... word."

I recognize the voice instantly. *Why is he slowing down?* My eyes widen. I slowly look up to find Dr. Kennedy standing right in front of my desk. Physics' Dr. Kennedy. The man. There he is standing in his cream shirt and brown tie with white, wispy hair looking through his glasses and down at me, then at my phone and then back at me. I freeze, praying that he doesn't recognize me but who am I to fool the Kennedys. I figure it out. They are married. Of course they are! Husband and Wife. Mr. and Mrs. Kennedy. *How did I miss that?* The entire class stop their chatter and stare at our interaction.

"Is everything okay Kyle?" Julie asks him.

"Is this your student?"

"Yes, this is Jennifer," she smiles.

"How long have you been coming to this class?" he asks me.

I'm still a statue. Merely breathing.

"Her attendance is decent, she's here almost every class," Julie kindly answers for me.

"She's a literature student?" he questions still glaring at me and then my phone, cooking something in his brain.

"Yes, yes she is." Julie, still smiling doesn't seem to understand what is going on.

If only the literature classes had more people in them, maybe I would've stayed hidden.

"Jennifer, follow me to my office. Immediately," he orders, pushing his glasses up and turning around. "Julie, please come along once you've dismissed your class."

I blink sharply and then pack my stuff away, quietly and fearfully. Julie or should I say Mrs. Kennedy looks at me confused. I hear her wrap up the class as I follow yards behind Mr. Kennedy. I am so dead.

We reach his office and he tells me to take a seat. I am scared but not as much as I should be due to my recent experiences, which in turn, is scaring me more. I try to think of an excuse, but I don't know what for! *Should I say I just attended astrophysics classes out of interest? Or should I say I attend literature classes for fun?* I can't say that, he'll see my details and that I'm registered to the literature course! Argh! What have I got myself into! It's all over anyway with the astrophysics, so I should stick to literature. That is what I came here for. I want my Literature degree. I want to graduate in that. I am sick of everything else. Yes, I will stick with literature. I prepare myself.

Dr. Kennedy takes his time. The wrinkles on his forehead are as deep as his thoughts. He looks quite intrigued but also pissed off. Obviously he's angry that I've been sneaking into his classes but that's not bad, *is it?* I still don't actually know why he has brought me here. Maybe he doesn't recognize me. Maybe it's for something else. He takes a seat in his leather chair, then leans forward, hovers his hand over the phone and then picks it up and dials a number as my blood pressure begins to increase rapidly.

"Vice Chancellor, could you please come to my office, this is urgent," he talks with firmness through the phone, "Thank you."

I feel like my heartbeat can be heard in the whole room, increasing so quickly that it may explode.

"Is everything alright?" Julie walks in and stands next to Dr. Kennedy's chair opposite me.

A few seconds later we are joined by the Vice Chancellor, I'm not even going to lie, I don't know his name. I can feel sweat dripping from by back and absorbing into my shirt. *All I have to do is explain why I'm in both classes. Make it quick and simple Jen. How bad can it possibly be? I just need to act confident and prove I've done nothing wrong.* I try and calm my mind and body to display a more self-assured look.

Dr. Kennedy begins, "Jennifer... your surname?"

My confidence goes bust as soon as he asks a question, "Err... Jennifer...sorry, it's... it's Kost... Jennifer Kostigan... Sir," I stutter.

"What do you study Jennifer?" he unsympathetically asks.

I look away from them and my eyes wonder for an answer, "Literature, English literature." I say it clear with a burn in my chest. *No more astrophysics! That is enough!*

Dr. Kennedy looks at the Vice Chancellor and his wife before looking back at me, "Do you attend your classes?"

"Yes Sir, I do," my gaze slightly turns to Julie, afraid she'll say that I don't turn up all the time, but my grades are good, so I pray she keeps her mouth shut.

"Do you attend any other class, Jennifer?"

I've been caught. I clench my fists under the desk, "Yes." I tell the truth.

"Which class? Or rather, which course?"

I gulp, *stay strong Jen*, "Astrophysics."

"Vice Chancellor, could you please confirm which course

Jennifer Kostigan is enrolled on to," he tilts his screen towards the Vice Chancellor.

"English literature," the Vice Chancellor frowns at the screen and then at me.

"Is Jennifer a final year student of yours Dr. Kennedy?" he asks his wife.

"Yes she is."

"Well according to the records, she certainly is not a student of mine, isn't that right Jennifer?"

I stay quiet.

"Vice Chancellor, is it acceptable for a student to be enrolled onto an English literature course yet study astrophysics?" his voice is getting angrier.

"No, it is not acceptable," Vice Chancellor seems disappointed but not angry.

"And it is not acceptable for a student to sneak into another class at all, let alone for almost three whole years. It is unacceptable to study any course other than what you are enrolled onto. It is also unacceptable to lie to the lecturers at any university. It is unacceptable to use resources and teaching that you have not paid for. Furthermore, Jennifer Kostigan, it is unacceptable to steal equipment and material from any school or building especially one that you do not belong to!" he shouts standing up from his seat and throws something onto the table.

My entire body loses its senses. All I can feel and hear is a light ting sound. *How? How!* I see what he threw, its Jupiter to Pluto. The other half of my phone case!

The Vice Chancellor and Julie gasp. Julie looks at me in disbelief. Dr. Kennedy sits back into his chair.

"That does belong to you doesn't it, because I'm sure if you pull out your phone we can prove it," he viciously smirks. "Would you like to see proof Vice Chancellor?"

"Yes, yes I would," the Vice Chancellor replies. "Miss Kostigan, if you would, please."

I unclench my fists into trembling hands and reach into my pocket and pull out my phone, with half of the smashed case still on – The Sun to Mars - thinking how injudicious I am to still have that on my phone. It quivers as I place it on the desk. Dr. Kennedy pics up his found piece and joins it perfectly to mine revealing the solar system and the planets in order, before chucking it onto the desk again, making me jump out of my seat. There's silence in the room. My breathing gets heavier and cold sweat takes over my body, hands and face. I feel faint.

"Miss Kostigan, this is improper behavior," the Vice Chancellor speaks softly. He is bursting with disappointment and looks ashamed. He seems like a kind hearted person, but the circumstances are such that I am causing him distress. "This has never occurred in our university before. You are not permitted to attend any other classes but the ones that you are timetabled to. I don't seem to understand how you gained access to the astrophysics class timetable. Furthermore, stealing? Breaking into the labs? This is not what I expect from a student, an academic. University is a place and a stage of life where people are allowed to make their own choices, because they are wise enough to do so. You, however have made some very ill decisions, childish and quite foolish. Education is supposed to lead you on the right path, a sensible path. We select our students very carefully upon application and we choose those that are highly intelligent, sensible and those that will bring a good name to our university, but you have done the opposite of that. You have taken the privilege of being a student here for granted. I don't know what to say. Did you not think about the consequences of your actions Miss Kostigan?" he shakes his head and fold his arms. "The protocol for this would be suspension or worse, but we are almost at the end of the year-"

"There are no excuses Sir. We are appalled!" Dr. Kennedy responds to the Vice Chancellor in a high tone. He points is fingers at me, "You have brought disgrace to yourself, your family and this institution!"

"Kyle, I think we should hear her out. Jennifer is there something you would like to say or explain? Why did you steal the equipment?" Julie touches my shoulder. Her eyes plead for an explanation.

I don't know where to begin to explain everything and even if I did, they would all think I'm crazy, including Julie. Nothing about this whole dream situation is logical, nothing is sensible, everybody on this planet thinks dreams are just dreams, we've all been taught to dream and then forget about them and move on in life, 'wake up and smell the coffee' or 'start living in reality'. Even my own parents have been saying that! These guys don't stand a chance at understanding, they're academics! They study what they love! My thoughts take time, too much time.

"She doesn't have an excuse!" Dr. Kennedy yells.

"Dr. Kennedy, we are so close to the end of term now-" says vice Chancellor.

"Simon, she stole from our labs! She's a criminal! This should be a police situation."

I feel nauseous.

"Kyle, I don't think we need to take it that far," Julie insists.

"We will not take it that far, Kyle," Vice Chancellor orders.

I exhale. My mouth is dry and I see the waterline in my eyes fill.

"However, I understand Miss Kostigan has made some grave mistakes, therefore since the two of you know her best. I will leave the decision on Miss Kostigan's consequences of her actions up to you."

Dr. Kennedy eyes me. I don't think Julie will have much of a say in this. I am suspended. I know it! I can see it in his angry face, he wants to break me.

"Jennifer Kostigan, your actions are unforgivable. You do not deserve to be here, you do not justify to be an academic and you certainly are unworthy of a degree. Hence, we have no other option but to... expel you... immediately!"

I look up at Dr. Kennedy in shock. *Expel!* It is like something has exploded in my brain. I can't even believe what is happening.

"No! Please!" I beg, tears find their way out of my eyes.

"Kyle, she has worked very hard, she's a bright student and her grades in literature are good. I can vouch for that," Julie appeals.

"She has committed a crime. If we were to let her continue and allow her to graduate with everything she has done, what influence do you think that will have on our students? Everybody will go around stealing, lying and sneaking into other classes and still expect to graduate! We will be setting a terrible example. This is a lesson for everybody! To teach the future generations to be truthful!"

I'm losing everything! I need that degree for me, for my family. My heart speaks out, "Please Sir. I only attended the astrophysics classes because… because I… I wanted to become an astronaut." I weep at the truth that now sounds so pathetic, I wish it never said it. "I thought I could. I did not mean for this to happen. Please don't expel me. I'm happy with literature."

"Ha! You wanted to become an astronaut?" Dr. Kennedy laughs a pitiful, icy laugh, "With what entry grade? A grade B in physics? She wants to become an astronaut with a literature degree!" he sniggers.

I am actually scared. I wish my friends were here, my mom, anybody! *God! Help me! Please!*

He stops the laughing and leans forwards seriously, "Dreams do not come true!" he shouts.

Now I get angry. I knew he would say that. That's what everyone says. But *why* am I getting so mad over it. He is right. That's the truth Jennifer. *Wake up!* Dreams do not come true!

"Does your friend, what's her name… oh yes, Kyara, have anything to do with this?" Dr. Kennedy questions.

My hairs stand on edge. My tears stop. I'm quick to answer, "No Sir. No. She doesn't."

"Not even in the stealing incident?" he cunningly asks.

I shake my head, "No. She doesn't know I study literature," I lie ironically.

"Alright, I'll tell you what Jennifer, give me the names the four others involved in that stealing hoax and you will not be expelled. We will allow you to continue to graduate in English literature and all of this can be forgotten. What do you say?" Dr. Kennedy proposes a deal.

Julie and Vice Chancellor sigh and wait for my response. I reflect on my friendships, my friends and what Brian said to me the other day. I feel the pressure around me. On one side is my graduation, my hard work and my future and on the other side is my friendship, their degrees, their hard work, their futures and most of all, their trust.

"Obviously, you used someone's ID to get into the labs and possibly someone helped you hack into the system. They all seem like students to me, the way they were wondering around the labs. What's you decision Jennifer, is it your degree or theirs?" he sneers swinging in his chair. "Friends don't last forever, you know."

I gently look at Julie and then the Vice Chancellor for help. They both seem sorry but helpless. The pain in my chest is indescribable. My head aches and I can feel blood thrusting through my veins. *God!* I scream in my head. I can hear his clock ticking on the wall. Time is running ahead and I've been left far behind it, so far that it has over taken me more times than I ever imagined.

"Well, Jenn-"

"I have no names Sir. This was solely my doing. I'm... I'm sorry," I cut him off and get over with it quickly.

Dr. Kennedy frowns, "Then you are dismissed. You will receive written notice of expulsion by tomorrow afternoon. You shall no longer attend any classes or exams. You are to leave immediately," he stands up and points to the door.

"I'm sorry Miss Kostigan," Vice Chancellor bids his farewell.

I begin to walk out.

"I think you're forgetting something," Dr. Kennedy calls holding my phone out towards me.

I take it and leave.

The world around me seems emotionless, my heart is distraught and my brain is traumatized. I find my way outside. I feel cold. I feel like I've lost, lost to life. The wind blows strongly but I can't feel it. Everything around me seems slow and motionless. I can't hear anything. My sight is blurred and I can just about see where I am going. *What have I done? Where will I go? What will I tell people? What will I tell my parents?* Questions bung up my mind. All my efforts have gone to waste. Worse! They haven't only been wasted they've been punished. I once thought I'd been coming out with two degrees, two subjects of knowledge, yet here I am coming out with nothing. Empty handed. I came here with such hope, then I found more hope and believed it, my dreams were coming true. I was so close. But those hopes and dreams have been shattered like a crystal glass shattering on a marble floor. Life has hit me hard, so hard that I can no longer feel it. Tears fall from my face. I am not able to show my face to anyone now. All hope is lost. It was all too good to be true.

I'm sorry, Diary. Forgive me, God.

CHAPTER TWENTY FIVE

KYARA

"Thank you very much for coming in Kyara," Angela says sitting in the middle of the long desk.

Rob and Donna are also seated accompanied by one of the producers, Steven Adaminski. Until today, I hadn't realize how big this movie is going to be, Steven Adaminski is an incredible producer! Initially they are shocked to see my leg, so I tell them about my accident, how long it will take to recover and the fact that I'm recovering much quicker than predicted. At first they seem a little hesitant, but then Angela and I have a ten minute conversation about *Lost Diamonds*, my short film. She actually watched it! That takes all the pressure off my leg. I perform the dialogue and then finish, unable to complete the fitness tests.

I wait patiently for Angela to continue speaking as I stand in the middle of the room on one crutch. I didn't need to use it much for the actual audition, *thank God*, my recovery is going quicker than we all had thought. I just balanced around on one leg, but now I'm standing for too long so I need some support. I see Angela and Steven lean back into their chairs, their necks arch further back behind Rob's seat as they discuss something in a whisper. Then they return to their normal positions. Steven looks directly at me with a sympathetic smile and Angela seems a little anxious as she gazes down at her papers before looking up and me.

"Kyara, you are our ideal actress, you fit the role perfectly and we are very impressed with your auditions so far," Angela talks.

I twinkle of hope lights up in my heart.

"However, due to your accident, which we are extremely sorry for, we have been unable to see your obstacle course and fitness tests. Furthermore, we will begin filming in a few weeks and your recovery time is much longer than that," she's genuinely sympathetic.

Steven takes over, "Kyara, unfortunately we cannot reschedule shoot dates due to the location and the scene is physical. Therefore, we are sorry to tell you that on this occasion you have not been selected. You were perfect for the role, but unfortunately we can't change the circumstances. We are deeply sorry."

The twinkle fades. *They would have chosen me? They actually would have chosen me? What the heck God?! Why did you do this to me?* I question everything in my head, speechless, unsure how to respond. I could plead with them but that's unprofessional and the situation is not the kind that can be pleaded with. I want to leave a good impression but I'm so broken after hearing that they would have actually selected me, that I don't feel like saying anything. My face turns sore and my eyes begin to water. I blink to counteract the tears. I actually had hope. My hope was right but what the hell has happened! I try to keep my emotions under control, *it's okay Kye. How can I be upset over something I never had?* A nod is the most I can respond with.

Angela apologizes again, "We are sorry Kyara, I've got your files on the system, if there's anything else we find you suitable for, we will be in touch. We hope you get well soon. Thank you for coming."

They all considerately nod at me. I want to thank them too, but if I open my mouth and relax my tense muscles, I'll cry. Words will not come out. So I just swallow and nod with a forced smile

My Friend's Dream

and then crutch my way out. Donna runs to help me with the door.

"Sorry Kyara," she whispers.

Deq and Rio told me to call them when I'm done so that they could come and pick me up. However, I am so disoriented right now that I decide to just make my own way back. The wind makes it hard for me to walk but my misery is so much that I push against it, hoping for the wind to blow it all away. My ears are cold from the gusts and I can just hear it howling. All my life, all I ever wanted was to become an actress, to be in a movie, play a good, inspiring role. I worked towards that dream every day, I took every opportunity possible and I always had faith that one day an opportunity would lead me right to my dreams. It's crazy where I am now, I took the opportunity, I got through the auditions, I even got selected but fate had other plans. *God, why did you bring this opportunity to me? Why did you get me so far only to have me rejected because of something outside of my control – an accident? This was in your hands God! What are you writing up there? What are you planning! I had faith! You broke it. You broke it, God!* I grit my teeth. I'm so fed up of everything. I feel like the fire inside me has burnt out so much that all that is left is smoke and soot. I need to let it all out but there's nothing there! It's as if my tears have ran out.

I crawl up the quiet stairs and walk inside my apartment. I throw down my crutch in the hallway and hop through the rest of it. I stop at Jen's door. I need someone to talk to. Usually this would be her. I lift my hand yet I pause just before I touch the handle. She's already devastated from the whole project thing, I'll only make her feel worse. Plus, I really don't want to argue right now. I turn around to enter my room but I hear the wind howling through the living room. I stop and listen. Then I walk through the arch. I look towards the kitchen, everything is fine. I look to my left. The balcony doors are wide open, wind gushes through and the curtains are blown inwards. I see the shadow. A figure through the curtains. I walk towards the balcony and gasp. Jen stands on the balcony rail, teetering on the edge. I can hear her shuddering breaths of anxiety and I hear her cries clearly past the roaring wind. My heart beats rapidly, forcing blood through my body and into my brain. I'm scared to call her, scared that she might slip. She pushes herself against the gales to stay balanced. She's... she's distraught. Not thinking right. God, what is she doing!

"Jen..." I breathe softly, frightened by what is happening in front of my eyes. Frightened of what she is about to do.

She turns her head only, still balancing, petrified and unsure of what to do. Her face is red and wet with tears, she finds her way into my eyes, crying. Then... her foot slips!

My feet move. My arms stretch out long. I leap. Her shriek pierces my ears. I close my eyes and for a split second, my whole world stops.

I open my eyes and feel my arm being pulled down. I slip, hitting my back on the ground. I'm being pulled forward by the weight. My casted leg finds a way through between the bars of the rail and my left foot pushes against the bars on the other side. I come to a sliding halt but I'm still being pulled as my hands hold Jen's arm. I put in every spec of energy I have left to pull her up. I push fiercely against the bar with my left foot. "Don't let go!" I groan as I push my leg, straightening it, sliding backwards as I pull her up. But I can't do this alone. I can't take her weight.

"Jen!" I shout at her to help me, "Hold on!"

Her other hand reaches a bar. I pull with all my might! She pulls too with the shattered energy that she has left. She scrambles over the rail with me still holding onto her. I slip back, past the doors and just into the living room pulling her with me. Jen falls onto me. She tries to talk but her voice is wheezy. I hold her head onto my heart. I breathe heavily. My face scrunches up and I let it all out. We both let it out. Tears remanufactured.

"Are you crazy!?" I yell, weeping. "Are you fricking crazy Jen! Don't you dare ever even think about doing that again!"

"I'm... I'm sorry!" she pants. Her speech is slurred from crying, "I...I got expelled! They found out Kye. They caught me. It's all over Kye. It's all over!"

She got expelled! *When...how...what?* Now is not the time to ask questions. I lean my head onto hers and she clings onto my arm.

"I'm sorry," she cries.

I slow my breaths down but I need to let out my emotions, my pain, my anger, my sorrow so I continue weeping, "Shh...It's okay. It's okay."

"Dreams don't come true! Who were we kidding? It's all over Kye. No hope! No faith! I have had enough!"

We release our emotions. There's no holding back today. Everything comes out. All of those tears, all that ache that has built up inside us, we let it out. If you could measure it, our tears could fill a bath and we'll continue to let the bath fill until there's no more water left. Then, we'll pull the plug.

***

Afternoon turns to night and we still sit on the floor. The plug has been pulled. Our eyes are sore and tears are dry. We have cried to our hearts contents and now we are empty.

Jen breaks the silence, "How did your audition go?" her voice is croaky.

"I didn't get the part. I would have, but my leg got in the way," I reply in my strained voice.

"Sorry Kye. I'm sorry for everything. I'm sorry for being a bitch and not talking to you. I don't know what came over me," she apologizes.

"I'm sorry too," I say.

Jen starts giggling quietly.

"What?" I giggle back.

She shakes her head, "Nothing, just… it's so weird. Look how far we've come. It's the final few weeks of university, well, days for me. And we got through almost three whole years of it. I just never imagined this happening. But it's strange because thinking about it now, I don't know what I imagined actually happening in the end."

"You're right. I didn't imagine this part either. Damn, has it really been that long? It feels like we started all this shit yesterday," I laugh pitifully.

"Just think about everything that we've done. Your scripts,

your book and all those online casting calls and auditions. All that medical training and flight training I did, then the big mission – which now I've been caught for. Just everything."

"About that, aren't we all in trouble?" I ask.

Jen shakes her head, "Nope. I didn't name you guys. You've done a lot for me. I wasn't going to drag you all down with me. And knowing Kennedy, he would've expelled us all."

"You are a crazy person Jen,"

"We've done some crazy shit Kye. And it's not even crazy shit like drugs or weed or something that kids do these days. This is like different stuff that people wouldn't really think of doing."

"Ha, yeah. Still, I'd rather do what we've done than all that crap. Everyone knows the outcome of that, poor health, rehab and regret. This outcome…" I pause.

"…What is our outcome?" Jen questions both me and herself. But we don't have an answer. "Do you regret any of this Kye?"

I wonder, then make a face, "Right now? Strangely, no. I don't. I really don't. Do you?"

"Having cried it out, no. The only thing I regret is doing what I was when you walked in-"

"Don't talk about that," I cut her off.

"Sorry. No, no I don't regret it either. I mean, we did something different, right? Like we've done something that we wanted to. We tried doing something that I don't think anybody has ever done before and we got pretty far."

"Yeah. Yeah we did."

"We worked so hard. It's funny how the bad things in life come for free and the good stuff you have to work for, and I mean work *a lot* for."

I completely understand that but I'm not angry about it. My mind and thoughts are clear, so clear that risks don't seem risky anymore, "I… I don't think we should stop."

Jen sits up and looks at me raising an eyebrow, "What?" she has a sparkle in her eyes as she smiles from them.

I raise my eyebrows back. "You've only got a few days left

here, technically, but realistically we have a few weeks left altogether."

Jen looks intrigued, "Well, I don't have anything left to lose but I don't see what more we can do."

"I do. And to be honest, it's you doing all of it. I'll still continue my stuff like I have been, my writing is mine forever and no one can take that away from me. And I'm going to tell you now Jen, that if you are getting expelled, then so am I. But, as it stands, I'm still here doing a master's next year. So to give this some context, I personally have a lot I could lose.

Jen waits for the plan.

"First of all, you will finish your final English assignment and you will hand it in. You will sit all of your final exams – the lecturers aren't allowed into the examinations so you'll get away with that. And finally, you will rebuild and finish your project-"

"In like three weeks?" Jen hypes up.

"In three weeks. Use whatever you have left, the essay is done. It's just the build, Jen. It doesn't have to be perfect. It just needs to be reasonable and innovative," I explain with determination.

Jen looks attentive. I know she wants to finish off her project and show it to NASA. She's motivated and this is her only chance.

"Jen, you've done so much. You might as well try and finish it off. Give it a go. Take your chance. What's the worst that could happen?" I motivate her further.

Jen nods with enthusiasm, "Yeah, I'm expelled anyway," she chuckles. "Oh boy, I'm going to need a whole lot of help."

"We've got our boys and Lia. And you've got me. Always."

CHAPTER TWENTY SIX

JENNIFER

My audience consisting of Kye – who has now almost completely recovered and doesn't need any assistance to walk - Lia, Brian, Marcus, Deq and Rio applaud me as I finish my last rehearsal of the presentation. The big day is tomorrow and my nerves cannot be tamed right now. Kye says it's good to be a little nervous and that when I start talking about the project my nerves will go away, which seems to be true since I've practiced. She knows what she's talking about, she can handle the stage. She dressed me up in a smart skirt and blazer with my hair in a bun. This was a dress rehearsal.

"That was really good Jen. I'm not going to lie, I don't understand some of the technical stuff you talk about but I'm sure they will," Lia stands and stretches her legs.

"Yeah well, law's terminology is quite different to astrophysics," Deq comments prior to receiving a playful slap from Lia, "Ow!"

"Thanks guys. Goodnight," I say as they begin to leave, arm in arm.

"I still cannot believe that you built that... with our help.

Like, we made that! And it actually works! You're good Jen. Good luck!" Marcus says waiting for the boys.

"It makes sense to me," Rio buts in. "I actually think they'll like the material change from your initial design."

"Yeah, I hope so. Thanks for the idea, Rio."

He has helped me a lot with the rebuild and gave me some great ideas along the way.

"No problem. I'll be there watching you tomorrow. Break a leg… not like Kye though," he chortles making us all laugh except Kye who's nostrils widen at the remark.

"You'll do great babe," Brian says hugging me. "I'll try and sneak in with Rio if I can. We'll all try and sneak in. Be you. Be confident. I know you'll put your heart into it. Do us proud."

We kiss with our friends squirming in the background.

"Goodnight." They all leave.

Jen and I stand looking at the project. I named it JK6. J for my name, K for my surname but more so for Kyara and six for the six of my cherished friends who helped me build this, but if anyone asks then six because it has six functions and coincidently it has six wheels.

Kye sits on the floor checking my essay one last time, while I change into my pajamas. I join her and just touch my project making sure it is perfect. I switch it off.

"Looks good," Kye says, placing the booklet essay neatly on the MDF board the project sits on. "No matter what happens tomorrow, I'm proud of you. This is going to get you to your dreams no matter what."

"Thanks Kye. Your motivational speeches got me here. I'm fulfilled. Even though I'm expelled already, I'm happy! I couldn't have done this anywhere else. I guess I owe thanks to the university too."

Kye admires the project, "I too feel accomplished looking at this. Look where we started, look what we've been through and look where life has brought us. I'm so glad you did this and listened to your heart. Life is too-"

"Short to not do what you want to," I finish her sentence. "We should live it how we want and do the things we love because who knows when it's time to go. And when it is, at least you'll have lived your dream. I know," I nod lost in my own thoughts. "You want to sing like Beyoncé and say 'I was Here', tell yourself like Imagine Dragons that 'I'm on Top of the World' and imagine 'How Far I'll Go" like Moana."

I smile gratefully and then begin to sing with my eyes closed. Tears fall from the corners of my closed lids and my passion glows from within me. I hear Kye joining in, crying, smiling and laughing, all the emotions together. I am ready. This is it.

* * *

I walk back and forth taking small steps as I nervously wait outside the Great Hall door. Kye peers through the window watching the rest of the project presentations. The guys and Lia made their way inside and now sit at the back of the lecture theatre, which is fully packed out! Dr. Hadfield sits with two more *judges* I suppose, at a long table right at the front. Alongside the NASA specialists are a few science and engineering lecturers and of course Dr. Kennedy, plus there are a few other lectures in the audience too. The contestants sit on the front row with their projects lined up along the side wall on trollies. My project also stands on a trolley, with my paper work neatly laid out, but it's not in the room, no, it stands right next to me, outside the room. I hold a folder in my hand along with my USB stick for the presentation. I am extremely anxious. My hands and body are sweating, I can literally feel my shirt wet on my back. I washed my hair as well, I bet it's already greasy from the sweat. Kye carefully looks around the corridors to ensure that no one comes along and questions us standing here. Apparently, she is waiting for the right moment. I am now feeling sick, I've been waiting for way too long just staring at my project, practicing my words and occasionally peeking through the window (but honestly that just makes me more nervous).

"Kye!" I whisper.

"Wait," she concentrates looking through the window and holds her finger up.

"Kye, how long man? I want to get it over and done with!"

"Shhh!" she says trying to listen, "I think this is the last one."

The last one! I begin to freak out. I have worked so hard on this project. It is my own creation. My heart and soul has gone into it, I just don't want to be disappointed. I at least want to show it to the judges, otherwise everything will be a waste. I still don't know how they're going to react when I just barge in. What am I supposed to do after that? Should I start talking straight away? I don't know what's going to happen. *God, help me!*

"Are you ready Jen?" Kye looks widely through the window. "Alright, this is it. You have got this. God bless you! Ready?" she asks again.

I grip the handles of my trolley with my hands shaking slightly. I blow air out from my mouth to calm me. I look back at Kye and nod. She gives me a confidence enhancing look and then, at the right moment, she swings the doors open.

I push my trolley into the middle of the stage taking a quick, unsettling look around the hall. The chatter of the audience and applause for the judges and contestants comes to a stop and the judges who were packing up to leave and discuss projects, pause, and stare at me. At this moment, I am supposed to say something but my words don't come out. Not after my eyes meet Dr. Kennedy's, who pulls down his glasses, his forehead creases into a raging frown.

"Sorry Sirs, there's just one more presentation," Kye helps me out standing near the door.

I swallow. Dr. Kennedy turns his head to look at where the voice came from and isn't surprised to see Kye. His face turns red and I can almost picture steam coming out from his ears and nose. He glares at my project with utter wrath. Now he knows exactly where that stolen material went. I look at Kye who tries to slyly tell me to speak through her facial expressions and her hand movements. I blink quickly and then take center stage.

"Good afternoon, I am Jennifer Kostigan. If I may, Sir?" I hold my USB stick up asking Dr. Hadfield if I can begin my presentation.

With all this anxiety I forget that I am standing in front of *the* Dr. Hadfield. This makes me more nervous, but it also reminds me how much I need to fight for this internship. It motivates me further. He is actually there in front of me. *Come on Jen. You can do this. God, let's do this!*

Dr. Hadfield smiles at my project, "That looks very interesting." I knew he was a nice person! He continues, "If it is okay with yourselves, Dr. Kennedy-"

"I do apologize Dr. Hadfield, however Miss Kostigan is not entitled to present any sort of project to our panel." Dr. Kennedy rudely cuts him off.

My heart beat increases. I cannot let this go, "Sir, if I could just present my project-"

"Jennifer Kostigan, I'm afraid that you have forgotten…something." He grits his teeth trying not to embarrass any of us, reminding me that I am expelled.

"Is there a problem, Dr. Kennedy?" Dr. Hadfield asks politely trying not to interfere too much with our discussion.

"No, no, not at all, it's just that, Jennifer is not actually a science student, you see, so I think this would be a… waste of time," he tries to put it politely in front of the guests.

"No! No it's not a waste of time," I stand my ground. "Sir, all I have ever wanted in my life is to become an astronaut. I have studied and worked hard. Please!"

"Dreams do not come true Miss Kostigan!" Dr. Kennedy raises his voice with anger but then realizes there are guests and an audience.

I panic! He won't let me do it! I see Kye getting worried and the guys and Lia at the back of the hall waiting anxiously.

"My apologies Sir…" Kye takes center stage, "…But that, is a false statement. Dreams… are there for a reason… dreams give us a reason to live, they are what drive us to continue into our future." She looks at me weirdly, trying to find convincing words.

I frown back at her, I have heard that before. I look up at Lia whose eyebrows are raised in surprise, she gently gestures with her hand at Kye to continue. Dr. Kennedy is about to say something but Kye overpowers him.

"We… we… we all have dreams, some seem bigger than others but for a person their dream is theirs and to them it's a big deal. For some, it can be to get married, or to have children, or simply to wake up every morning in good health. For others, it's a profession or an achievement like becoming a lawyer or going to university, winning a medal in the Olympics or even just taking part in the Olympics. They are our goals in life. We only have one life." She talks with confidence, her speech is sharp and moving. I get lost in it once again and from what I can see, so is everyone else, the audience and the judges. I can imagine that motivational music for a second time.

"One life, to make our dreams come true. You know, it's funny because whether you admit it or not, you all have a dream or have had a dream. Especially when you're young and you really want something in life or you want your life to go a certain way, but then life itself gets in the way; our families, friends, relationships and money. And then we forget we even had dreams, trying to compete in the race of life. But who are we to get in the way of dreams? I ask you, think back to when you were young, what was your dream?" She pauses. "Has it come true?" Another Pause. "I didn't think so. Why didn't it come true?" Pause. "Because you didn't have the guts to pursue it." She points directly at Dr. Kennedy.

Strangely, he looks exposed and… wounded.

"How often do you meet a person who is living their dream? Anyone you ask will say, 'I wanted to be this, but then I ended up doing this'. Why? Because they didn't have the determination to pursue it or because their parents told them something else. Everybody has the right to live their dream. They give us freedom, they lead us on the right path. They give us an aspiration in life. Without dreams, we wouldn't look forward to the future. And you know what's crazy? Everybody has them; the rich, and the poor, the ill and the healthy. You know, some people say money makes the world go around, yeah maybe," she laughs gently, again. "Most will say that love makes the world go around, also quite true. But I say *hope* makes the world go around because hope gives us faith in the world and with faith dreams come true. So who are you to get in the way of Jennifer's dreams?" she now improvises. "Yes, she came here to study literature. And you know what, she did that, but she also studied astrophysics on her own accord. This girl has worked her ass off to produce something that is literally out of this world. She has gone and done that without any supervision of a teacher, without any help from the science department and all solely from her own research! *That* is not a waste of time! Don't you think that at least *you* deserve a chance to see *her* project?" She finishes with a rhetorical questions in a soft yet powerful voice.

There's silence in the room. It is as if everyone is holding their breaths waiting for an answer. Dr. Kennedy doesn't speak, his eyes are low.

Dr. Hadfield clears his throat, "If you don't mind Dr. Kennedy, we would like to hear Jennifer's presentation."

I feel a rush of adrenaline pump through my chest. A single clap is heard at the back of the room and then the whole audience is applauding. Dr. Hadfield smiles and gives me the go ahead to set up on the computer. I burst into an uncontainable smile and clap for Kye before she moves away. She looks relieved.

"Thank you for that," Dr. Hadfield nods at Kye as she stands back against the wall acknowledging his appreciation.

The audience settle down, I load my presentation on the screen and hand out copies of my essay to the judges, then I take some deep breaths. Kye says take your time, I already know what to say, it's my passion so it's not about remembering, this is about telling. So I relax my mind. I take a moment. Then, I begin.

"Good Afternoon, I am Jennifer Kostigan, thank you for this opportunity. Let me introduce you to, JK6."

I finish with an applause from the audience but most importantly a standing ovation from Dr. Hadfield and his coworkers. My emotions get the best of me and I let tears role down my face – I feel like I've won a TV talent show.

"That is originality," Dr. Hadfield compliments my project. "Contestants, we shall meet back here in an hour for the results. Thank you everyone."

I roll my trolley to the side where the rest of the projects are displayed. Dr. Kennedy has not said a word since Kye's speech. The judges take all their notes and our essays and head into the room behind the Great Hall. A few people leave the hall, but most stay and find their contestant friends. I hug Kye and then we walk up the stairs to the rest of our gang. I get compliments along the way. Apparently my project is original and innovative. There are some aspects of my project that I know need expert work, but from a lot of the comments I'm hearing, mine is the simplest and most valuable. I was too nervous to hear or see anyone else's so I don't have a lot to compare it too, but the audience does.

"So proud of you Jen!" Brian embraces me.

They all compliment and comfort me.

"Nice speech Kye," Lia winks at us.

"Man, I don't even know what came over me, it just all poured out!" Kye says.

"Hey, you smashed it Jen, don't worry about a thing," Marcus hugs me.

I am a little quiet right now, but I think that's more to do with me talking so much for the past twenty minutes.

"Thanks guys. Yes, I would love to be selected, that would literally be my dream come true, especially if I have the chance to go to space. That's all I've ever wanted. I'd be fulfilled. But no matter what happens, I'm so glad that I finished that project and got the chance to present it today in front of NASA and Dr. Hadfield! All thanks to you guys. I'm happy. I truly am."

An hour later, the audience is back and the judges are back in their seats with hidden expressions. Julie Kennedy is also in the room, she sits behind the judges with a laptop. I am suspicious but who cares, I'm expelled anyway. The contestants including me stand at the front, in a line. There's twenty one of us all together. According to the gossip during the break, over one hundred students from our university applied for a supervisor but most of their project ideas were not realistic or already existed, so they were turned down. Dr. Kennedy stands up. He is still miserable from my entrance, I bet he hates me even more. Then again, he hated me so much anyway that I don't think it matters. I've come to terms with that. What more can I lose.

He begins, "First and foremost I would like to take this opportunity to thank NASA for selecting our university to be part of this internship opportunity. We are truly grateful. I would like to personally thank Dr. Hadfield for coming in to tell us about this opportunity and for bringing a prestigious team with him today to judge the projects," he applauds as does everyone else. "Furthermore, I would like to express thanks to all of our supervisors who have assisted our students in the design and build of these projects." Another applause. "Thank you all," he sits back down.

Dr. Hadfield takes over, "Yes, thank you all very much. Also thank you to the contestants for producing such innovative projects. This truly is proof that our future is bright and that the young people of today have the passion and the determination to advance our findings and technologies. No matter who we have selected for the internship, I believe that everyone we have seen today has the power to make our future a better place. So really well done to everyone. We will be keeping all your project files and your projects with us at NASA for possible future development, and of course if and when the time comes, you may be contacted. So don't change your email addresses," he jokes.

I giggle. There's always *hope*.

"Right, let's get to it." Dr. Hadfield pauses as he catches my eyes, "Oh yes, and thanks to our dreams, for they *do* lead the way." He looks down at his notes, "Jennifer Kostigan, we found your project innovative, original, useful and achievable. We love it. However, you study literature here, am I correct?"

"Sir, I am enrolled on the literature course and have completed it. However, I have also studied astrophysics for the past three years at this university. I have taken and passed all of the examinations so far. You can check this on my records. I have taken all the assessments. Hence, technically, I have also completed an astrophysics course. It is just that… my graduation is in the hands of the schools… for both subjects." I stutter the last few words.

"What is your average grade in astrophysics?" Dr. Hadfield asks.

"Around eighty percent."

"And in literature, if you don't mind me asking."

"Around seventy percent."

Julie shows him something on the laptop.

"Ah, both quite high. I'm going to be quite frank Jennifer, you are our ideal intern. Your project is great, your essay is professional and your enthusiasm and determination is commendable!"

I'm the ideal intern! I get excited but I wait for the *frank* part to hit me.

"However…"

Here is comes.

"… We need evidence or a witness in the form of a lecturer to prove that you have studied astrophysics, we require graduates and therefore you will ideally need to graduate in a few weeks' time in astrophysics. More importantly, we need a reference for you and since you didn't have a supervisor, we don't have a reference."

There's silence. I don't know what to say. I can't argue against that.

"I will be the reference," a voice enlightens the hall.

It's Dr. Kennedy's. Kyle Kennedy. Science Kennedy.

"I can guarantee that Jennifer Kostigan has studied astrophysics and… and she will graduate in both subjects in a few weeks' time, of course on the condition that she passes the current examination season." Dr. Kennedy now slowly looks up. His voice is empathetic and his anger has turned into sorrow.

"Very well, then I am happy to announce that the first intern position goes to… Jennifer Kostigan!" Dr. Hadfield declares.

Applause fills the Great Hall and I hear cheering at the back. I stand in surprise. The happiness of me getting selected has been whitewashed by the utter shock that Dr. Kennedy is willing to be my reference! He is letting me graduate in both subjects! *What the heck is going on! Oh God, is this real?* People either side of me nudge and congratulate me prodding me into reality.

"You know, I once dreamed of becoming an astronaut. If only I had the courage to pursue it." Dr. Kennedy stands up to shake my hand. He actually smiles. It's as if something from his past has finally been forgiven. I walk forward and shake his hand. "Well done Jennifer, for proving me wrong," he smiles and nods his head genuinely.

"Thank you Sir," I humbly say, getting emotional, now the happiness of getting through is coming back. "Thank you so much!"

I got it! I fricking got the internship! *Thank you God! Thank you!* I move on to shake Dr. Hadfield's hand.

"You've seriously got some bravery to study two subjects, Jennifer. Your project will make history and so will your determination of fulfilling your dream. Congratulations. We look forward to working with you at NASA."

I squeal with excitement and happy tears, "Thank you Sir!"

I move along the panel receiving congrats and shaking hands and then as I move to the side I catch Julie Kennedy's eyes, which glitter with pride and joy. She raises her thumbs at me and I express my gratitude back. They reveal the second intern, who jumps with delight. His project looks fascinating and he himself seems like a hard worker. With all the joy in the air, I take everything in, in slow motion. The cheers, the applause, the smiles on my friends' faces. It's beautiful. I feel accomplished. All the happiness has been handed to me all at once. I couldn't have asked for more. The graduations for both subjects, the completion of my education, the success of my project achieving this internship and the belief that my dream has come true. The feeling is indescribable. Out of this world. Magical. Dreamy. But it's real. *Thank you God. I am grateful for the years you have given me, I am grateful for believing and I am grateful for the friends you have made me meet. I am grateful for Kye, because if it wasn't for her, none of this would ever have happened and my dream would have stayed a dream. It is surreal.*

Yeah, I made it.

CHAPTER TWENTY SEVEN

KYARA

Two Years Later.

It has been two years since we graduated. Everyone has gone their separate ways and are doing great! *God Bless*. Brian is an editor for a news publishing company. Rio is an automotive engineer for a luxury car company. Lia is now a lawyer at the firm where she did her internship – she's now doing a sponsored PhD. Deq is a cybersecurity analyst working for the government. Marcus graduated last year and now is a real junior doctor. And Jen, Jennifer Kostigan is an astronaut – a mission specialist! Six months ago, Jen made history as the youngest person ever to go to space! She made it! She's in the news and all over NASA. And guess where she is right now? Yep, in the International Space Station! The JK6 is still in development and hopefully one day it'll bring us knowledge from deeper space. My friends are all succeeding in life and I'm over the moon for them. Deq and Lia have tied the knot! I can't wait for their wedding next summer! We've all grown up! I'm going to be a bridesmaid! On the other hand Brian and Jen have split, but they left on good terms, she's not around much physically so they thought it was best to just keep it friendly. We all try to speak at least once a month but to be honest everyone is so busy that sometimes we can't all make it on a video call. I mean, I am always available. However, Jen and I are still like crossed fingers. We talk all the time. I have literally seen space though her camera! It's crazy how far we all are in our lives. I am a proud friend.

I still live here, in apartment 403, on campus. Actually, I moved rooms since the new girl moved in. I moved into Jen's, 403A, which was originally mine. The new girl is okay and the new people opposite us are nice too but they're nowhere near as close as we were, in fact they don't talk to each other much. I don't talk to them very much. They all have their own, different friendship groups. It's weird having our front door shut. The hallway is a lot quieter too. I have gotten used to it, but I miss the noise and nuisance so much! I haven't changed things around in my room, it still is the way Jen decorated it with the addition of my Oscar statue. The room still smells like her and I still find random things of hers lying around now and then.

I completed my master's last year and now I'm a research student at the university. My effort towards achieving my dream is still strong. I still apply for online auditions but it's not the same without everyone helping me. Now I just do them myself. I have written lots of work, scripts, novels, short stories, poems and of course I have finished 'A Dream within the Stars'. I am in multiple casting directors' books and in inboxes of publishers. Now I'm just waiting for my big break and I think it's about to happen.

"Jen, will you stop moving the camera around, I'm trying to talk to you! Show me your face!" I yell at my computer screen. We have to use a special software to communicate with the astronauts.

"Sorry!" she swings around in mid-air and holds the camera to her face. "It's my last day I just want to see it all! Take it in. I have seen it all Kye! I am now at peace," she exaggerates but she really means it.

"Nice. Nice. Anyway I have some news for you!"

"What? You finally got published?" she eats something by squeezing a long, thin straw-like packet.

I squint my eyes, "Maybe!"

"No way!" she says with surprise.

"Well, almost. I hope. I'll come back to that later but there's more…"

"What? What? What?" Jen hovers in excitement.

"I got a call from Angela yesterday!" I say to the camera, with the cheesiest smile.

"Angela?" Jen tries to remember. "The casting director?"

"Yes! Angela Weir! She called and didn't say that they were auditioning… she said she wants me for a side role in an action movie sequel! I had a screen test yesterday and she called earlier today saying… I've got the part!" I burst with happiness. I have been waiting so long to say those words, so long to taste the joy of gaining a movie role! A good one too! She's even sent me a sample of the entire script to read!

"Oh my God! Kye, that is awesome! I told you good things will happen for you! I told you! Hey, we are dreamers, because our dreams have come true. I'm so proud of you Kye! The first thing I'm going to do when I get back, is travel to you somehow, because, well, I won't really be able to walk or drive for a while and then we are celebrating! My girl! You did it!" she explodes with joy and summersaults in midair.

"And that's not all… back to the book. I have a final meeting with the publisher tomorrow! I think they like it but they are going to confirm and tell me tomorrow if they want to publish it!"

"A Dream within the Stars?" she asks impatiently.

I nod holding back tears.

"Kye! I'm so proud of you! I am so happy, words cannot describe. I've seen you want these things and now it's all happening. You were right the whole time. God is there, above me, listening to our prayers and keeping our faith. I knew it would happen one day. We knew it would happen. Though, I still think 'My Friend's Dream' is a better title," she smirks.

"Hey, I may not get the publishing deal. But I have faith in whatever God does. I just can't believe this is finally happening for me!"

"I know that feeling! I'm sure you'll get the deal, Kye. I have

My Friend's Dream

a good feeling. This is your time. We have worked so hard to get where we are today and we both know from experience that when good things come to us, they come all at once. My good things have come to me, now it's your turn. Embrace it! Good luck with both of them. Smash it up Kye! I know you'll do all of us and your family proud. Ah! I can't wait to see you on the cinema screens! Can you tell me about the movie? Or is it secret?"

"Thanks!" I say unable to retract my smile. "Hmm, it is a secret, but I'll tell you when you get back."

"Yeah you better! Hey, what time is that meeting though? Are you not going to watch me land? It's broadcasting live tomorrow, remember!" Jen reminds me.

"Oh yes, I know. I should make it back in time. Don't worry."

"Cool cool. Alright, I have to go, my break time is over. I have to be prepped for tomorrow's landing. I'll speak to you when I get back! Break a leg! Not literally. Do us proud Kye!"

"Haha! Good times, good times. Cool, see you tomorrow!" I wave.

"See ya! Muah!" Jen gestures, blowing kisses to my screen and then ends the call.

It feels so great to tell Jen about my life right now. In fact, my life just feels great right now. I'm relieved. *Thanks God, for everything. I hope I get this publishing deal tomorrow and I'm slightly nervous for the movie but I can't wait to start! This is what I've wanted!* I told my parents and they are over the moon too. They think I've already got the publishing deal, it's hard to explain things to them and keep them from getting overexcited. Things are finally working out for me. Hard work does pay off. I have faith.

CHAPTER TWENTY EIGHT

KYARA

"That is a deal Kyara, we are certain that the book will do well." The publisher and his assistant sit opposite me at a grand desk.

"Thank you very much!" I squeal trying to control my excitement.

"This is the contract, please read it, take your time. If there are any changes you would like to make, then do so and highlight them. Once you have read and checked everything we can go ahead and start the publishing process. Is one day enough for you to read through the book and contract? Could you come in tomorrow afternoon to sign the papers?" he asks as the assistant hands me a copy of the contract and a copy of my book.

"Yes of course. That is absolutely fine." The sooner the better in my opinion. I take hold of the papers.

"Is four p.m. okay?" he asks.

"Yes, four is perfect. Thank you very much once again," I shake their hands as I get up to leave.

"Thank you for such an amazing story. I hope the people empathize with it," he expresses his gratitude with his hand on his heart.

My Friend's Dream

I got the fricking publishing deal! I jump in the air on my way home after safely putting away the contract in my bag. Finally! Finally, everything is going to plan! Hard work and patience certainly pays off. I got one of the best publishers in the world! *Thank you so much God! I love you! I hope it's a best seller!* I can't wait to tell everyone! I can't wait to tell Jen. This was her idea! This happened because of her! I race home to watch Jen's arrival on earth. Life is finally on the same page as me.

"I'm late! I'm late!" I shout out loud to myself as I run up the stairs and into the apartment. I place my bag carefully on the kitchen counter and take out the papers to make sure they are there. They are. I then wildly look around for the TV remote searching all over and under the couch. I find it tucked under the cushion. I grab it quickly, point it towards the TV sensor. I bang on the power button three times until the TV switches on. I type in 101. The channel it is being broadcasted on. I wait. Then I see the sky. It's dark. I see a red strip at the bottom of the screen with words in capital letters gliding across it. I hear gushing. Then, I see it. I see flames. Not the good ones. Not the ones that are supposed to be propelling off the spacecraft. Then... I wish I had gone blind before my eyes see what they are seeing. The spacecraft peels to bits. Parts wildly fly off it. An explosion in midair. I now see what is written on the red panel. I now hear what the presenters are saying.

Repeating. "The spacecraft has exploded! This is unbelievable. This has not happened in fifteen years. NASA have confirmed Astronaut Jennifer Kostigan, Mission Specialist is deceased. We can confirm, Astronaut Jennifer Kostigan is dec-"

My finger switches the TV off. I stand still in the middle of the living room, unable to think. My knees are weak. I take a moment. I blink my eyes a couple of times. Then, I laugh. I chuckle. To myself. *No. No, this is not right. I probably got the wrong channel. Ha! God, you play some funny games. It's really not funny, you shouldn't do that. It's okay. Jen's okay.* I switch the TV back on. The tragedy continues. The spacecraft now disintegrated as it gets closer to the ground. The presenter still says the thing I do not want to hear and the red strip still shows what I do not want to see. I turn it back off.

I am stunned. I laugh again, this time louder. I am not willing to believe.

"No. What is wrong with you Kye?" I ask myself, politely giggling. "Jen is fine. I'm going to tell her I got the publishing deal. Yeah, I'll call her in a bit. Give her some time." My giggles turn sour, I lose control of the muscles in my face. I bite my hand and feel pain. I'm already awake. Tears travel from my heart to my eyes and excrete without me giving them permission to. "I'll... call... her," I stumble, unsure what to do. Unsure how to feel. "No! No! No! God no!" I scream, irritating the back of my throat. "What did you do? God, what the heck did you do! This can't be happening, God please! Please!" I beg, shouting to the empty air that surrounds me. "Please tell me it's all a lie. Please God!" I now weep still talking to the air. "God! How could you do this to me?"

I switch the TV back on and point at the screen in rage, showing God what I am talking about. Somewhere deep inside me, I still pray and I still hope that this is all false. I hope that God has turned this around. But as I see it again, the space craft is in pieces on the ground. There is further confirmation of... of... death. It is true.

"What is this, God? What did she do wrong! Huh? She had faith in you! I had faith in you!" I realize something, "This is all my fault! This is all my fault! If we never followed our dreams this never would have happened! If I hadn't persuaded Jen to pursue her dreams and become an astronaut, this never would have happened! It is... all... our..." I grab my publishing contract papers in fury and scrunch them up, "... It's all our fricking dreams' fault!" I throw the scrunched ball. "Where did we go wrong!? Why, God? Why!? She was happy, living her dream!" My voice tires from shouting. My energy drained. My face soaked. My eyes scrunched with non-stopping water, leaking from them. Pain sores through my head. "Why, God?"

My knees give way. I fall to the ground, questioning everything I ever believed in. I cry wiping away my tears but they keep falling. I still hear the news on the TV in the background. I listen to it and continue to weep, soaking my clothes. Fluids find a

My Friend's Dream

way out of my nose, my entire face is red and hot. My eyebrows hurt from the frowning. The more I cry the more I realize what has happened, and the more I realize what has happened the more my heart aches.

I get up, still crying and walk into my room. Jen's room. Anger takes over me once again when I see her poster of the solar system. My body uncontrollably lashes out at everything. I throw things, smash things and crush things, turning the room upside down. One is so much more powerful when fueled by anger and sorrow at the same time. I push and shove things out of place. Objects tumble onto the bed and floor. I kick and stamp on things. I scream and shout until my lungs dry out. I fall onto the bed, hugging the pillow I cry some more. This cry is different. It's not the quiet one that you try to hide from people or try to stop yourself from doing. This is the loud one. The one where you don't care if people can hear it. The one with nothing to hide. It is not embarrassing. It is pure sorrow. Pure sadness. Uncontrollable grief. My whole body shakes as I wail. I huff and puff trying to catch my breath but I keep bawling. My life with Jen flashes past my closed eyes. All the good times, all the bad times. Our happy times and our sad times. The times we dreamed, the times we believed and the times we achieved. Now, all a memory.

* * *

Hours pass by, I open my tired eyes with a struggle. The wet tears have dried on my lashes to form a seal. I can still hear the news from the living room. *It wasn't a dream.* I lay still. My dry, salt-burnt face lies on the soaked pillow. I move my hand to feel my face but as I do, I hit a small hard surface. I hold onto the object and slide it up to eye level. It's a small hardback notebook, with a starry sky printed on the front and back. I flick through the pages. It is Jen's diary. I read through it, with my soul still aching. Each new entry has the date and time written and each entry begins with 'Hey Diary'. She wrote about all the things that had happened in the three years that we were at university. My memories illuminate from Jen's point of view. She's written about everything! The first day we met, her first sneaky physics lesson, her first literature lesson, my first audition, the mission, my accident, our fight, her project, everything! And in every entry no matter what it was about, she always wrote about our dreams without fail. Every single entry ends with 'I have faith, that one day I will become an astronaut and Kye will become an actress. I just know it.' In her last one she writes;

'... So, to summarize! We made it! We've all graduated. I'm packing for my NASA internship and I can't wait to get started! I'm really going to miss everyone. I can't believe it's been three years! I love them all so much and I thank God for an amazing life. If I get to go to space while at NASA, my life will be complete. My dreams will have been achieved. That is all I want from my life. So, yeah, I hope I get to go to space soon! Now it's Kye's turn to publish her book, 'A Dream within the Stars' I still prefer 'My Friend's Dream' but whatever. I can't wait to see it on the shelves! Anyway, got to go, we're having our last get together in this apartment. Good night Diary! I had faith that one day I would become an astronaut and here I am today – Astronaut Intern Jennifer Kostigan. And I still have faith that Kye will become an actress. I just know it.'

I close the diary and hold it close to my heart, finding breath through my swollen lips and blocked nose. Crying clears your mind. I know that. I've experienced it enough. And now my mind is clearer than ever. I kiss the diary and push myself up from the bed. My arms and legs are stiff. I know my Jen. She'd be disappointed with me and I know that this is what she would want me to do. I take it back, I'm glad she lived her dream. That is all she ever wanted. She lived it. She is happy. I will never truly understand why God did this, no one knows his ways. I will probably always question it, but I won't ever forget that in the end, Jen lived her dream. I will never forget our journey and I will never forget what we both wanted. I use the walls to help me to the living room. The news now shows images of Jen when she first started at NASA. She looked so happy. I search the living room, but struggle to see through my blurred, sticky vision. I pick up my keys from my bag on the breakfast bar and switch on the torchlight that Rio and Brian bought me for Christmas. I shine it behind and under the couch to find what I'm looking for. My scrunched up publishing contract. I neaten it out and place it on the coffee table rubbing my hand over it to remove the creases. I find a pen on the table. *For you Jen, we were and still are in this together.* I draw a line through 'A Dream within the Stars' and write in capitals above it, 'MY FRIEND'S DREAM'.

EPILOGUE

KYARA

"And the Oscar for Best Actress goes to... Kyara Averoni for My Friend's Dream!" The presenter calls out in her strong voice from the grand stage as the venue is uplifted with applause and cheers.

I stand up from my seat in my blue glittery dress and my glammed hair and makeup. I turn to my husband who embraces me and helps me out of the row and into the aisle. I walk to the stage being congratulated along the way.

"Kyara actually wrote the book and the script! Can you believe that, John? She's a tremendous actress. This is her first Oscar. Here she comes!"

I climb up the stairs carefully and greet the presenters. They hand me my first golden man, smooth as ever with some weight to it. I hold it with both hands looking at the accomplishment. They gesture at the stand with the microphone in front of me. I place the award on the stand but continue to hold onto it with one hand. I look out to the audience far, far away, the hundreds of people waiting for me to speak. I take in the moment. This is more than what I ever wanted. God has given me so much more, I am lucky to have been able to fulfil more than just one of my dreams. I am grateful. I'm nervous but I'm ready.

    I lean into the microphone, "Hi." I take a breath. "I would like to thank... God first of all, for keeping my faith. I want to thank my parents, my family and my husband for their ongoing support. I want to thank the academy, my agent, the director, the producers and my coworkers for teaching and guiding me through this project. Also, thank you Angela for casting me in my first movie because you gave me my big break. Of course I would also like to thank the fans and the audience, for without you, our job would not exist. And I would like to thank my friends, you know who you are, for getting me through tough times and for staying sane during the time we tried to insanely chase our dreams. But this award, this golden man, I would like to dedicate to someone special, a friend of mine, a friend who most of you know by name as a woman who made history. But I knew her a little differently, to me she was a dreamer, a girl who had courage, motivation and determination. A girl who was a little crazy but the opposite of her stereotype. She taught me to follow my heart, she taught me that life is about dreaming and believing and achieving, and that if you put your heart to it, you can do anything. Have faith she said. Faith gives us hope and hope keeps us going. You all know her as Astronaut Jennifer Kostigan. I knew her as Jen. This, is for you Jen."

.

ABOUT THE AUTHOR

Manisha Kaur Rathore is the author of My Friend's Dream. She began writing her first short story and poetry at the age of ten. She's an actress/model, playwright and writer. As an actress she trained at the National Youth Theatre of Great Britain and as a model she won the title of Miss Eco-Birmingham 2017/18. In her other life, she's a chemical engineering graduate from Aston University.

Printed in Great Britain
by Amazon